A
TRANSCENDENTAL
HABIT

A TRANSCENDENTAL HABIT

JAMES CALLAN

Queer Space
New Orleans

Published in the United States of America by
Queer Space
A Rebel Satori Imprint
www.rebelsatoripress.com

Book design: Sven Davisson

Paperback ISBN: 978-1-60864-248-9
Ebook ISBN: 978-1-60864-249-6

Library of Congress Control Number: 2023930058

for Sharman Russel, whose teachings,
like miraculous seeds, brought life to barren rock.

1
HE CARRIED A SWORD

Nyvyn was a real heap of shit. The place I lived. The place I was born. The place I didn't want to be. Nyvyn, which means 'little saint,' or 'nephew,' or 'saint worshiper,' was a stack-upon-stack, multi-layer collection of filth and degradation. I loathed it, as did we all.

Nyvyn. No one calls it that. At least we don't, the people who live here. Flip the letters around and you get the same thing; Nyvyn. So we who live here call it Palindrome. Or 'the Dome.' Or 'Drome.' Or 'the Saint.' Or 'Shit stack.' Or sometimes we don't say anything, we just sigh and become wistful about places we'd rather be.

I ducked my head under some rusted grating that served as a walkway above me. A hobo or a drunk or a drunk hobo cascaded warm urine down to tinkle upon my shoulder. I sighed and moved on. I traversed the alleys, I sidestepped the vomit, the refuse, I kicked the occasional rat.

The malaise was eating me alive. And the boredom. That too.

But the boredom, in the very least, was about to subside for a time.

'You carry a sword. How quaint.'

They were the wrong words, spoken at the wrong time to the wrong man. The tone of mockery, particularly, was a mistake. The man who said those words would forever grieve his right leg, his left eye.

|

'Woah,' I said, while watching next-level violence enfold before me, one stranger casually maim another. 'Wicked sword.'

They were the right words, spoken at the right time to the right man. The tone of genuine amazement, particularly, was a good call. Not that I made any conscious choice. They just came out, those words, genuine amazement and all. They spilled out of my mouth just as the rivers of blood spilled from a severed femur, a gouged-out eyeball, onto the street and down a sewage grate to entice the fevered rats.

They squealed as loud as the dying man who wallowed in the curb-side filth. The rats, they soon drowned out the man's piteous howls as his consciousness ebbed and faded, their own peaked by the taste of fresh flowing lifeblood.

'Rats,' the man with the sword said.

'I know,' I nodded. 'So many of them.'

'No,' he shook his head. I looked over, confused. 'I mean, "rats." As in rats, look at my shoes.'

So I did. And I saw what he meant. Pristine white sneakers stained with smears of dark crimson, blotches of bloody rain.

'It could be worse,' I offered and he looked my way, waiting, hoping I would say the wrong words so he could do to me what he did to the man on the street. Only maybe this time a left arm, a right ear. I gulped. 'I mean… at least you're not *that* guy.' I indicated the heap that was nearly a corpse, now gnawed at by greedy, long orange teeth. Presently, a couple came to aid the savaged being. He may be passed saving but it was good to get him off the street. The rats would disagree.

'You going in there?' I pointed to the glare of neon, yellow and pink, that spelled out in lavish cursive "The Bee and the Lily." The question was merely a tool to keep our conversation alive. He was already three steps down the stairwell. There was no question as to where he was going.

But there *was* a question. And it came from him. 'You coming?' Four steps, five, six down the stairwell. He was gone. Nearly. *Am I coming?* Now I asked myself. 'Yes.' I nearly shouted. 'Yes I am.'

Another question: what the hell was I doing!?

But he had me hooked. This guy. This guy with a sword. This guy that cuts off legs at the hip and pinpoints pupils in a blink if you say the wrong words at the wrong time. He had me hooked like a fish on a reel. Except I wasn't pulling away. I wasn't fighting. I was swimming with the reel. I was begging to be scooped out of the water and thrown onto the deck of the boat. Why? Because I was hooked. Because in all of Palindrome, over all my many years of walking her heinous byways, her sordid and salacious streets, it was this raucous encounter that lifted me, just a little, from those onerous icky vibes of existence.

For the first time in years I wasn't bored to death. I owed that to him. This freak stranger. This hot-tempered, kill-you-quick, yet cool-headed, bummed-about-those-stained-new-shoes maniac. Sure, I might die myself, like the man outside who fed the rats. It's conceivable, I'll grant you, I could snuff it while hanging with this guy. I could die inside of midnight and it's 11:32 p.m. But I'd not be yawning just before my death throes. And besides, I was already dying. Like I said, for years I've been bored to death. Dying.

The Bee and the Lily had us bathed in a wash of aquamarine, hues of Neptune blue. The neon lights and venetian blind lampshades an assortment of teal and mint, summer sky and swimming pool water. I could almost smell the chlorine. But Hotel Nostril didn't have any vacancy for the imaginary. My olfactory was fully booked out, aromas of booze and smoke, the sweat of a tightly packed hothouse pub. And the lilies. Those too. A dozen or more erupted from wine or spirit bottles placed on each tabletop, at intervals along the bar. The last thing I smelled was fear. It came from those that glanced in our direction. Or is that stale chicken wing? Pub fare? I think not. The fear was real, and it had nothing to do with me. It had everything to do with the guy I was with.

There were actual bees. Real ones, neither holographic nor mechanical. They were buzzing from table to table, one lily profusion to the next. Doing their pollination thing. A whole lot of buzzing. And soon I'd be buzzing, I hoped. I didn't wait to order a drink. I stole a sip from my pocket flask.

'Vodka?' I offered my murderous friend.

He shook his head. We took a seat. All that buzzing to fill the silence, all that low tone drone and hammering bass from speakers, a chorus of chit chatting drunks, it all amounted to a whole lot of noise, but the silence was still deafening. If you know what I mean. Just me and this guy with a sword and his blood-stained sneakers well within the space beneath the booth that should have been for my own clean pair. His blank stare added to the loud silence.

'You know…' I blazed the trail for conversation. I took another sip from my flask, I waved it in front of him. 'This flask is probably the most valuable thing I own.' That wasn't saying much. 'I had it enchanted, you see. Doused in green. Emerald fern and sea foam, moss and olives. Green magic, replenishing hue. It cost me a fortune. A year's worth of wages working at Taco Nirvana. That's where I work. Low pay. But I was thrifty for a year and saved up.'

'A little bit of green magic,' he smirked. 'What does it yield?'

I was grinning now. I was stoked I had him talking. Now we were chit chatting like the other patrons, the drunks. Like the winos and the rats outside the door. Soon we'd be buzzing, too, with the bees.

'For every bit of drink I take from this flask it replenishes thirteen percent.'

'Pfff.' He pfffed.

'Hey man!' I complained. 'When you drink as much as I do, that's saving a buck. Hell, it's getting *more* for your buck. Only annoying thing is… I always have to transfer from a bigger bottle into this tiny flask. I often spill a little. Especially when I am drunk.'

'I wonder if you spill as much as thirteen percent?'

I frowned. Had I wasted my money on that little bit of green?

The waitress came and gave us some sass. Like she was annoyed to be serving us. Annoyed to be a waitress. I'm annoyed that I work at Taco Nirvana — more so still after seven years of service — but I'll make a man's taco when he orders it. I'll shovel on extra cheese or toss in additional packets of fire sauce upon request. I do it with a smile. No sass. Now I was the one annoyed.

When she walked away I huffed a bit. 'What a bitch,' I ventured my opinion.

'That's my little sister.'

Oh, fuck! Was I going to lose a leg? An eye? I winced and tensed and waited. Nothing. Then it came, a wash of relief. 'She is a bit of a bitch.'

We laughed. Then laughed again when his little sister came back with our drinks and we assured her nothing was funny. 'No really, it's nothing.' We laughed all the harder as she walked away, suspicious.

'You know,' he initiated for the first time, 'I've my own bit of magical infusion.' He tapped the pommel of his sword.

I leaned forward, interested. I sipped from my pocket flask and smiled, knowing thirteen percent of what I swallowed would remain, magically, within.

'My sword,' he began, and hoisted it up onto the table. The bottle with the profusion of lilies rattled, the bees buzzed in annoyance. 'It's a seeing-sword.'

'A seeing sword?' I echoed.

'I call it *Witness*.'

'I see.' I didn't. But apparently the sword, by some magic, did.

He tapped a slender finger. He did so for a duration I found irritable. I thought it was a tick. But then I noticed it. He was indicating a strange feature embedded near the base of the long blade. An eyeball, of all things. I stared into it with morbid curiosity. It glistened, as if alive, sentient. It blinked. I shuddered and recoiled. Gasping with a rapid heartbeat.

'That's revolting,' I said without any thought of etiquette, without any strategy to preserve my life from the wrath of an insulted madman. 'But very, very cool,' I assured him, holding my breath, then exhaling at seeing his grin.

'*Witness* sees, observes, watches; a sentinel and ally. In battle, we are two, but we are one.'

'Uh-huh.' *Wack job. Total wack job.*

'It is a human eye,' he remarked.

'How lovely,' I upended my flask, then upended it again to consume the thirteen percent of dregs that now truly was dregs. The last drops.

'It is, in point of fact, my own eye.'

'Your *own* eye?'

'Aye.'

We laughed. His little sister came back and deposited our drinks. Vodka martini for me, big old olives speared by toothpicks, some fruity looking cocktail for the oddity on the other side of the table. He stirred the contents of his golden drink with the little paper umbrella jutting from a wedge of citrus.

It was then that I noticed it. That optical quirk. With a backward flick of his long dark locks he revealed his bionic eye. It shone green, binary code trickling vertically, running a script that did, what? Reveal ultraviolet spectrum? Detect heat signatures? Ultra zoom with picture capture mode? X-ray vision? Or did it simply see things as I do, plainly, the mundane world all around us?

But there was nothing mundane about it. That eye. Or him. That man. I looked at him look back at me, one eye long-lashed and blue and fleshy gelatin, beautiful, the other a green matrix of computer who-knows-what? He smiled slyly, perhaps even flirtatiously. It was then I realized I had my mouth wide open. My jaw had dropped down to the sticky-with-beer table we sat at. I snapped it back into place. I blushed and then hid my face in my martini.

'My real eye was gouged out with a stiff finger.'

I spat the eyeball sized olive I was playing with in my mouth back into my cocktail. 'Ouch.'

'Indeed,' he attested the memory of pain. 'I lost it in conflict with a certain man.'

'A fight?'

He took a long, slow sip from his Mai Tai or Bahama Mama or whatever the hell that thing was. 'Such was its severity,' he explained, 'that I should sooner call it a battle. A war. Pent up feelings exploding all at once. Volcanic eruptions of rage.' Again, that slow, thoughtful sip. 'If I am being entirely honest, it was a lovers' quarrel. When he became batshit mad I didn't stop loving him. I was mad myself,' he admitted. 'Mad for him.' He returned to his alcoholic fruit punch and downed it in one gulp, grinding ice cubes between molars and chewing on lime rinds. 'Love is a mistake,' he concluded.

Damaged goods. I did not voice my thoughts.

'I lost something else that day,' he continued. 'I lost a lot of things, actually. I lost my left eye, as is evident and noted. I lost my lover, the wildly ingenious nuthouse kook. I lost a measure of dignity, for myself and for the world at large. I lost my temper that day, which led to this series of other losses. But what I refer to when I say that I lost something else that day, I refer to *this*.' I followed the sound of knuckles wrapping on metal and looked under the table.

'Your leg.'

'My leg.'

'Your right leg.'

'Right, as in *correct*. Right, as in my *right leg*.' It was an odd time to make a joke. But I sort of laughed when he did. I thought of the man outside, the one that mocked that strange sword, the man that carried it. The one that fed the rats a gallon or two of blood and a rolling sphere of optical tissue. His left eye. His right leg. He took from the man on the street what he himself had lost. Certainly no coincidence. It was chagrin for his own losses. It was the rage that he harboured, always, continuous, a molten hatred within. Hatred for himself, for the world around him, for his lover that left him maimed.

'I gathered up my eye and limb, strewn upon the floor. I left, howling, glaring with my remaining optic organ. But I did not allow death to fall upon me. I slammed the door on the reaper. I turned the bolt. And I yelled an emphatic 'fuck you' through the obstruction between us.'

He waved to his little sis for another round. I finished my martini so I could have another. I was starting to notice a buzz that did not emit from the bees on the lilies, but from within my guy. Real pleasant. Real nice. I was going to nurture that. See where it led to.

Sissy brought the booze. She unloaded some tude and sashayed

8

back to the bar, hips and ass like a pendulum. I let my eyes linger. I smiled and sipped.

Then came the continuation of that bizarro narrative. 'I survived the savage ordeal only by the sheer stubbornness, a will to live fueled with hate, that engulfed me, filled me. Like scaffolding around an empty husk, I was held in place by it. That will. That need to make it through. And I did.'

I held my martini by the rim and rolled my wrist. A little vortex formed to whirlpool two perfect cubes of ice, two oblong olives the size of testicles. I took a long sip through my teeth and nodded, not knowing where this was going.

'My eye was a crumpled, ruinous thing. The rejuvenation vats that rebuilt it, revivified its cells, its structure... that cost a fortune in and of itself. The black magic to keep it alive while detached from my body, the meticulous shamanistic prayers, the voodoo hymns and seance, the injections and rituals, the devotion to daily practices, dances, otherworldly routines, all the many disciplines and ingredients to see the enchantment through; that cost yet another fortune, and a larger one.'

'You made of money?' I asked.

'I am made of many things, as are we all. In my case, some of those things are now bionic.'

Literal. Go figure.

'Anyways...' he carried on, 'The most challenging thing — and yes, yielding up yet another fortune to do so — was manipulating the black magic just enough into blue magic so that my eye, living while separated from my body, could transmit images into my brain, all the while infused within the blade of my sword.'

'A seeing-sword.'

'Witness.'

Long pause. 'Jeez, mate. You are an exceptionally fucked up individual.'

He smiled and drank deep from his beach-vacation beverage. 'Incidentally,' and again he obliterated both the ice and citrus wedge of his cocktail, creating a suspended silence. 'Incidentally,' his mouth now free of obstruction and busywork, 'my leg, too, is merged with the sword.' He held it up and I blanched to see what appeared to be a femur playing the part of the hilt, the kneecap acting as the pommel, the appendage of bleached calcium worked cunningly into the metal. Leathern straps entwined the bone to improve the wielder's grip.

The eye. The leg. It was all rather macabre. Over the top. A bit of those old icky vibes that are the sad gray world we live in was in that sword. But still, rather theatrical, entirely eccentric, the murderous device was, in my estimation, pretty fucking wicked besides.

'What *was* that conflict about?' I asked, staring at that strange sword that had come into this world as a result of a lovers' quarrel. That is *some* quarrel. I've broken up for spilled milkshakes, let alone severed limbs, lost eyeballs. 'What in the hell got you cutting off legs and poking out peepers?'

He got up without warning. He took up his sword and sheathed it over his shoulder into a long strap of black leather that slashed diagonal across his back. His bionic eye flashed. He looked like a comic book hero, or villain, some vengeful warrior from a pulp serial. Taking strides towards the door he stopped and turned his head, his back still facing me. 'Care for a nighttime stroll?'

Walking the Dome wasn't my idea of a good time. It was my idea of a necessity to get from point A to point B, as quick as possible, while avoiding a myriad collection of vile detritus. Still, my curiosity for this weirdo was off the charts. It had only grown. I jumped to my feet to follow.

'On my tab,' he shouted out to Sissy. *Sweet, free drinks.*

He held open the door for me, all chivalrous, and together we ascended the stairwell into the late night crudity of Palindrome, Nyvyn, the little saint that has fallen from grace.

2
A TEMPORARY BUZZKILL

'Bit of Squidge?'

It was music to my ears. I hadn't had any in weeks. He took out the little tube and squeezed the yellow goo like eye drops into his single living optic. Well... the single living optic on his face. Let's not forget that sword.

I took the tube that was offered to me and did the same, two fat drops, one per eye. The sad, grim city suddenly brightened, looked nicer, as if viewed through rose tinted glasses. You could see better, which meant you saw all the shit in its ugly detail, but you could see the stars through all the smog, the neon light playing off the gloss of a pretty girl's lip. You could see all the little gems, otherwise concealed, scatted here and there among the midden heap.

One drop on the tip of the tongue. Why not? Squidge would have me tasting nice for hours. It would go well with the booze in my bloodstream. I'd feel a better man, *be* a better man, until it wore off. Until I reapplied.

Squidge hit the streets a year or so back. It was an awesome new drug. A bloody miracle. It enhanced the world around you. It made everything better. Spread it on toast, you got toast that tastes like ambrosia, food of the gods. Lube up your cock, you're the best fuck in town. Wipe it through your hair, you got yourself a good hair day. Dribble a drop on the lips of a hopeless stutterer and you have the world's most articulate orator, for a time.

Wires shorted? Circuitry bust? Slather some Squidge and your device, your robot, your electric toothbrush, it runs like new. Drink some, feel alive. Your immunity and cellular health will be prime. Douse some on that car engine next time it does the old chug, chug, chug; you got yourself a race car, mate. Top notch vroom.

Get my point? It enhances. It makes better. It is genuinely divine, or is to me, who worships nothing but a good time, a happy day. Squidge is the cure to depression, cancer, bad style, or mechanical failure. It just takes what's wrong, somehow, and makes it better. Lifts what is low. Tickles what itches. Holds the hand and pats the back of whatever ailment is there, lends support... for a time.

Well worked into my eyes, the Squidge had me seeing the world like it should be. A version of Drome that was ugly as hell, as it well and truly was, but had bits that were tasty, morsels worth eating. There were a few sparkles among the drab if you could smell them out. And a bit of Squidge in the system, I was smelling them out.

He took my hand, 'This way,' and guided me along a thoroughfare lined with garbage sacks and dead cats, sleeping (or dead) men and women that seemed to favor the apertures billowing steam from warm currents of shit below. They huddled next to them. Like worshipers haloing a shrine. They looked like carbuncles or hemorrhoids rimmed around an angry anus. From beneath the steaming grating I swear I heard a whimper or the sound of crying. Maybe I imagined it.

The narrow byway we traversed opened outward and widened into a street with a ceiling of multitudinous crisscrossing metal grates that served as walkways. The traffic was light. But the echo of footsteps above indicated that other nightly creatures prowled.

'Hey, lover boy.' It came from the shadows.

Some roborgs threw themselves at us. Offered us their mostly metal bodies. They flashed what little bits of skin they still had, a nipple on a breast of indeterminate sex. Hairless, but muscled like a gym body. I reckon a man. But a roborg is more machine than anything. Besides, we didn't have the downloadable drugs they wanted for the sex favors they were offering. We walked on without a second glance, without a word.

We reached the Flow, the largest river in Drome. It looked like chocolate milk, or diarrhoea when you weren't on Squidge. It was a silly name. The Flow. The water moved, but at a paralytic snail's pace. The wrappers, the rubbish, the bodies floating on the surface; they moved with the current slower than we were walking.

'So, where are we going?'

'My place, I suppose.'

His place. Dandy. A bit more Squidge, methinks. Maybe something else. *His* place. Whoever *he* is.

'Hey, what's your name?' I'd have to wait to find out.

Without warning, a mean looking pair a of rozzers rolled out from around a dark corner. Big and bold. No nonsense. The man cop was tattooed in the style of high rank among the police guild. Red and blue motley, the arms, neck and face. The woman cop was huge. Seven feet tall, no joke. She was pretty, but maybe that was the Squidge. Her hands could crush my skull. She was all muscle. The cops before us were elite crime killers. And they weren't in a good mood.

'You.' She pointed to my companion. Her voice belonged to a bear. 'You with the sword. Drop that thing. Put your hands behind you head and knees to the ground.'

'Don't be a dead man,' the advice from the other. He was confident. In charge. 'Do as the lady says.'

Sword man was calm. Even easygoing, friendly. 'Some confusion about your request...'

'No funny shit. Drop it, fuck face.' Lady cop.

'Do it now.' Man cop.

'I shall,' my friend assured, 'but as it is sheathed and not currently in my hand, to drop it, I'd have to unsheathe it first. I will do this,' he reasoned, 'but I do not wish to receive several flying bullets for reaching for my blade.'

The cops looked at each other. 'This has got to be the guy. I mean, the sword alone is conviction.' 'No doubt. You saw what he did to the other guy, his leg?' 'I saw that *and* a street red with blood.' 'So I'm not getting anywhere near him. Not until he drops it.' 'Me neither.'

Then, to my friend, 'Unsheathe it, and drop it. Better yet, throw it into the Flow.' Even bold and badass crime killers, police elite, they still had a measure of fear for the guy with the sword. It wasn't like a cop to willingly ditch the murder weapon. Murder... if that guy ended up dead.

'As you command,' it was what he was hoping to hear. His movements were so quick I couldn't distinguish between start and finish. All I know, the sword was out and the cops barely avoided the assault. The swing chipped brick from over their ducking heads. A gun fired and bounced off the blade. The ricochet had been planned. The angle of the blade sent the bullet back into the flesh of the woman cop's thigh. She didn't seem to care. She growled and shot forward, picked up my friend and threw him. He collided with an erstwhile sleeping homeless man who had presently received the worst rude awakening of his life.

Then my friend's hand was on mine, tugging, and we were running. Gunfire woke the rabble that had crashed for the night on the curbside. In confusion, they stirred and rose. They unwittingly blocked the path for the rozzers hot on our heels. The icky vibes were fading the further the coppers trailed behind us. The buzz had been killed, but resuscitation is a miracle true to this world. I've seen it work on wasters that flatlined for several minutes. They crossed over, probably to hell, and maybe made a deal with the devil because some thud on the chest or a borrowed breath brought them back, blinking at the dim world like it was blinding them with some light that wasn't there, shook off the feeling and got back to it, fed their back-to-life systems more of whatever it was that had killed them in the first place. We could bring it back to life. Our buzz. With resuscitation. Or a bit more Squidge.

Sword guy read my mind. 'Here.' He squirted some of the yellow goo into his hands, rubbed my calves and thighs, a massage that now had me running faster than a cheetah with a firecracker up its ass. He amplified his own pegs. Lubed up, all shiny, in Squidge. His brand new sneakers, befouled in gore, my own old plastic boots, they were hammering 16 beat city-street-music, splashing puddles and angry car horns. Now we were flying.

But we didn't need to. Not with his equine construct to carry us. A brindled mare, she arrived as if summoned by magic. And shrouded in a veil of lilac mist, perhaps she was magic, or maybe the Squidge was fucking up my mind. I marveled at the artistry of her mechanics. Chrome skeletal frame, jagged metal ankles and planks of wood, circuitry and recycled or stolen organs, a digger bucket ribcage, slabs of syntho-meat injected with preservatives, some real meat too, but not a whole lot. She was a beauty.

With Bee, I mounted the pseudo-animal. We straddled the machine-beast of burden and rode off into the night. And the sound of clip-clop was a dandy one on the wet, ugly streets of Palindrome. We couldn't even hear the gunfire. We'd outclassed those cops that much.

Sword man had the reigns. I was sitting backseat, holding onto his hips. I stole a glance at the stars through the smog and smiled at a beautiful, ugly night. Breathed a satisfied breath of foul air and leaned into my man to drown out the stench. I took in his sweat, his musk, his long dark hair. The Squidge made it smell real nice. But you know something? I think it would smell nice even while sober.

3
SQUIDGE

His apartment wasn't half bad. And why should it have been? This guy had enough dough for a black magic seeing-sword, tainted with a bit of blue, no less. He had enough dosh to dunk his eye in the rejuvenation tanks, check into a five star while he waited for the job to be done. Enough coin to jingle loud sums with plenty to spare, even after that installation of high-tech bionic optic. This pretty little enigma that kills people on the streets and offers out Squidge to strangers like it isn't hard to get, isn't pricey... this fucker was loaded.

Poked out eye? No worries. Dunk it. Fork over what most people won't make in their lifetime. Bada bing bada boom. Oh, and you want it living, functioning, fused into your sword while still transmitting images to your brain? Not a problem. I'm on it, says the doc, the sorcerer, the bionic shaman. Just fork over, if you will, a sum that could change the lives of hundreds of refugees, or down-and-outs, or regular joes. Signed, sealed, delivered.

I'm the guy that started a conversation about my hip flask. Bragging about its green magic that replenishes thirteen percent of the contents. I'm the guy that saved up for a year while working at the Taco Nirvana and thought I was hot shit for my little magic trick receptacle. So yeah... all that money, all that magic. I was next-level impressed.

The apartment wasn't as flash as you might expect. It was only on the third floor, for instance. You could still hear the city squabbles from the streets, the urban shrieks and moans, the car horns and automated adverts, the rats fucking in corners, squealing in delight. But the glass had an opacity filter that could make it all go away. Just blot out the city in whatever hue or shade struck a chord. And the furniture was new, or well taken care of. The smell was clean, a faint trace of eucalyptus or lemon. It was spacious and tidy. It was, by comparison to my own apartment, a Sultan's palace.

Okay, so it's a nice apartment. But what in the fuck was I doing here? I mean, if there is more Squidge on the menu then I am not complaining. Hell, I'm not complaining even if there isn't. I started this, after all. I initiated it. This wacko batshit evening. And for the first time since the last time I was on Squidge I wasn't bored to tears, morose, choking on all the future regrets that was my life to come, the tallied disappointments that was my life that had already passed, drowning, as it were, in malaise and contrition. But still… standing in this apartment, smelling that nice fresh eucalyptus or lemon, staring out onto a street of the Drome I'd never seen, it all had me wondering; why am I here?

And there was the thought to run. Turn tail and just too-da-loo. Walk away. And I could have, too. I was waiting while he was taking a shower. He was washing off the stink of Palindrome and the sweat of the mad dash running from those rabid rozzers. While he was sudding up with soap and washing out those long curly locks I could slip out the door. He probably wouldn't even miss me.

There's the door. Just walk through it. But I wouldn't. I couldn't. Intrigue is an element in my life about as common as kaleidoscopic skies or the pigs that fly through them. And man-oh-fucking-man, was I ever intrigued.

'Your turn,' he came out in a towel.

'Alright,' I wasn't going to say no to a scrub-a-dub-dub in a fancy shower. A rare chance to get truly clean. As I passed him I stole a glance at his perfect fitness, his many scars, his remarkable beauty.

So now I was washing up, shedding off all the shit and stink of the city of Drome, soap suds and pretty pink bubbles in a shower belonging to man whose name I still had no knowledge of. I laughed at the notion, discarded whatever awkward feelings came with the amusement of it all and just enjoyed it. I turned up the hot so the water with all its high pressure almost burned my skin. My own shower trickled a pathetic, tepid drip drop. So I was savoring that heat. I was soaking it in.

I came out of that little hotbox cleaner than I'd been in months. A warm, rainforest waft and the smell of soap followed me out of the bathroom. Still drying my hair, the instafood 'dinged' the moment I entered the room. I guess we'd be dining together. If this is a date, weirdest one I've ever been on. I took a seat and tucked into a burrito that was filled with genuine food. Instant or not, it gushed with goodness. Hardly a trace of syntho proteins or the chewy scraps of rat I was used to. Rat scrap and Drome Bowls, syntho steaks, and insta-dins, the unsold scraps at Taco Nirvana at the end of the shift. That was the usual fare.

'Damn, that was tasty.'

'It was alright,' he shrugged. 'You're the one with a drop of Squidge on your tongue.'

'Oh yeah,' I had forgotten. 'But even so, that was prime grub. No icky vibes.'

'Bit a Squidge for your digestion?'

'Absolutely.' He threw me a pack. I went hard, emptied half the tiny tube into my mouth and swished it around, gurgled, swallowed. I was left with chocolaty mint breath and a smile that flashed whiter than it ever had before. My mouth ulcers dwindled, shrunk back, stopped stinging. And as the goo crept down into my belly my bloat ebbed, my gas vaporized, and I was feeling light on my feet, giddy, quick to flash my brand new white smile.

My companion worked his own Squidge into his hands and fingers, combed them through his hair and left strands of lubricious locks looking like a mega-model's on a billboard for some shampoo ad. He pinched the remaining residue into his eyelashes and now he looked like some child's doll. Too beautiful to be real. He batted them and they sparkled. Even the code streaming down his bionic eye carried an alluring, liquid rhythm. I could get lost in those eyes.

'You know much about Squidge?' He asked me.

'Yeah,' I told him. 'I know that it's fucking fantastic.'

He chuckled, and began to wipe his blood-stained sneakers with yet another application of Squidge. He nodded in satisfaction as the mint condition, pearlescent white returned to his footwear. It was as if the slaughter had never occurred. Yeah right. Just tell that to those trigger-happy rozzers with their big guns and angry, tattooed scowls.

'Do you know where it comes from?'

'Squidge? Heaven, I suppose.'

'Heaven is a lie,' he declared. 'But if there was a heaven, Squidge would be prevalent within it. Do you have any notion regarding its source? What it actually is?'

'Love, perhaps, extracted from the purest of hearts? Virgin's tears? Stardust from the super nova of a giant ball of perfection?'

'Caterpillars.'

'Excuse me?'

'Caterpillars. Little wiggly worms, sleeves of goo, a walking mouth and stomach, a voracious eater, hatched from eggs and metamorphosing after stages of growth into moth or butterfly. Butterfly, in the case of

21

the species responsible for Squidge.'

'So… it's what? Something the caterpillars excrete?'

'It's simply them, the little wiggle worms, all squished. All squidged.'

'That's revolting.'

He shrugged. 'Meat is meat. You just had some in that burrito. But Squidge isn't just meat, it's a miracle.'

'Caterpillar guts…'

'Shall I take back that Squidge in your hand?'

'No!' I inadvertently raised my voice. Clung tight to the tiny tube, like a mother with a baby, safeguarding that which is precious. '*Ahem…* I mean, no. I do not mind. Caterpillar guts. Whatever. Squidge is Squidge. It could be anal gland excretion from a baboon, I'd still savor it.'

He smiled and nodded. 'Out of interest, did you know… caterpillars go through five instars before shrouding themselves in silk cocoons?'

'What the hell is an instar?'

'It's the stage between two phases of molting in the development of the larva.'

'Sorry?'

'Stages of development. Put simply; tiny worm, small worm, medium worm, big worm, very big worm. Five distinct stages.'

'Then it becomes a butterfly.'

'Or a moth. But yes. Quite right.' He poured a drink of brown booze and circled the rim of his glass with a Squidge-soaked finger. 'Whiskey?' He handed me the drink. Made himself one and took a long, lingering sip. 'The first instar, the tiny worm, the Squidge inside is at its highest potency. Really, at that early stage, it is something unfathomably miraculous. It could raise the dead, I am sure of it.' He got up, paced the room, 'Of course, at this stage the caterpillar is very, very small. What it has to offer is legendary, but it offers so little of it. With each advancing instar, or stage of development in the caterpillar, the volume of Squidge increases with the size of the creature... so too, its potency diminishes. By the time the caterpillar is in its fifth instar, you have a relatively weak potency of Squidge, but you have the largest volume on offer.'

I licked the rim of my glass. Took a ginger sip. Then a big-boy glug. I was heady with good feelings. Not a trace of icky vibes. 'Guy like you,' I ventured, 'made of money and all... what are you passing around? First or second instar?'

He laughed out loud. A good and long guffaw. 'Most of whatever Squidge you'll ever find on the streets is synthesized. Heavily synthesized. It's Squidge, but hardly. It's like a third cousin. A distant relative. It's taken from a fifth instar pupa and the result is a much greater quantity of a watered-down substance. Weak Squidge, if you will.'

'And that's *this* stuff?' I waved my little tube back and forth.

'That is a slightly upgraded version of what you'd typically find among the rabble of the Drome. But yeah. More or less. It's synthesized, bastardized caterpillar juice.'

'Fuck me... Imagine a trip on first instar Squidge.'

He became dark. Foreboding. His posture sagged, slumped, drew inward. 'Yes...' he upended his bevvy. 'There are miracles, and then there are miracles. And then there are curses, abhorrent transitions.' I had no idea what the hell he was on about. Half the time I didn't with this guy.

'I was on an expedition,' he suddenly changed the subject. 'I was a member of a team of prospectors. Mostly looking for potential mining sights on asteroids. Nickle, Iron, Ice. The usual stuff.' He poured himself another drink, a drop of Squidge and wedge of lemon. He made the same for me and I marveled at all the free drugs and drinks I'd scored in the past three or four hours. 'One day we were scoping out a dead planet. Eight Ball. It was the eighth planet in the solar system and it was almost entirely covered in black, barren rock. A colleague of mine — more than that if truth be told as we had been sharing a bed for the length of the expedition — left on a scouting patrol on his flying construct and came back with a miracle. He came back with Squidge.'

'Your coworker, the guy you were fucking, he discovered Squidge?'

'Avid Argyle.'

'Holy shit!' I nearly spat out my drink. 'You were lovers with Doctor Avid Argyle?!'

He put down his own drink. Got animated, then morose. 'He's not really a doctor. He just calls himself that. He was a mining prospector that found a few bugs. Some caterpillars that couldn't possibly survive among that bleak, lifeless wasteland, but did. As if a miracle. It was luck of the draw that he found them. It was luck of the draw that it was his turn for patrol. And in a way, I'm afraid to say it, all of our luck ran out that day.'

Again, I had no clue what this crazy guy was talking about. Then it hit me. *His lover?* 'Wait…' I hesitantly ventured. I was tiptoeing on eggshells with my words. I didn't want to piss him off. You know… lose any eyeballs, any legs. 'Was Avid Argyle, the world-famous scientist, the creator of Squidge… was he the guy that… the one who… your eye, your leg… was he the lovers' quarrel?'

His grim face, the silence that engulfed the room, it said it all. 'Come,' he ushered me across the room to a shelf full of books and scattered papers. 'Here,' he rifled through the shelves and found a sheath of papers bound with brass rings. He threw it on the table. Pulled out a chair and told me to sit. 'This entry will tell you of the expedition, the day, the moment the world had entered its next instar. The moment mankind came upon Squidge.'

24

So I begin to read.

4
FROM THE DIARIES OF
AVID ARGYLE (I)

The meadow was an anomaly. More than that, a miracle. For it to be there... that alone was strange. Yet strangeness such as would pale all other strange tidings before it was yet to come. But for now, the meadow, it being there... that alone was enough.

In the midst of desolation, an otherwise barren and seemingly endless stretch of sterile rock, the skeletal remains of a vast region bereft of life, here, a verdant carpet of purple heather and russet switchgrass flourished. It was startling to come upon. It was unnerving to witness. Not because it was an unwelcome sight, but because it made no sense. It defied nature. It raised questions about the condition of one's mind. It brought doubts to one's sanity.

Strange enough was the fact that I stood on the edge of a meadow. Not for that mere fact alone, but for where I was, a planet called Eight Ball, a scorched, ruinous wasteland where meadows like this simply could not exist. A dead zone of insurmountable acreage. An impoverished landscape, unbroken, unending, free of even the slightest of variation. Strange enough was this impossible pocket of isolated grassland, a living, fertile thing. But stranger still was when the heather and switchgrass came alive, dancing in a wind that was not there.

Like blades of grass, leaves of weeds, that are bombarded by raindrops; the initial dip with contact, the spring back upward, bent and stooped then erect once more. Repeat. Again, again. A yo-yo motion of up and down. The heather looked almost antsy, nervous. The switchgrass, over caffeinated.

Yet not the gentlest of gentle winds to stir even the fine hairs upon the back of my hand. No rain to speak of. No reason, whatsoever, for these blades of grass to bob and fidget like toddlers holding in the contents of their full bladders.

Or so it seemed at first.

When I dismounted from my avian construct, a vulture, more or less, compiled by recycled metal parts of machines, motors, pistons, gears and spokes, coils and springs and pliable well-greased sheets from this and that, I walked gingerly towards the moving vegetation. I marveled at its unexplainable pulse. It breathed, or seemed to. Again, I likened it to the shoots of grass in a meadow under the frequent tinkling of rain. Again, looking to the sky, I noted an atmosphere devoid of precipitation. Indeed, I looked into a blinding ball of white-orange flame that cooked the bare rock that was as if an immense ocean surrounding this small, inexplicable island of life.

Hazarding I knew not what — exposure to some soporific spore? Vibrating scorpions in an aggressive stance of territorial defence? A tiny, yet mischievous fairy with a malicious spell at the ready? — I crawled to my hands and knees to better observe the heather and switchgrass that defied the natural world.

And all at once the miracle of motion became simplistic. The stirring wonder, almost fear, of an unknown element became in an instant a thing of cogent explanation. Yet still I looked on with no small measure of fascination. The grass that did not move from a wind that was not there moved instead, with authority, by the vigorous contortions of hanging pupae. From within their sleeping bag sacks of garishly decorative chrysalises, whatever unknown species lay within wiggled in spastic thrusts and jerks. In what

27

was perhaps the late stage of its metamorphosis it had become agitated. Or so it seemed to me, no entomologist, while gazing from down on my hands and knees.

The miraculous element to this whole episode still holds firm. While the mystery of the grass that moves is well behind us, solved in a rather logical manner, the great riddle of the grass being there in the first place remains very much unanswered. It edges on the impossible. And not just grass, but some caterpillars or moths or worms that pulsate like corn kernels on a hot skillet. It was hot enough, I'll give them that. But why the fevered wriggling? Why — and how — are these aberrations here at all?

I collected a pupa from a stalk of heather. I did so with the utmost delicacy. I did not know what I was dealing with. And besides, I am benevolent to all living things. Except mosquitoes. Those, I crushed or swatted on sight. And sometimes ants, if they caught the trail of sickly fruit smears on the kitchen counter or grains of sugar cast upon the tiled floor. Still, it can be assured, I am a benevolent man… in most cases. In others, I'll admit, I am rather far from. Perhaps I should withdraw the original claim. But still, more often than not… I am a benevolent man. Ahem. And so I handled the pupa, exacted its removal, with surgical care. First one, then two, then perhaps a dozen or more. I cradled them in my cupped hands and looked down upon my collection.

It is likely I had been distracted by the concentration required of their delicate removal, for I had yet become aware until this instant; the pupae, the dozen or so chrysalises I carried… they were beyond the standard notion of beauty. They gleamed with off-the-charts magnificence. Spread out between my fingers were many dazzling baubles of uncanny glamour.

Metallic magenta with streaks of parrot green, almost luminescent. Gold and bronze bands, rivers of precious metals, outlined so finely one had to look close to notice the purest of black edging. The horizontal bars

28

encircled that plump protective sack that nurtured whatever life within, an arrangement of complex intervals that repeated a series of three times. Towards both far ends of the pupa, stamped in brilliance, a circle of peacock blue haloed within by a mesmerizing icing-on-the-cake of canary cream.

Whilst mounting my avian construct, the vulture-like, scrap-metal condor reared its rusted head and wailed a piteous moan of discomfort or dissatisfaction or both. It did this every time I mounted. It did this all the time. With or without reason, who is to say? Though the way it chugs and sputters black plumes of exhaust and coughs and wines in heaving, hot breathes of laborious dismay, I would venture its wailing was a product of discomfort first, and dissatisfaction as a result of the former.

Quite frankly, I did not care. Or did, but only with concern that the damned machine would run. That the beast would fly. Like the man who turns the keys in the ignition and listens to the woes of an antiquated car gag like an old man's perverse, breathy laughter. Such was my own predicament that moved me to care. Two, three attempts. Four. Five. And she sputters to life!

Transportation should never be a fickle thing. Least of all while situated deep within the boundaries of a barren expanse of scalding basalt. Plastic soles, my footwear would not survive the journey. Much more to the point, neither would I.

I leaned forward to stroke the bare patch of exposed soft flesh that was not yet sheathed in metallic husk. One of the few signs that my avian construct bore living parts, an exposed, pink tissue that drooped and sagged, sandwiched between metal plating. I lovingly caressed its rough, wrinkled underbelly. This was reward for not leaving me stranded to die as a result of an ineptitude to fly. The sentiment was offered sincerely. And the perverted compilation of parts that was the sum of the bird-like-thing that I rode upon crooned in a satisfied spill of sounds; one part cute, two parts revolting.

My forward motion to reach down and tickle the scabby portion of skin beneath my saddled thighs inadvertently crushed one or two of the pupae I had been carrying. The biological juices of pulverized worm trickled down my fingers in a river of yellow snot. I blanched and recoiled. Held my hands outward, extended, eventually wiping them free of the mucus by smearing the contents on the flank of my avian transportation.

The vulture's rigid, graceless motions smoothed out at once. A tight, aerodynamic posture was instantly adopted, employed for speed, and wings beat in long, artful flaps that made for a comfortable, well-paced ride. It's hideous crooning, those irksome, piteous moans, ceased. A shame to lose two pupae, I had thought at the time, not knowing that their destruction was the catalyst to my construct's instant upgrade.

The speed at which I now traveled, saddled comfortably on a beast that performed no wasted motions, all efficiency and grace, I found myself approaching our spacecraft well ahead of schedule. I docked and decontaminated, unloaded and reported. I presented my find to a team of fellow prospectors.

My teammate, my lover, Bee, was young and beautiful. 'Wha-wha-wha-wha-whawha-what wh-what did you f-f-find?' But he carried with every word a terrible stutter that left him sounding like a simpleton. A complete fool. This was not the case, my sweet, smart Honey Bee. But his impediment did make discourse tedious.

I put a finger to his lips to silence him. Soft lips that I preferred for kissing than for conversation. Yet in an instant that would change, not so much my desire for kissing, but for conversation, as unbeknownst to me my finger that rested upon Bee's lips withheld a trace of caterpillar goo. At once, and forever, Bee's stutter had vanished. He spoke with eloquence, with authority, his words like poetry. He was cured, instantly, of his impediment.

It was then that I had an inkling of what I had truly found. Not a strange and beautiful insect, a curious life form paradoxically living in a place that could not bear life. It was more than that. More than mere insect. I had found a miracle substance that mended any faults it came into proximity with. The gooey innards of a wiggly worm that probably created the impossible environment of heather and switchgrass in the first place. This of course then raised the old conundrum; what came first? The chicken or the egg? But I was sure of it. Without any doubt. These caterpillars, the miracle juice that is their strange biology... they — it — created that patch of life on the dead planet.

Dribble some on the lips of a man with a heavy stutter, a daunting speech impediment, he will be a world class orator, an opera singer of the finest calibre, a silver-tongued wordsmith. I had seen it myself. It worked on Bee. Spill some on an avian construct past its expiration, beyond its expected lifespan and it suddenly flies as if a peregrine falcon in the prime of its health.

Later, as I discovered with glee after crushing a plump cocoon and rubbing the expunged fluids along the shaft of my penis, I found it improved love making. Improved... ha! It turned sex into an erotic extravaganza that made me feel young again. Made me the best to be had. Made me a monster worthy of my name, Avid. Made Bee beg for more then plead to stop. Made me the king I always knew myself to be.

Squidge, I'll call it. And I'll keep it a secret. I'll keep it all to myself. I'll quit this prospecting gig and harvest more caterpillars. Eight Ball, a dead and unwanted world. No one will find that little patch of miracle. And when I come back, after I strip the heather and switchgrass of its population of critters, I will set that tiny utopia afire. The miracle will be mine. Patented. Sold. Under my authority. My control.

The day man found Squidge the world became anew, better. The day man found Squidge, man became god. That man's name is Avid Argyle.

5
KILLER BEES, ROSES, AND LILIES

'You're Bee.' It wasn't a question.

He spread his hands, a gesture of admission. 'Buzz buzz buzz.'

'And an apt name, I'd say.'

'How's that?'

'I've seen how you sting.'

He smiled. Sighed. Took up the papers and put them back on the shelf. 'And your own name?'

'How is it now,' I marveled, 'after so many hours, after so many drinks, so many indulgences of Squidge, a hand-in-hand nighttime stroll, a galloping high-speed chase down the streets, gunfire blazing in the backdrop, angry cops and clean showers and yummy burritos, a 101 course on Squidge, its origin, a detailed, personal account from the past… how is it *now* that we are exchanging names?'

'It's that kind of night.'

'And I didn't even mention the maimed man, skewered eyes and severed legs.'

'Or blood-stained shoes.'

'That's the least significant detail.'

'Not to me,' he said. 'I love those shoes.'

I had to laugh. This guy… Bee. He and all the substances that came with him had me buzzing. Buzz buzz buzz.

'So…' he said.

'So…' I echoed.

'Your name?'

'Oh,' I chuckled. I don't know why but I was hesitant to offer it up. Was I nervous? Shy? Scared? I think it was the little schoolgirl in me. The one I always knew was just beneath the skin, even if on the outside I was all… me. 'Jarred,' I told him.

His delight was no little thing. Bee's amusement was plain to see. His laughter was warm, satisfied. 'What is it?' I asked.

'Jarred,' he told me, 'is another name for rose.'

'Oh. My mother always told me it meant descent.'

'Names have many origins, many meanings.'

'Well, for my mother, the meaning of me is descent. A downward spiral. A toilet flush. And I think she may be right. I mean, sometimes I feel exactly like that little piece of flotsam circling the crapper. Me, the bit of shit. And Palindrome, the can.'

'For me, Jarred, your name means rose,' his eyes were sparkling with Squidge, dreamy like the cover of a romance novel. 'And roses, I'll have you know, are a favorite among bees.'

The man with the sword. Bee. The guy that dodges cops. Dismembers the odd passerby. The hard edge, badass, mean maniac. Now he shows me eloquence. His calm demeanor. His soft side.

Bee. Fuzzy and soft. Bee. Venomous and aggro. From one pretty flower to the next he flits, all grace, all elegance, and occasionally, when the mood strikes, he'll pause to sting, to kill, to destroy.

Then it hit me. An understanding of sorts. A realization. A strong supposition. 'The Bee and the Lily,' I declared. 'That's you, Bee. And Lily, she's your sister. Isn't she?'

Bee flashed a wink. 'Spot on, baby. Spot on.'

'So, she's not just the barmaid. You guys own it, run it together? Big bro and sissy sis?'

'Lily owns it, really. Me? I just frequent it.'

'It's a stellar joint. No icky vibes.'

'Drink?'

It was well into the night. My tank was full. 'Yeah, hit me.' Okay, so there's always room for more. The whiskey and the wedge of lemon, the single large cube that took up more than half of the glass, his signature drink. But then I remembered that Caribou Lou or Piña Colada, that topical, white sand beaches and palm trees in the sunset sort of drink. And now I watched him from behind the bar, doing this and that, concocting some sort of complex, fruity, surfs-up sort of bevvy.

'Hey, what is that?' I asked, happy with my simple whiskey and lemon. 'You had one of those earlier. It looks like a beach holiday sunset.'

'It is,' he assured me. 'And more. It is paradise and pleasure, passion in a glass. My very favorite cocktail.'

'What's it called?'

'A Killer Bee.'

And then I remembered I'd heard of those before. 'Well, of course it is!' We laughed and emptied our glasses. My head was just about spinning and morning was so close that I'd call it early rather than late. 'Hey, Bee. I just have to crash. Hit the hay and hit it hard.'

The gray hue gradually staining the cityscape before us advertised a new day. Just when the grays were budding into perky pinks and cheerful orange the opacity filters did there thing. Killed the new day. Bathed us in the comfort of shadows and a snooze-friendly gloom.

We shared the same bed. It was spacious. Probably a king. Heaps of room for outstretched arms and legs, shifts and shimmies without

34

disturbing your neighbor. It was nothing like my little twin mattress at home. The one thrown on the floor in the corner. The one with an ever growing tear, a great chasm of fluff, a wide open wound. This large and spotless mattress had none of the familiar stains, those various collections that showcased sweat, blood, food and semen. The foam was supportive, and it lacked that squeak when you moved, that sagging depression, a testament to decades of me passed out from my nightly attempt to escape the ugly world of Drome.

There was plenty of room for the both of us. There were inches or more between the end of my body and the beginning of Bees. But even as we lay there, faced away from each other, back to back, I sensed things getting borderline intimate. It was just a place to sleep, but still…

I thought of his bratty little sister, the bitch from the bar, and I touched myself a bit from under the sheets. She was all freckles and pigtails. Jailbait, but only by design. Faux youth. I mean, she was young, no doubt, but she wore that style with intent. That I'm-sixteen-and-I'm-wild look. That can-you-handle-my-teenage-mood-swings swagger. I'll tell you this; you don't own and run a bar if you're a kid. She was early twenties. Maybe twenty-five. But still, I loved that she looked like seventeen.

I turned over and was startled to see Bee already facing me. His bionic eye lit up the pillow with a soft, green glow. He stared into my eyes. 'Don't take this the wrong way,' I braced him, 'but your sister is a real cutey.'

He kissed me and I let him. I actually wasn't all that startled. I had felt it coming, and I was already hard thinking about Lily. So I rode that wave and just went with it. Got into it. Let Bee kiss me and kissed him back. I gave as much as I got.

It escalated, and soon we were running round all the bases. I'd rather it was his little sis. But I'd take him. I swing both ways. Nine times out of ten it's a girl, but from time to time a bloke sways me to romanticize, to want that other flavor. He wasn't half bad. His kissing. His deft hand. But that bionic eye was a little strange so close to my own natural ones. I focused on the living tissue of his other eye. I got lost in it. And we kissed some more.

◆ ◆ ◆

Palindrome's rooster heralded the new day, police sirens and car horns, broken bottles, slurs and curses. It wasn't really the new day. It was well into the arvo. Just about whiskey o'clock. But first; breakfast.

Bee was already up. He was frying up something that smelled like bliss, that would crank down the hangover to something manageable. I stretched and rubbed my eyes and got my ass out of bed. Before I was even dressed a third party came bursting into the room. All sass and spunk and sauce. All freckles and face piercings, fire-engine lips and an unapologetic sneer. Itsy bitsy cut-off jeans, an inch of ass, and long, long legs wrapped tight in neon fishnet. Sweet little sissy-sis. Welcome home.

'Who the fuck is he?' She didn't even look at me. Just sat down and ate what I think was meant for me.

'Don't be rude, Lily.' He tsk-tsk-tsked. 'Here, have mine.' Bee surrendered his own breakfast to me. I was looking down at a mountain of hash brown, some fried eggs and salsa. 'Thanks, babes.' I got busy with my plate.

'Filthy pig.'

'Bitch.'

'Stop it, you two,' Bee was stern but he was smiling too. He begin

36

frying up a new batch for himself. 'Lily, I'd like you to meet Jarred.' Lilly stuck a finger down her mouth, made a hideous noise. 'Jarred, I'd like you to meet Lily.' I smooched the air in her direction, big wet puckered lips, and winked. She made more retching noises.

Bee laughed, threw some hash on the skillet and sizzled it brown. Bloodied his plate with some salsa and slapped the overdone eggs on top. And we ate. One big, happy family. Not a bit dysfunctional.

'You know, you shit-for-brain morons really fucked up last night.' Lily said through a mouth of hash browns.

'How do you mean?' Bee asked.

'Yeah, how do you mean?' I did the same.

'Shut the fuck up, cheese dick.' Lily.

'Lily...' Bee.

'Whatever you two were up to last night, you brought two cops into my joint. You know how fucking *bad* that is for business?'

'Two flatfoots came busting into B and L?'

'Yeah, and they were red hot,' Lily told us. 'No "excuse me ma'am." No polite explanation. Just to-the-point, angry asshole no-nonsense. The size of that fucking woman! And those rozzer tatts sent my clientele packing. It's no good, Bee. You guys can't send that type of shit my way.'

'Sorry sis. I'm afraid that one's on me.'

'Oh great, did you kill someone again?'

'Undetermined.'

'But you cut him up good? Is that it? For fuck's sake. Don't tell me it was right outside The Bee.'

'Sorry, sis.'

'Well that just puts me in the perkiest of moods, doesn't it? Please, next time just dribble my tits straight into the blender.'

37

'Where's the blender?' I asked.

'And rid me of this scumbag shithole,' she shot me a withering look and I just smiled, lapping up all that sass that turned me on. She left the apartment in a real huff. A black, angry storm.

We finished our hash browns and hot salsa, our over fried eggs in silence. 'Come on,' Bee finally said after a long gap of sullen nothing. 'Let's go for a stroll.'

6
DAYTIME WALK

We had drenched our eyes, our noses, our ears. No stinting, we had squidged up each orifice real nice, real generous. We were seeing, hearing, breathing the best of the worst, because even the best in Palindrome is rotten. We had squidged up our calves, our knees, our feet for comfortable walking, ergonomic strides. Lubed them up, all shiny. Like a porpoise or a wad of phlegm.

I was getting used to the idea that Bee had no end of the stuff. It was an idea I was happy getting used to. He could paint the walls with it. Squidge. He could redecorate his home in pure pleasure. I watched him as he squidged his eyebrows. And why not? Such was his excess of that fine narcotic lubricant. And looking at him now, those brows, like two fuzzy caterpillars, like the little critters that Squidge comes from, they glistened in the gloom of another gray day in Drome.

We walked the humble streets hand in hand. His hand was so warm, my own like ice. I'd like to think this has no reflection on our dispositions, our characters. We disengaged our locked fingers to point at a holographic child chase a holographic ball across the street. His cyborg parents came rushing after him and winced when the taxi cab barrelled through their child made of light. We all sighed in relief when the moment of panic subsided and logic took its place. One of the benefits of holographic children....taxis can't kill them. One of the many,

I'd say. I reckon the food bill is right at the top of that list.

It was the answer to overpopulation. Digitized babies. At least that's what they say. I think it was just a scheme to sell product to the borgs, the bots, the mechanized sect. Now beings of circuitry, of software and metal plating, now they too could rejoice in parenthood. There was a void in the market and it was hastily filled. Now holo-kids were a dime a dozen. Common as piss puddles and sacks of crap. The streets were filled with digitized laughter. Hollow kids, most of us called them. That way we made the mean joke and got away with it at the same time. You could say it right to the parents' faces.

Above us, a lattice of metal grating zigzagged the somber sky. Pathways led from one dreary corner to the next, a transitioning network connecting countless cesspools, a cat's cradle of filth. Laid out before us, a grid of shadows, like an endless checkerboard or citywide scrap of graph paper. Footsteps echoed with the falling drops of moisture, yesterday's rain or today's vomit, and a rusted spiderweb of tetanus sprawled upward, outward, everywhere. Ahh… Nyvyn, you cheeky little saint.

'So did you *really* stutter all that badly?' I asked Bee as we dodged dead rats on a rubbish strewn street.

'Oh my god, Jarred. Like you wouldn't believe. Each sentence was a marathon of effort. I was like an android with a glitch.'

'You'd never know it,' I told him. And it was true. The way he spoke was streamlined, artful. His words, his diction, the nuance of applied timbre that came with each syllable. It was much like Avid had described in his diary: "a world-class orator, an opera singer of the finest calibre, a silver tongued wordsmith."

'I just can't believe a little bit of Squidge made such a big difference,' I marveled at the notion. 'I mean, just a teensy-weensy bit on Avid's finger pressed against your lip to silence you. But it didn't silence you. It silenced your stutter… forever.'

'Squidge isn't just *like* a miracle. It *is* a miracle.'

'Still… it's a tall tale. I'm having trouble believing it wholesale.'

'That day, back on planet Eight Ball with Avid. That Squidge… it wasn't like the type of goo you buy off the corner. It wasn't of the same grade you see shared among the destitute. It wasn't squeezed out from a little plastic packet, a synthesized product, a knockoff.' Bee stared out passed the metal grating, beyond the murk and smog. He had that distant, thousand mile stare. He was swimming in it; those icky vibes. 'The Squidge that took my lisp was third instar. Straight from the insect. No synthesization. No added elements. Nothing to water it down.'

'*Third* instar? Surely first.'

'No, Jarred,' Bee went dark, became withdrawn. His squidged up eyebrows furrowed a troubled expression. Then he took me by the shoulders and spoke in a hushed though impassioned tone. His fervency was startling. It was as if he were an enlightened conspiracist in a crowd of the zealously blind. He had wisdom to share but no one would listen. 'Just as I said before, Squidge isn't just *like* a miracle. It *is* a miracle. But I hesitate to call it that at all. A miracle.' His eyes, both flesh and bionic, took on a somewhat crazed aspect. The biological wide and desperate, the computerized streaming code at a frantic pace. 'How shall I put this?' He carried on, a mile a minute. 'The bastardized stuff that wasters employ for a good time, the watered down Squidge of the common layman, the type of Squidge we are using right now… while that may well and truly be a fraction of the miraculous, the further one climbs back down the instar ladder to the *truly* miraculous, the closer one also gets to something akin to ruin.' His grip on my shoulders strengthened. I winced at his digging fingers. 'Imagine fire. Its discovery.

41

This has elevated the caveman. It sends him projecting towards modern mankind. It is, in its discovery, miraculous. Fire!' Little flecks of spittle erupted with the force behind each word. 'Now imagine fire with its wild rage. Its capacity to devour, to decimate, to singe all before it leaving nothing but ash in its wake.' He was panting like a Labrador. 'Fire, its discovery, is everyday Squidge. It's a caveman's campfire that cooks his meat, warms him while he sleeps. Fire, when truly out of control, beyond hope of stopping, a sweeping grass fire or a ragging forest fire or a blistering asteroid heading towards the world... *this* is first instar Squidge. I have seen it.'

I blinked. I stared. The pure savagery of his conviction, this outpour of firm and rigorous belief; it had me startled and silenced. He released his grip and let me go. He became inward. Morose.

We walked on for a time in silence.

A gang of teens was all rowdy on the side. Half of them were making out, hands groping under shirts and skirts. A few were downright fucking. Others were throwing refuse at a parked tuk-tuk and a saddled animal tied to a post by its reigns. Old food and broken bottles struck the camel construct, a complicated working of fetid curtains of meat, woven rope and rubber haunches, outmoded circuitry and PVC pipe. The poor creature moaned but could do little else. When we walked through the crowd of youth the smarter ones got wind of Bee and read the signs well. They ushered others away, gave the signal to make nice, to stay quiet.

And still we walked on without sharing a word.

'Oh look,' I said to break the silence.

The street cleaners came by and killed a man again. AG. Automated Garbage. Can't tell the difference between a sack of rubbish and a sleeping man. The big machines just clean the street as they know how. Slow

42

but sure, steady as she goes. It happened once or twice a month. The red smear on the street brought a little color to the gray city of Drome.

Later, when the sun gives up on trying to cast some cheer down onto Palindrome, when the bright ball in the sky cashes in its chips, slim pickings, gives us all up for a lost cause and nighttime comes rolling around, then the city will come to life. Little red smears in the street won't be the single tally to denote life, or in this case, death. All sorts of colors, sensations come out of the metalwork and breathe a little life into the rusted husk that is Drome. Later, when the roborgs are peddling whatever inch or two of flesh they have left, when call boys and girls are throwing themselves at strangers under a warm wash of street lamp, all of us mulling it over, whether its worth it, that roulette wheel of good time or venereal misfortune, all under a barrage of neon script, heady music and shouting. Nighttime. The right time. The wrong time. Just another time, like all times in the Dome.

We wallowed in daytime. Hand in hand. Our feet trudging. Carried only by the Squidge all over our bodies. The icky vibes had us dragging our heels. The silent treatment was killing me slowly.

'Tell me something,' I finally said. My words came out like a breath of air I had been holding in for minutes, aching to exhale. 'How the hell are you so goddamned rich?'

We turned down a narrow alley with scraggly cats fishing in a dumpster. Someone was all nuzzled up, recumbent in the filth, so out of it from the night before that the cats didn't even disturb their sleep. 'We struck gold,' Bee told me. 'Back when I was a prospector.'

'You found a goldmine?'

'We found Squidge.'

'Oh, of course.' But I was still scratching my head. 'I've heard all about the famous Doctor Argyle...'

43

'He's not really a doctor.'

'...But I got to say, Bee, I've never come across a tale about a crazed bastard with his own living eye for an ornament in his sword.'

'It's not just an ornament.'

'My point is, I never took Doc Argyle for a charitable fellow. He doesn't seem like the sharing type. And, well... *he* found Squidge. Not you.'

'We were lovers.'

'Yeah, I've had my share of those, good and bad. But whatever the spectrum, from "can't wait" to "can't wait for this to be over," I've never felt obliged to forked over a portion of my Taco Nirvana wages. So, what? Were you and the Doc serious? Or were you just two prospectors contracted by the same outfit, stuck on the same ship, passing some time and having a little fun? I guess what I'm really asking you is if you are employed by Argyle. Are you like the, I don't know, *co-founder* of Squidge?'

Bee took in a long, deliberate breath. Personally, I don't know how he did it while keeping a straight face. The alleyway smelled so strongly of piss my eyes were on fire.

'When Avid found those caterpillars on Eight Ball he became a changed man. Like one instar to the next, he became something new, something different. His ultimate metamorphosis produced a man I could no longer claim to know. Too different. Too altered. Like a butterfly from a wiggling worm, only I'd not use that comparison as it paints him in colors too comely, too clean.'

'The change in Avid began as obsession. A zeroed in, unaltered focus, a fevered drive, to explore and study what he had found. His obsession only grew with time. It was tempered with greed, with secrecy, with experimentation.'

'Later, when the business aspect came to fruition. When 'Squidge' was patented, made weak, and sold to make millions of addicts and hundreds of millions of credits, Avid underwent further changes. For starters, his arrogance became overbearing. His egotism, rife. He was bloated with self-importance, saturated with hubris. It was brimming over the edge. It was actually revolting. But before it went rotten I was smitten. Smitten by the man that Avid once had been. And for full transparency, I'll admit it, I enjoyed the cash flow, the high-society living, the potent grade of Squidge on offer.'

'In the end, the change that repelled me the most was Avid's keen fascination of testing Squidge's limit. The over application of first instar caterpillar juice. It was only the squidge wing's limited population, the tiny size of the first instar worm, that held him back from doing something drastic. Which he did, in the end. Something drastic… ha! Something catastrophic!'

We turned another corner. We stared down another bleak street decorated with sad figures, bent heads, forlorn and bereft. 'This "something catastrophic,"' I chimed in. 'was this what led to your lovers' quarrel? The eye… the leg…'

'Aye.'

And despite the mood we laughed again at that bad, asinine joke.

'But to answer your question, Jarred; how the hell am I so god-damned rich? It is simple, really. It is merely the leech effect of living with and sleeping with a man who has such epic excess. In what was sort of seen as quasi partnership in the business I had been given my own accounts. It was gifted to me. I was in no way part of the business. Not really. Including my name on the payroll… call it Avid's great sugar daddy gesture to his young lover. It was just a really sizable bauble. Like a bone thrown to a dog. His bitch. But with a business empire like

Squidge, Argyle was throwing me a pretty fucking big bone. Let's just say I'll not need to worry about earning credits ever again. Nor need to spend wisely. I could spend like a fool for decades and I'd be safe by a fair margin. If nothing else, I still have *that* out of my relationship with Avid, if but one less eye and one less leg.'

'And even those you have, really,' I remarked. 'Even if some of them are stuck in new places.' I eyeballed his sword as I said it. It's the only sword I've ever known to eyeball me back.

'I certainly haven't lost everything.'

'So that "something catastrophic,"' I tested the waters. 'That lovers' quarrel of yours.' I pushed the boundaries. 'You want to shed some light on that one for me?' Curiosity killed the cat. Although the one we just passed looked more like it was thrown from a window.

'Not yet, Jarred.' Fair enough. It hasn't been twenty-four hours yet.

'But I can say one thing about it all,' he added after I thought the conversation was behind us.

'What's that?'

'I'm going to stop that megalomaniac, motherfucker. I'm going to take dog shit to his doorstep and make him eat it. I'm going to put out that fire he started, the one that may otherwise eat up the world. I'll snuff it, and him, out. I will stop him. I will…'

'STOP HIM!' It came from behind us. We turned our heads and looked at the meanest pair of rozzers you'd ever see glaring at us through the steam clouds coming out of their flared nostrils. Seven foot tall blonde bombshell, rippled with muscle. A tattooed checkerboard face of red and blue and a gun primed to turn us into Swiss cheese. Lady and man cop. Dynamic duo from the dimension of pain, police elite. 'DON'T MOVE A MUSCLE!'

So we ran like fucking hell.

7
DAYTIME RUN

The overcast sky sure looked like it was about to rain. But it wasn't the usual acid rain of Palindrome that showered down upon us. It was little lead pellets encased in copper jackets. Rozzer slugs with our names written on them. They were whizzing, screaming, banging by, those bullets. A horizontal rain, each droplet aimed for me and Bee's asses as we ran.

The lawmen weren't stinting. Trigger happy, and happy to pull the trigger, they weren't reading their magazines or counting the tally. Their police issued pieces were blessed with a replenishing douse of green magic, rejuvenation juju, courtesy of the military occult. Ammunition would be added to their clip at a rate almost as fast as the rounds were fired. Fifteen shots from those spell woven green guns and a fifteen round magazine may hold fourteen bullets. In other words; fire away! And that's what those cops were doing. Their trigger fingers will be aching tonight. Cause man, those projectiles... they were coming down on us just like rain.

Thank god our legs were lubed up in Squidge. We had done it for the ease of our walk, but we were needing it now for the breakneck jolt of our run. I turned a corner, real sharp, and felt the Squidge save me from what surely would have been a rolled ankle. My sneakers were pounding the 16 beat. The music of running for your life.

I dashed forward, doing my damnedest to keep up with Bee, who was flying like graceful getaway needs to be. Pellets whirred by my ear and ate through the wall in front of me. Through an explosion of pulverized brick and mortar, a cloud of confetti made from chipped-off building, I sprinted onward while dust and debris sprayed into my face. Lead balls, like tiny meteorites, chiseled away at the urban world around us. One hit a rat and the sickly thud and brief cry of surprised agony was a sound that encouraged me; just keep fucking running.

These were icky vibes at their worst. As far as you could get from fun. Those red-hot rozzers were rabid and go-get-em. And meanwhile, the bullets just kept on flying.

I stole a backward glance and wished I hadn't. That seven foot swimsuit model with biceps to spare, thighs like coliseum pillars; she was wearing her serious face and was closing the gap between us. And I thought *I* was moving fast. Just behind her, a mosaic of blue and red angry face, top cop, the head honcho. He was fiddling with his gun while he ran, tweaking or tinkering. And it didn't take long to realize what he was doing.

Incendiary rounds. Each projectile, the hundreds of them, now carried a trailing cloak of flame before exploding on impact. Dark corners lit up to reveal hidden dimensions of filth. Scorched curbside and city structure charred black and steaming. One bullet whizzed so close to my ear I heard it singing its fiery song as it passed. I smelled the singe of my hair. Another bullet flew over my shoulder and hit a hobo between the legs. I've heard the term "fire crotch" before, but this was fucking ridiculous. If he lives, no chance of kids. Maybe that's for the best.

Now I was jumping hurdles over sacks of trash, complacent rats, and dead dogs. Bee was flying like an angel, way ahead. I was happy for him but unhappy he'd left me behind. I could hear the laboured breathing of that beast woman behind me. All eighty-four inches of her gorgeous bulk. Even the Squidge couldn't save me now. I was done for.

Then all that speed came to a sudden, screeching halt. Her alternating red and blue lacquered fingernails on the tips of long fingers from mammoth hands gripped around my shoulders and the rest was history. Her iron grip was herculean. Her strength, mythical. And now boss man was coming to join the fray. Gun in hand and teeth bared, a yellow streak to divide a square-jawed blue and red chessboard face.

I'll say it again. I was done for. Finished.

Then Bee flipped the script right onto its fucking head. Put a spanner in the works. Put a whole toolbox in for good measure. Hell, now he was adding a kitchen sink just cause no one ever does; it's always everything but. And just like true heroics his actions happened all at the very last second. Just when that iron vice was starting to grind the cartilage right off of my bones, when those pretty painted fingers started to dig mischief into my threshold for pain, there he was.

And good god, what a sight. What a dreadful, horrific thing to face. What a fantastic thing to have come to your aid. That gleam in his good eye that spoke promises of pain. That cascading code in his bionic optic that let you know he was seeing it all with mathematical precision. His third eye, wide open, guiding the arms and wrists and hands just so, deflecting oncoming projectiles of flame, providing sight coming from a wielded instrument of death, a monolithic cleaver. A seeing-sword. Bear *Witness*; Jarred's rescue.

His calm yet murderous focus, that well disciplined rage, his intent to maim, all of it amplified by thick applications of enhancing narcotic... he came at us as fast as those fiery balls came at him. Well placed shots from Top Cop, but not well enough. Precise and oh-so-deft, subtle movements of footwork and body contortions left Bee free from bullets. And now he ate up all that distance. He was on us. And I was free.

The lady cop let go of me in an instant, and met fire with fire. She sidestepped a downward swing that would have otherwise cloven her neatly in two. She lowered her silver bomber shades and revealed a pair of wild eyes, enhanced by magic or drugs or both. They swirled and roiled, as if mercurial pools disturbed by movements under their surface. She was probably seeing in any way she damn well pleased. X-ray vision, ultra violet, slow fucking motion. Take your pick. But however she was viewing the world, she assessed a threat in Bee and she did her damnedest to take him out.

She slipped on a pair of iron knuckles and was now freely deflecting Bee's furious attacks with his blade. Top Cop came to Big Girl's aid and showered some more flame out onto the urban stage. Bee was dipping and ducking, darting and jumping like only ninjas or freaks can leap. Running up walls and back flips. Low crouches and splits that would leave me in the hospital if I tried to do the same. He was a ballerina. A gymnast. A kung fu monkey.

But then he took one square in the face. A knee from She Beast. It had him spitting blood and howling but then suddenly he was smiling, laughing. I hadn't noticed before. He took a knee in the face, but she took two feet of sword through a shoulder. She looked at the blood seeping out like it was a nuisance, an irksome condition. She grabbed Bee by the shirt and pulled him into a headbutt. He was on hands and knees. His world, no doubt, was spinning.

So I picked up some pieces of bricks and started throwing. Re-enacting my days of youth, playing catch in the alley with my pops. You know, those rare weekends when he wasn't down and out, wasted on this and that. I was giving those cops my fastball. Not aiming for strikes but aiming for the batter. One nasty piece of chipped brick hit

50

Lady Cop right on the nape of her neck. She turned around with those splish-splash eyes and gave me a look that withered my spirits. That glare practically neutered me on the spot. But what else could I do? So I threw some more.

Man Cop shot them each. *Bang! Bang! Bang!* Right out of midair. Then he trained his pistol on me and... *click.* Guess those magical bullets just ran their course. Didn't stop me from standing in a puddle of my own piss, dark tally down my trousers. Now wasn't the time for embarrassment.

All that brick throwing and rozzer rage and pissing in my pants bought Bee enough time to find his footing. He pranced to his feet and kicked up a puddle of oil-slick water into Big Girl's face. She took it like a champ. Hardly even blinked. But we didn't see what she did next. Once again, we were running.

Bee plunged into pockets and took out fistfuls of Squidge. He shoved some at me. 'Where?' I asked him.

'Everywhere!'

So we ran and Squidged wherever we could. Legs and feet for speed. Hands for agility, to better push away the roborgs or beggars that stumbled into our path. We were Squidging so hard we were laughing, loving life, even while in the midst of this dire crisis that threatened to end it.

We turned a corner and barreled through a holo-kid. We ran right through her. She, made of light. Incorporeal. Bullets passed through her too. Just passed my face. I guess those flatfoots found their footing, flat out running, back on the chase. The hunt was on.

Then we heard it through a break in the gunfire. A ghostly, haunting whistling. Constable voodoo. Police magic. Cop whistles laced in purple enchantments, the sound waves summoning beings long out of earshot, miles away, sometimes from different dimensions altogether. What awaited us… what was coming… it didn't bear any fucking thought. Run. Just run.

But running wouldn't help us any longer. Not a chance. I saw what had now arrived to stand by those fearsome gumshoes to assist them in our capture. Constructs of menacing demeanor. His and hers. Top Cop saddled a monitor lizard festooned in armored scales and tattered hide. Its neck frill was corrugated iron. Its talons, flagpoles whittled into spears. She Beast now sat upon the bulk of a heavyset tapir. It was all muscle and meat and bristles. It looked more animal than machine, and smelled it too, but its dead eyes indicated no actual life. It probably had recently deceased, kept animated by black necrotic magic and marginally fresh by rejuvenating green.

Looking at the pair of cold blooded cops astride their beasts of burden, mean eyes and promises of torment, my morale was at an all-time low. I was wading, sinking, drowning, in thick icky vibes. And then a sound turned my head to a sight that turned my mood. Bee, with a silver flute at his lips, played a whimsical melody that carried purple notes on the wind, across the cityscape, to find the ears of a brindled mare, an equine construct of swift and sure stride. Shrouded in a plume of lavender hues, she clip-clopped like an arrow to our side. Summoning magic. Add *that* to Bee's repertoire of odd quirks and fine abilities.

And while that monitor lizard had talons that could tear us to bits, teeth that could dismember us, a tail that could leave red lashes of open gore with each whip upon our bodies, it shall never get the chance to do so. And while that tapir, strong as an ox, could trample us into flat stamps upon the pavement, could break our bones into a shattered constellation of calcium fragments, could kick us across the city and leave us little more than bloodied lumps of dead flesh, it shall not have the means to do so. For while both lizard and tapir are impressive and deadly, when it comes to speed, they are second rate, nothing compared to a horse.

Mounted upon a machine-beast of burden, we galloped off smiling. Both of us holding our arms high above us, four erect middle fingers silhouetted in the late afternoon sky.

8
FROM THE DIARIES OF AVID ARGYLE (II)

When we got back to Bee's we did what we do. We washed off the stink of running from cops. Except this time we skipped the polite formalities. We shared the shower. Saved some water. Pressed our porpoise-slick bodies up against each other. Rubbing with suds. Squeaky clean.

Bee told me to make myself at home. Have a drink. A whiskey. A Killer Bee. Rub in some Squidge. Go nuts. Have fun.

It suddenly dawned on me that coming back to Bee's joint was about a smart as coating yourself in honey and getting frisky with a mean old mama bear. The law was sure to come crashing down upon us. And when it did, it would come with a whole lot of pain. I looked to the door, expected it to be broken down by two rabid cops any moment.

'Should we be here right now?' I asked Bee. 'Aren't you worried those rozzers will be showing their ugly, tattooed faces any second?'

He waved his hand, all casual. He dismissed my concern. 'I've got a dozen places scattered around town, nearly one in each rotten borough. I buy under false identity. False faces.'

'False faces?'

'I'm chummy with a shape shifter. Makes dirty dealings a whole lot cleaner.'

At some point I'll stop getting surprised, but I sure as hell wasn't there yet.'A *shifter*? Fuck, that's cool. I've never met a shifter.'

Bee looked at me and smiled.'That's the thing, Jarred. You probably have.'

He left to go check in on Lily. Little sis. He was worried about the bar. The Bee and the Lily. He was worked up thinking that those coppers might bust the joint, disperse the drunks. Stop the cash flow for his sister's biz. So he buzzed off.

I poured myself a vodka, threw in some olives, a splash of vermouth and one of those big old cubes Bee liked to dip in the drink. I kicked up my heels. Grabbed Doc Argyle's memoir, and had myself a wee read.

I excitedly awaited the arrival of the first butterfly. If the caterpillars are little wiggling parcels of miracle juice, what would their final form entail? My expectations were lofty. In truth, they had no bounds. So, needless to say, I was beyond disappointed when I found the adult butterfly, the "Squidge Wing," was utterly worthless. And while rather pretty to behold, of no use whatsoever.

I experimented, of course. I tried eating them. I tried crushing them into my flesh where I had dry skin or scabs or fungus. My ailments remained. I tried first removing, collecting, compiling the dust from many squidge wings until I had formed a substantial mound of metallic magenta. Pixie dust. I sniffed the stuff and achieved nothing but an excess of sneezing for the remainder of the day.

In the end I gave up on the mature butterfly form of the squidge wing. I only kept them around, tolerated their existence, for breeding purposes. For their egg laying. Those minuscule, precious orbs from which the miracle worms wiggled forth.

At first I was only using Squidge from the final, largest stage of development in the caterpillar. Its fifth instar. My thought process dictated that the worm was larger, a sack of greater size to carry greater contents, more narcotic gore. I was particularly interesting in enhancing sexual pleasures, performance, and prowess. I was delighted, you may imagine, to discover that Squidge, when applied in the form of mist and focused primarily on the erogenous zones, acted as a rather potent aphrodisiac. I often strolled around that cramped ship turning heads. My ears, lips, neck, nipples, thighs and cock slick with caterpillar mist.

Our captain, Liara Shepard, a half human, half bionic, holographically enhanced woman of enticing charms was particularly swayed by the allure of the Squidge-mist that decorated my hot spots. I had been sharing a bed with the young, no-longer-stuttering, beautiful buffoon, sweet honey Bee, and had no interest at all in women. Yet even so, I used Liara's intoxication, her fevered desires to devour me, to satiate her lusts upon my Squidge-soaked form, for further analysis. To test the waters. To see just how strong this little love potion really was.

And oh, the things she was willing to do! The many adventurous activities that went well beyond the boundaries of common decency that she willingly, joyfully partook in. Just a hint of suggestion and the deed was done. Whatever it may have been. I, myself, was ashamed by the end of it. Liara? It was only many days later, when the aphrodisiac dwindled to nothing, that her own shame entered into it. Like an avalanche. I had guessed the memories were hitting her hard. Knew that they were when her routine vomiting, shower taking, became excessive, obsessive. Poor woman. Well... all in the name of science!

In a matter of weeks since the discovery of the squidge wing butterfly and its much more remarkable larval form, I had determined that applications of Squidge enhanced areas where applied. In cases of injury, it worked miracles of healing. Closing fresh wounds, knitting broken bones, warding off fungus and sores. In the case of illness it was as if a strong tonic. A health booster. A 'cure-all' at best or a 'aid-all' at worst. It did so many things, had so many uses, but all cases underwent what I would more or less determine to be an enhancing effect.

This same enhancing effect extended to inanimate, non-living things. After hours of tinkering with the ship's corrupted star-hop, half a day of hold-your-breath, deft and subtle tweaks of circuitry, all to no avail, no solution to the problem, I threw my tools in frustration and moaned curses to my drunken shipmate who had spilled his Killer Bee into the vents that led to the heart of the complex machine. Bee had been giving lessons on concoctions of tropical cocktails and the result was a lot of the fruit rations running low and bumbling idiots half drunk or fully inebriated while on the job. In the end, in experimental frustration, I squeezed a caterpillar into the crux of the problem and the sizzling circuitry suddenly hummed a low drone of well-working machine.

From the infinitely complex, such as warp drives for faster-than-light interstellar travel, or the ever simplistic, a mechanical pencil or a coffee grinder, the Squidge would fix any existing issues. Bring faulty gadgets back to factory setting, broken appliances back to mint condition. For man and machine alike, Squidge was a fixer upper in all aspects, to all degrees.

But in most cases it seemed to wear off. Particularly in the case of man. While that patched up mechanical pencil may remain fixed until some future mishap happens to break it again, on the other hand, the removed fungus between toes, the departure to that bad case of dandruff, increased sexual prowess or how it thickens that thinning patch of hair above my forehead, those cures or enhancements seem to fade over time. Like a buzz from a case of beers or the dulling of pain from some opioids... the effect would fade, diminish, and eventually disappear altogether.

And then there is the case of Bee and his oh-so-terrible stuttering prob-
lem. How it just vanished. The most minute of applications. And thus far,
many weeks at this stage, he still speaks as eloquently as a practiced politi-
cian, but without all the lies and obvious, intentional misdirection. If or
when his stuttering will return, who's to say? But it had me thinking. The
whole scenario. And it led to my most recent discovery.

I have now determined that each subsequent stage in the developmental
process of the squidge wing larvae, each advancing instar, weakens the po-
tency of the Squidge within the creature. This is an important discovery, but
also a sad one, or in any event, bittersweet. While I now know that the max
potency can be targeted in a simple way, a potency I have yet experienced or
witnessed, I also am faced with the disappointment of realization that max
potency comes in tiny, tiny packages. The first developmental stage in the
larvae. First instar Squidge.

In the case of Bee's stuttering, its complete and utter disappearance, I
would postulate that whatever residue from my finger touched his lips — the
same residue that enhanced the performance of my avian construct — was
Squidge from a fourth or third instar pupa. Postulation, but firm conviction
that it is correct.

In any case, I certainly look forward to exploring the effects of max po-
tency Squidge. Now that the star-hop is online again it will become possible
for our crew to move on, one step closer to voyage's end. I am most eager to
return home. To exploring the benefits, the many miracles of Squidge, not
aboard a cramped space-bound vessel, but on terra firma. The real world.

It shall be, I postulate, a lot of fun.

9
AZALEA REN

I dropped Doc Argyle's manuscript when the door burst inward. Real loud. Real forceful. Heavy breathing and hurried footsteps. Turning to anticipate some home invasion, maybe some smash-and-grab hooligans or a rozzer raid, I saw, instead, little sissy Lily. Her and some other character that had my eyebrows up and all who-in-the-hell-is-that?

'Oh my good fucking *god.*' Lily slammed the door.

'That was batshit manic.' The stranger.

'Totally fucked. Just — I can't even — seriously, just throw some Squidge at me. Right now. And a big drink of whatever is closest.'

'Coming right up, babes.' They hadn't noticed me watching, all quiet and recumbent, slouched and half hidden behind the back of the sofa. Lily was all slick with sweat. From all that heavy breathing, I'd guess she had been running. Her hair was wild, even while in pigtails. Complete disarray. That, and all the shiny sweat she was wearing, the semi see-through tank top, the flushed checks; I put a pillow over my legs and crossed them, nipping what was growing in the bud.

I turned my attention to the stranger. A curious fellow. Gracefully, hypnotically, he moved his hands and took artful strides, light on his feet, making first a plain Jane vodka, neat, but then took on the complexity of a Killer Bee, with all of its ingredients, its steps and measurements, each movement a deft performance of perfected poise. He topped it off with a wedge of lime, of kiwifruit, and a twist of cracked black pepper. He raised the sunshine amber glass to his lips, almost as if in slow motion, and sipped a long and meaningful intake of what may have been the finest tropical cocktail to ever enter this world.

In mid-sip his eyes met mine. Me, concealed behind the couch and cushions. His surprise at seeing me came out not in the form of wide eyes or spat up Killer Bee cocktail. Instead, his well-tanned face flickered, a microsecond or two, to luminescent hues of porcelain white. Then back to normal, well-tanned, or perhaps even tanner than before. My own face probably looked like a holo-kid who had been run over by a bus. The shock was there, the surprise, the fear, but knowing seconds later that it ain't no big thing.

'You've got a stowaway,' the stranger said to Lily, gesturing to me with a head tilt.

Lily looked over. Rolled her eyes. Downed her vodka. Showed me the interesting, electric blue color of her lacquered nail on one extended middle finger. Then suddenly went soft, kind of nice, and came over to sit on the couch beside my own. Guess that vodka hit her tummy really warm and pleasant. The lioness retracted her claws, squidged her lips and they went all glossy, perky, pretty, pink.

'So what the fuck are *you* doing here?' She asked me, only mildly venomous.

'Bee and I had a run-in with the law, some elite red and blue.'

'Yeah, no shit!' Some of that fire was flaring back up. 'Those pork fuck bobby bastards came into the BL, guns out and gingham tattoos rubbed up into other people's faces, my patrons, asking this and that and not being gentle about it. Being downright hostile pig pricks.'

'They were looking for Bee,' the stranger said, suddenly standing behind me. He was leaning into the sofa, hands on either side of my head, propping himself up at an angle. He was relaxed, but totally in my personal bubble. I kind of liked it but kind of felt intimidated. Arching back my head to look up at him looking right down at me, one eye winked, then both eyes went green, then blue, then brown.

'This is Ren,' Lily told me, and then told Ren to take a seat. She patted the cushion beside her own. Ren walked over, opalescent bomber jacket with a big pink flower sewn into the back, white denim trousers as tight as a vice, pretty pink shoes, good looking pair of sneakers, not a splash of gore upon them. When he took a seat he plopped down with obvious intent and when his ass hit the cushions he was suddenly someone else. Boy turned girl, pigmentation jumped from dark to light, and that wild hair from running went smooth and straight, turned from black to copper, and then those winking eyes, like a slot machine of rapidly changing images, all colors of the rainbow. They settled on hazel. She smiled. 'I'm Azalea Ren. But everyone just calls me Ren.'

'Hi Ren,' I said and gulped. Now looking at two girls that made me flicker through all sorts of sexual fantasies and would-ifs. Ren turned back to a boy, but left the copper hairdo, the hazel eyes. He/she put an arm around Lily and the two kissed like there was no tomorrow, like I wasn't watching them right there with a cushion over my crossed legs.

Azalea Ren. A Shifter. Sexless. Interchangeable. A condition sometimes found among the mutated destitute who have grown up or have spent too much time in the heavily irradiated slums of Drome's west end. Chameleonic, able to take on different shapes, sizes, colors; Ren could transmogrify at will. All in all, much luckier than the mutations that more commonly result in extra or missing limbs, blindness, cancer, or brain decay. Manipulating form, interchanging faces, bodies, size, a never ending menu of flavor-of-the-day, or hour, or minute, or bloody fucking second. All in all, pretty damned cool.

'So, those madhouse flatfoots came busting into the B?' I asked.

'Busted in and busted up. My patrons were out the door, the ones that didn't get the bad cop, bad cop interrogation.'

'It was a rather fine slice of bedlam,' Ren contested.

'A rank fucking slice!' Lily fumed.

'We'd been running from those ragging rozzers earlier today. This afternoon,' I told them. 'Mean looking constructs, summoned with lilac copper whistles, lizards and tapirs, five million fucking bullets, most of those on fire.'

'How'd you live?'

'Bee,' I told them.

'Bless the Bee,' said Ren.

'Bless his beautiful hide,' I concurred.

'So where the hell is he?' Lily queried.

And on cue, like he'd been waiting at the door for his moment on stage, sweet Bee came in on long strides of here-I-am! And we all said it at once from down on the couches, 'Bee!'

He flashed us a wink but walked right by us. Straight to the window. He had a peek, did a wee scan, nodded and strolled on over to join us. 'Kill the windows,' he signalled to Lily. She punched a button on the side table, toggled with the settings, and the ugly view of an ugly street in an ugly skyline vanished in a curtain of the purest of black ink. Transparency, nil. Opacity, full blast.

'So like, what the fuck, Bee?' Lily was well worked up. Wanted the deets real bad.

'Just a minute,' he held up a hand for silence, to ward away anymore would-be questions, exasperations. 'Before we get right into it, I'll be needing one of those.' He pointed at Ren's half-drunk killer bee. 'Would ya, Ren?'

'I'm on it.' And he was. In a jiff he was up off the couch and in the kitchen, doing the whole concoction thing all over again. He made it look like poetry. Like dance. Ren had the moves when it came to making cocktails. When it came to sunshine in a cup and wedges of tasty fruit.

'Little crack of black pepper… and *voilà*.'

'Cheers, Ren.' *Bee got busy with his drink, took in all that passion fruit and rum, crunched down on those big ice cubes, pulverized shards making loud noises of crunch between merciless molars. He took the wedges of fruit, lime rind and all, and just gobbled the things up. Like a cocktail monster, he devoured his killer bee.*

'Squidge,' *he held out a hand to Lily and then he was holding two packets. Bee tore them open at the corners and just squeezed them till his hands were slick with slime, then rubbed all that caterpillar shit into his eyes, nose, mouth and hair. Sniffed up some dribbles through his nostrils, inhaled some to coat the lungs, breathe the breath of life. Then he ground his teeth, rode out the moment of maybe-that-was-too-much and howled in exaltation. Bee got himself in the mood. He was in his happy place. Drunk on drugs and drink, insect gore and tropical punch. The icky vibes were way at the back of the bus, long forgotten.*

'So…' *he let that hang in the air. We exchanged glances, the four of us. Looking to Bee, the leader of the pack, and also to each other. Apart from me, who had been reading Doc Argyle's memoirs, the rest of us had come in from some heavy action. Cop raids and chase scenes. Today had been a wild ride of what-the-fuck. So what now? What were we going to do?'*

'So what now?' *Lily asked.* 'What are we going to do?'

Bee stared into his empty glass, probably wishing it was full. He set it down and sighed. 'Well, I can't be running from cops every time I leave my door.'

'And I can't run a bar when cops are up my ass every other happy hour.'

'And I can't be dating a girl who's a nervous wreck,' Ren playfully nudged Lily.

There was a brief void in the conversation and the three of them all looked my way. I guess it was my turn. 'Yeah,' I stumbled for words, 'and I can't afford to miss another shift at Taco Nirvana or I just may be out of a job. I've already missed two since meeting you lot.' They just stared at me. Like I was speaking encrypted Androidian or in ancient Nyvynese. 'Actually,' I added. 'Losing that job… might be a blessing in disguise.' They went on staring at me for a moment before each one broke their gaze. Subtle head shakes and perplexed or disgusted expressions were all around me.

'Well, one thing is damned clear.'

'What's that, Bee?'

'Those flatfoots have got to go,' he said without reservation, without room for anything less. 'I don't mind a little cat and mouse and running around town with bullets at my back… I can handle myself. But what I won't jeopardize, what I won't have those gung-ho gumshoes tamper with, is the smooth sailing of the bigger picture. The main objective.'

Huh. I thought. What's all this? Bigger picture? Main objective? I kept quiet, but put it all in my what-the-hell-was-that-all-about file within the old noggin.

'We've got to snuff them out,' Bee concluded.

'Hear! Hear!' Lily agreed.

'It won't be easy,' Ren lamented.

'Yeah,' I agreed. 'Look, I don't know about you, but that Bigfoot babe with the bomber shades and capital ass, she scares the hell out of me.'

'And that checkerboard, fuck face with all his red and blue gingham and yellow teeth; he's all guns in the face and bad attitude. And bad attitude… that's my department.'

64

'Amen, little Sis.'

'A-fucking-men.'

Presently, Ren transformed into a kind-faced, black skinned man of distinguished style. 'I've just the thing to get the job done.'

'What's that?' We all asked as one.

Now I was looking into the sly expression on the face of a matronly lady, all hips and tits, balancing a towering beehive hairdo of silvery-gray above her well-wrinkled forehead. 'Let's just say it's a nice, heady cocktail with a couple classic ingredients.'

Passion fruit and rum?

'A bit of bait to lure them in... and more than a pinch of ambush to knock them out flat.' Ren transmogrified into a fair semblance of the tattooed bull with the red and blue picnic table face. He mocked wrapping a noose around his own neck, pulled upwards and rolled his eyes into his head with a lolled out tongue. 'Bait and ambush, the perfect cocktail.'

Bee grinned with a glint of Squidge shining from a mischievous eye. 'Well, it's never been in any doubt, Ren. When it comes to cocktails, you make the best.'

Then Azalea Ren turned back into himself. And he gave us the deets.

10
BAIT AND AMBUSH

I was looking over at Bee. Doing the head to toe. And man alive! Was he a beauty! Tall, erect posture. Alabaster skin tone, celestial nose, flanked by crystal blue jelly protein peeper, green glow of computerized eye. Long curlicue locks flowing downward, trickling, splashing between wide set, athletic shoulders, a black spiral waterfall ending at the small of his back. And then that ass. That perfect ass. Begging to be squeezed. But me, poised on the opposite side of the street, I'd make do by squeezing with my zeroed-in gaze. His legs, concealed behind a balance of high fashion and protective armor, defensive chic. But I know those naked legs. One warm and organic, pulsing with life, the other cold and silicone smooth, prosthetic mastery, a work of well-crafted art. I'd seen them. Felt them. Been straddled by them. Those glorious, long and shapely tennis player legs.

Taking in the Bee like that, his beauty, his prime, on point sex appeal... I was foaming at the mouth. Gnawing on my knuckles. Wishing I was somewhere private so I could release the tension. Unload. But here's the real batshit thing about it. I wasn't looking at Bee at all. I was drinking in the best ever pulled-off job of any look-alike contest there had ever been. The man I was undressing with my eyes... the man that most certainly *had* to be Bee, because, you know, it *was* Bee. Uh-uh. Nope. From across the street I was staring at the impeccable handiwork of irradiated, mutative talent. The work of a shifter. A freak. A bloody artist. I was looking at none other than the uncanny Azalea Ren.

His plan was a good one, a simple one. An age old trick that usually worked. And while I'd trust Bee or Ren with my life, I'd not trust Lily as far as I could throw a holo-kid. And me? Well, I knew my intentions, but I'm just a guy who works at Taco Nirvana. So keeping the plan simple, keeping it classic, not getting too cute with all the deets and nuance and whatnot, I reckon that was a good call.

In layman's terms, it was your basic bait and bash. Lure them in, a sweet piece of meat on the end of string. The *coup de grace*, an alleyway ambush. Ren would be the bait. The genetic corruption that lent to him potent powers of transmogrification made him perfect for the crucial role. To lure the blue and red while in the guise of Bee, weaving through crowds choked with the masses, changing form in the confusion of it all, when things get hot, when things get hairy, just when Top Cop and She Beast think they've got him they'll be looking through a trained gun at some fear-stricken lady, some teenage riffraff with a constellation of acne. They'll be looking at anyone but Bee. Then when they think they've lost him, that the fat lady has sung, then the fat lady stops singing and turns into Bee, makes himself a nice slice of bait all over again. Dancing, waving, dangling little scraps on a fish line, luring them in... until the real Bee pounces from the shadows. Does the deed and walks away.

Or so we assume the operation will go.

We left Ren to get the ball rolling. Me, Bee, and little sissy Lily walked hand in hand, Bee in the middle, down Ribald Row. The houses were all rust and rot, drip-drop acid rain and stained with smog. The roborgs were rife, suggestive and bawdy from open windows. Open legs to reveal a mess of something almost human, an aperture warm and wet. What else could you want?

We had taken Squidge. What else is new? We were slick with it. Slimy. And we were doused in confusion brew, a blessed or cursed or poisoned mixture made and sold by the witches who dwell where the Flow meets the Puddle, where its wide delta fans out to pollute the great brown bayou. Confusion brew is rarer than Squidge, but not half so much fun. Still, it aided the mission. It made each of us seem that we were something we were not. Slightly paler, taller, darker, wider, uglier, sexier, more simian, more reptilian, more arachnid than our actual, true selves. It was camouflage, in a sense, while remaining in plain sight. Through the occult narcotics of herbs and curses, an old crone's ancient craft, we had become completely, adequately incognito.

Ribald Row turned into the Drizzleway, the path before us now dotted with scabbed dogs and skinny cats, mange and abscesses so bad some of them looked like burn victims or alien creatures from some unknown hell. The Drizzleway rose at an incline that ascended from the dark depths below, affording us with a fine view of one of the ugliest cities you'd ever see, if unlucky. Passerby wallowed as much as they walked, mumbling or cursing beneath their breath, and all to a backdrop of metallic metronome, footsteps echoing on zigzag grates, the urban labyrinth of Drome.

'There,' Bee pointed to nothing in particular. Brown and gray brick buildings, gutters off kilter like hang nails or late-stage scabs nearly come off the skin. Between the two rows of dismal buildings was a narrow chasm, an alleyway that led into a dead end. And there it was to be, after two bluecoats lay dead among the rubbish, the end of all that looking over your shoulder for a brace of bobbies hot on the hunt.

Bee reached inside his coat and tossed Lily a purple piccolo. A tiny flute. She flashed a grin and played a series of somber notes. Then there was like this beating drum, no, whooshing, or heavy breaths but from off beyond the clouds. And looking up to those very clouds I saw their murky structure part for a winged beast heading directly towards the precarious position of our lofty, rusted walkway. I cowered. Bee smiled. Lily laughed. Then presently I looked into the beady black eyes of a great, leathern mass of loose-fitting flesh.

A chiropteran construct. A fruit bat. Its body, the size of a small woman, but its wings... by Squidge! When outstretched to full extension they became a widespread semitransparent plasticized membrane that spanned — what? — ten, twelve, fourteen feet? In any case, whatever the length, I imagined She Beast, that massive, sexy rozzer splayed out for a nap and if those wings were her blankets she'd have plenty to spare. This bat was freaky, off putting, and oddly, kind of cute. But one thing about it that was glaringly worth mention; its wings were big as fuck.

We took turns holding onto its rubber-coated ankles, its black feet with hooked wrought iron talons. One by one, we sailed on massive wings, parachuting gently down from the high-rise narrow walkway to the roof of one of those dire looking brown and gray buildings. We assumed position. Made a few preparations. Got poised for the upcoming ambush.

Lily took out a pair of pistols that gleamed expensive in the dull light of the rooftop gloom.

'That's a pretty pair of pieces,' I remarked, admiring their silver sheen, their grooves of digital light that indicated what type of ammunition was loaded, how many rounds remained.

'They are,' she agreed. 'But prettier still is how well I shoot them. My shot is tops. I never miss.'

I rolled my eyes. Gave her a some sarcasm to match her sass. 'Yeah, I bet it's about as pretty as the bottom of the beef skillet at Taco Nirvana. About as pretty as the rim of the toilet seat at the end of the long day's shift.'

Lily stuck out her tongue. Made her usual offer. Gave me the middle digit, this time glossed up in sea foam silvery green. I think I was growing on her.

'It's true,' Bee gave me his two cents. 'Lily could shoot a wart off of a rat's ass.'

'Hell,' she said, all smirk and snarl, 'I could shoot your little pecker clean from the rest of you, no target is too small.'

Bee laughed. And I have to admit, so did I.

'But seriously,' she went on, 'I've got your back. I'm no ordinary marksmen, and these guns, they're no ordinary pieces of kit.'

She told me about them. Those bling bling blasters. Those pimped up pistols. How they were embedded with a desire to kill. How they were tempered with personality magic, literal personification. It was an odd practice developed and honed by the Mystic Creeps, cave dwellers and idol worshipers that are illusive and unfriendly. Or so it is told. I've never met one, and I doubt I ever will. The Creeps live well beyond the borders of Drome. Far north across the Gray Fields, their lands are a frozen wasteland. Ice and rubbish and aggregate dunes, the collective ruins of what was, and what will never be again; a well reputed empire, a decent home.

'And that's not all,' Lily goes on to boast, then gives me a whole other sermon on why she's the best. Why her guns are so top of the pops. Why she is queen bee, even if her name is Lily and not Bee. I was hearing it all. How the raw magic that gives the guns their hunger to shoot and kill is linked to an A.I. program that guides her hand with subtle movements, little nudges, pointers and tips for assisted aim and pinpoint targeting of enemy vitals. How the handgrip carries a collection of tiny retractable needles that inject her hands with adrenaline at opportune moments, sharpening her hearing and sight, sending more oxygen to her muscles. How those same needles could inject strong barbiturates, inducing coma or death, if unregistered hands were detected holding the guns. Down to the very last deets, even the silly gimmicks, like how small speakers in the firearms could play her favorite music or sing death dirges over the corpses they created.

'Want to hold them?' She offered.

And I almost reached for them before I remembered the lethal barbiturates. Unregistered hands and all. 'Bitch,' I muttered.

'Eat me.'

'You know I would.'

And then we were done talking about guns. Bee was telling us to shut up. Telling Lily to send up the bat. Telling me to give him a good luck kiss. Lily whispered commands into her construct's ear. Bee stuck his tongue down mine. Then it was all whoosh and whoa, clouds of debris and the giant silhouette of one big fucking bat against the moonlit smog.

'She'll keep watch on Ren,' Bee informed me. 'She'll watch with her nighttime eyes, her nocturnal know-how. That bat knows the fruit salad she'll be getting if she does a good job, and that bat... she *loves* a good fruit salad. She'll come through for us.'

I thought of all that passion fruit and pineapple, those wedges of citrus and kiwifruit, I thought of all those tropical beverages with all of their tropical fruit needs. Bee wasn't playing it down. That bat is going to have one hell of an epic fruit salad.

...If it comes through for us.

'What exactly is the bat supposed to do? I mean, other than watch?

Can it protect Ren against those madhouse coppers? That gingham-faced gumshoe and his sidekick, that behemoth babe.'

'No. Not from those two. Batty is good but those two are better. They'd tear her apart. But that bat is far from useless.'

'Yeah,' I agreed. 'I've always wanted to go paragliding. Now I have.'

'That's not what I mean.'

'Oh?'

'Batty has an eye like mine. The exact same, actually. My bionic one, of course. I had two made. You never know when you may need a spare.'

Seriously, is this guy literally made of money? If so, I've been sleeping in a bed with haystacks of cash. 'So it can — like what? — transmit images to your brain? Like you're the one looking down on Ren?'

'It could do that, yes,' he told me. 'But I've something else in mind. Something that will allow you and Lily to get in on the action. To see how things unfold as they happen. So all three of us are up to speed, fully updated, ready for the moment when our own turn comes to join the fray. Come, I'll show you.'

And there we were, watching Ren through the computerized optic of a giant fruit bat. A live digital feed playing from the portable holographic projector that Bee had brought along. We were watching Ren, the three of us, a mile or more away in another part of Palindrome. It was as if we were there. Almost. Like we were at the holo-cinema. Everything but the popcorn, the irksome silhouettes of bad hairdos between you and the show. We were watching Azalea Ren, a perfect copy of Bee, from Bee's spare bionic eye embedded in a giant bat construct. Reality was an odd thing the most of times. Tonight, it was batshit, madhouse fucked in the head.

It started to rain in the holographic feed. Ren looked up to the heavens, hands in pockets and leaning nonchalant, letting the acid-tinged droplets fall upon his closed eyes, into his open mouth. Then, from where we were watching, little driblets fell from the sky slowly, then a little faster, as the rain caught up to our corner of the city. Ren — though he looked exactly like Bee — glanced directly at the giant bat that he knew would be watching him. He smiled. Nodded ever so slightly. A mile away, through little unspoken gestures, he was more or less saying 'Hey guys. Where the hell are those cops? I'm starting to get bored.'

But suddenly all boredom was out the window. It was out the window, down a few dozen stories and a splatter on the pavement below. Boredom was finished. And now it was all action.

There was no lead-up to it. The bullets just went flying. Cryo slugs chipped brick and left frozen patches of frost inches from either side of Ren's head. A stray bullet hit some woman's kneecap and the gore that popped out was a frozen rain of crimson shrapnel. Little blood crystals. All ice and never-walk-again pain.

Top Cop. His magic reload bullets flying through crowds. I guess he wasn't the cautious type. More's the pity for that lady, less so for the holo-kid who just ate five bullets like they were no big thing. As for Ren, it was time to run. And run he most certainly did. He ran like a greyhound with a rocket strapped to his back. Legs all squidged up. 16 beat sneaker soles smacking the pavement. Ren was going for gold. He was kicking up some major dust. Pushing folks over, left, right, and center.

She Beast ate up some pavement real fast. Her long legs vaulted into action, covering substantial ground with each stride. She had Ren sweating. Running like a track star just to keep pace. Tearing open packets of Squidge and squirting lube juice everywhere. Doing anything, everything, to pull off something that would give him an edge.

He turned a corner like a jackrabbit. An instantaneous shift of direction, no loss of speed, a ninety degree angle manoeuvre. No way to dodge those garbage bins. He sent them flying, along with the refuse within. A cacophonous clatter of aluminium disarray filled the narrow aperture. Sacks of trash, broken appliances, dead cats and last week's meals. It was enough. Just enough. To slow down that giant po-po pin-up girl while Ren sprinted on, turning yet another corner, not wishing to lose the cops but to obtain a nice blind spot for some brief respite, to change form into a destitute roborg, to flash some ass, the rest of him gleaming metal, to slur as if strung out on lunchtime narcotics, and to tell those cops he saw a man with a sword go that way. Just down that lane. And watch them run off, laughing. Manipulating cells, changing form back into Bee at his leisure. Then setting up the bait all over again.

Cat and mouse. But this mouse had other plans. And those cats, they were chasing that mouse right into a pack of angry dogs.

Ren did the old shapeshifter shimmy. Biochemistry getting busy on the dance floor, going nuts, throwing a party. Now he was a fat but cute middle aged woman. Icing on the cake, he threw on a pair of thick glasses. In this guise, he walked right past his pursuers. Right back into the thick of the crowd, the soup of moving heads and shoulders of Ribald Row. He watched with a heavily dimpled smile, chubby cheeks with charming deep craters, and giggled in falsetto. He examined those two cops scratching their heads and scanning the crowd, trigger happy but with nothing to shoot. The image had me smiling too. And Lily. But not Bee. He was all deadpan and focused. Gazing into that holo-show like it was the entire world.

The rain picked up, both down on Ribald Row and up here on the rooftops beside the Drizzleway. We watched as Ren turned back into Bee. His eyes never left those gumshoes, and when their eyes met his it was pandemonium, part two.

Ren was dipping, ducking, diving, pushing people out of the way, pumping his legs manic through a throng of pissed off people, ragged breath and heart pounding like pistons in a sports car. He changed his visage as often as he could. Dramatic alterations of hair style, skin tone, or height. Losing layers to appear as if dressed in a different outfit. He was pulling off the stops. Taking advantage of blind corners, the confusion of urban herds. Mingling, melding, disappearing, reappearing. Now you see me now you don't. All the while taking on an arsenal of cryo bullets that came so close they turned the droplets of rain in front of Ren's face into beautiful crystals of frozen aquamarine.

If you could stop time you'd appreciate the beauty of it all. The way the neon lights of Drome's wares and whorehouses played off those tiny cascading ice crystals. The way the oil slick, blood puddle turned to a cherry hued ice rink. The way the smell of fear masked the smell of shit, of rubbish, all around you. If you could stop time… if you could pause to admire it all… but there was no time to stop. To slow. So Ren just kept running. Ignored the burning fire in his lungs and tried to ignore the freezing ice pellets whizzing in his ear. And just kept running. Running all the faster.

All that running and all that chasing was getting Ren and those cops pretty close to the moment of truth. The moment of ambush. Bee ripped open a packet of Squidge and lathered up his hands and arms. He hefted up his sword by its human femur hilt and gripped it with zest and vigor. Lily slicked up her guns in caterpillar guts, dribbled some down the barrels, rubbed it into the grooves. Me, I just sipped the stuff like a tasty treat. It made me forget the fear. It made me confident in my friends' abilities. And it had me buzzing for a good time. It washed away those icky, icky vibes.

'Here they come,' Bee let us know as we begin to hear the growing sounds of hysterical footwork, lunatic strides of 16 beat, rapid run-for-your-life on the pavement below us. And moments later the holo-feed went dead as we didn't need it anymore. We could see it for ourselves. The real thing. Ren running for his life. Cryo bullets punching holes in brick, ricocheting off of metal grating, leaving splashes of white frost the size of dinner plates. Lily's bat construct came into view and perched on the rusted walkway zigzagging above us. I just prayed the guano wouldn't find my head.

Now Ren took a left, ducked and dodged a bullet, just, and sprinted onward deeper into the dead end. Closer and closer to us until the time to act suddenly became now. The grand finale. The end to all this cat and mouse bullshit. Right. Commence with the ambush.

Down below in that dark chasm between two drab buildings Ren hit a wall. He had nowhere to go. The bullets stopped flying because the rozzers thought they had him cornered. Easy pickings. Just walk up to him and rough him up, real casual, billy club over the noggin, slap some chain bracelets on him and throw him over the hulking shoulder of a seven foot maiden in blue. The constables getting confident, getting cocky, that's what made what happened next so damned special. So very lovely to behold. It'd have me grinning for days.

Bee stepped off the edge of the mildewed brick cliff face and let gravity do the rest. He fell, flew, downward and true, sword first. And *slice!* One pistol, and the hand that had held it, lay in a puddle of blood on the dirty dead-end pavement. Top Cop, maimed and mutilated, cringed to make an ugly face even uglier, yellow teeth barred in pain, red and blue plaid ink scrunched tight over his distorted features. But this guy was rozzer elite. The tattoos said it all. Told the tale. Let folks know he's high up in the police guild. Gumshoe royalty. So he took his lumps and gave them too.

With his remaining hand he shot bullets from his spare pistol, sending a swarm of cryo slugs flying. Two of them hit Bee. One deflected off his sword, frosting up the metal blade and sailing to the side to hit a sack of trash, freezing the gooey remains of someone's old, discarded insta-din. Another had hit his leg. It bored through pockets of silicone, synthetic meats and fibers, rubber ligaments. It grazed metallic bone. Freezing, but not feeling it, Bee examined the hole in his prosthetic limb. His right leg. Lucky for him.

No time to assess the damage, he dodged a battering ram dropkick aimed for his head. She Beast missed her mark, went flying. Bee scrambled, stumbling. Lily, up above, shot projectiles with deft precision, bullets with a personality, a fondness for murder. They found their flesh. Rejoiced to penetrate the foot and thigh of Top Cop, who most certainly had seen better days. Ren did the transmogrify boogie, turned himself into something inconspicuous and found a dark corner. I was watching it all from above, doing my brick throwing thing. A nice half brick with sharp corners plunged downward to clip She Beast on the temple. Bomber shades shattered, she glared up at me with those liquid eyes and no doubt saw through the wearing effects of the confusion brew, marked my face and stashed it in her your-so-dead file for any future run-ins.

Bee wasn't hurt. Not really. But his manufactured limb wasn't exactly running mint. He got out his last packet of Squidge and worked it into the hole going straight through his leg. Dribbles of goo went down a hollowed-out plastic tunnel, coating the sizzling circuitry within. It wasn't factory new, but it would work in a pinch. Like a band aid, the Squidge patched things up. Bee was back on his feet.

Top Cop was in worse condition. He was bleeding pints from the stump at his wrist, his punctured foot, the hole in his thigh. He was applying medi-gel, police-grade salve. It was swimming with probiotic microorganisms, nanobots with healing programs, personality magic to emotionally strive to aid their patients. And it may have worked, that fancy healing goop. But meanwhile the bullets kept flying, bricks kept falling, and wads of sulphur-smelling guano were splatting left and right.

Taking his chances, Top Cop did something utterly bad ass and hard edge. 'Incendiary,' he voice-activated his gun to swap from ice to fire. He shot the pavement at his side. *Bang. Bang. Bang.* Then rubbed his bloody stump right into the molten red surface like a slab of pseudo-meat on the beef skillet at Taco Nirvana. It sizzled, that stump. Not that you heard through the screaming. In and out of consciousness, finally together, fully there, Top Cop emerged, upright, fully cauterized. And even Bee, if he had one, would be tipping his hat.

But it was all for naught. All that bravado. That showmanship. The next murder-hungry bullet that came flying from the rooftops found a blue and red mottled forehead. The brains nestled behind it scrambled like tomorrow's breakfast that I'll probably skip while thinking of this moment. And that was it for the boss man. There's no coming back from that. Brain matter and skull fragments were already being collected and carried away. The industrious rats of the 'little saint.'

She Beast was wary, maybe a little scared. On second thought, not a fucking chance. Looking at that face, the veins bulging out of her thick neck and super strong arms, she wasn't scared. She was big-time pissed. Madhouse angry. And now *I* was scared. Looking at her processing the loss of her boss, her partner, and funneling all that rage for his death into a concentrated absolute need to kill us all. Even from up here on the rooftop, way out of reach, my knees were doing a wee wiggle, jiggle.

But her day was done. She Beast was *way* outnumbered, if not out-classed. And now Ren rubbed salt into the wound just to prove he was in a position to provoke her and remain safe. He shifted his outward guise to match the recently deceased. His face turned gingham blue and red, his mocking smile was yellow. Next he made a pantomime of chocking, of dying. Then flipped the giant blonde rozzer the bird. Stuck out his tongue. And shifted back to pretty old Ren.

As I say, her day was done. And she knew it, too. But that didn't stop her from trying. Trying to take out at least one of us who had helped to snuff out Top Cop once and for all. Once she made her move she was under heavy fire. Lily was up above, adrenaline pumped, raining down bullets that yearned to find flesh at the end of their short flights. Big Blonde took a few in the back. *Thud. Thud. Thud.* She hardly seemed to notice, to care. She straddled a fire hydrant and worked her mythical thighs, her iron abs and arms and back, and heaved the thing from the pavement, bits of crumbling cement shooting out with the upheaval of water.

She Beast, in one last gesture of I-hope-you-all-die-in-horrible-ways, tossed the fire hydrant like most people would toss a baseball. It sailed like a fastball. And in this game it ain't three strikes you're out. It's one fire hydrant in the face and next thing you're in the obituaries. But it missed, narrowly. And only because Bee was there to intervene with his sword. If not… well… the world would be deprived of the very best Killer Bee cocktail. Because Ren, master behind the bar, he'd be the one in those obituaries.

It turns out that fire hydrant stunt wasn't solely for offensive attack, or even primarily. That was just an added bonus. What She Beast was really trying to pull — and she did indeed pull it off — was escape, or something to aid her in giving us the slip. All that water shooting up, filling the alley, coming back down with the rain that was now falling hard, it was loud, chaotic, and hard to see anything. All our eyes were on that fire hydrant that took a flight. Once we breathed a sigh to see that Ren was still alive, turned back to She Beast to finish her off, only then did we realize; 'That bitch is long gone.'

Lily was right. That cop was miles gone. She Beast, three bullets in a well-muscled back, had turned tail. Lived to fight another day. And that's what scared me. Scared me a whole fucking lot.

'What do we do with head honcho?' Lily floated down to join us, hanging by the ankles of her fruit bat construct.

Face up, staring into all that water falling from the sky, the acid rain, the hydrant's ceaseless ejaculations, Top Cop lay, a heavily tattooed, largely dismembered corpse.

'Leave him,' Bee made the call. 'It'd be unkind to deprive the rats.' And it ain't no joke. At the end of the block I turned to look back. And Top Cop was concealed. Totally covered. In a thick, black blanket of big city rats.

When we get home I'm going to need a big fucking drink.

11
COCKTAILS AND
QUESTIONS

We all deal with stress in different ways. Me, I rubbed one out in the shower. Let the hot water and high pressure wash away the sins and stink of the Saint. Bee was on his third Killer Bee, Squidge up every orifice. Lily and Ren were fucking in the spare room. Shape shifting kinks, living out fantasies without the risk, the work. Someone remind me to pick up girls and boys in the irradiated zones of Drome's west end. Even if they're not a shifter, maybe they'll have that third nipple, that second cock. Shit, I'm easy.

But was I even single? I wasn't sure myself. I thought about Bee and willed out another rub. Okay… now I need that drink.

Bee was on his fourth. His handprint decorated the frosted bottle of vodka he had fetched from the freezer. He was sipping it neat. Freezer fresh. He'd pretty much eaten a fruit salad after downing three Killer Bees. Passion fruit and pineapple, and all the rest. I guess he'd had enough of all that surf's up snack platter and just wanted the alcohol at this point. Which suited me. It was all I was after in the first place.

'Pour one up to rim, will ya?'

'Done.' He handed me a night's worth of booze and I nicked a good dent off my bevvy. Felt the ice-cold liquid slither down my tubes, hit my tummy like a cryo slug, a ripple of frosty pleasure expanding in my gut. I counted the seconds... six. There it is. It hit my system. That first drink of the night. Make it a big one. Get things off to a good, fast start. Then slow it down. Nurse that buzz that's warming my soul. Making me feel like tonight wasn't a tenth as batshit madhouse as it actually was.

'Good shower?'

I blushed, thinking of all that slip and side with the soap, my stress relief and erotic thoughts. 'Sure thing,' I told him. 'Good suds. Good warm water.'

'It was a hell of a night tonight,' Bee walked his drink from the bar to the sofas, plopped himself down like a sack of bricks, collapsed into the cushions. I took another sip of my own drink and went over to join him, a cozy lounge in the corner of the room with a small library of books.

'You did well,' he commended.

'I threw a few bricks is all.'

'May have been the difference. Could've been the little thing to tip the scales. A timely brick, or just that distraction in knowing that bits of building would keep falling for their heads... could have been what gave us the edge we needed. That wasn't a fucking barn dance we were having out in that alley. That was life or death. And that's on me. I factored things wrong, Jarred.'

'How's that?'

'I figured element of surprise, outnumbered like they were, bait and ambush, *the perfect cocktail*. Well, turns out an ingredient may have been overlooked. Or maybe I've no stomach for drinks at all.' He partook in a hearty quaff of his booze.

'Well, we all know *that's* a big load of bollocks.' We both chuckled but Bee wasn't completely free of those lingering icky vibes. His grin quickly returned to that morose, pensive expression he had been wear-ing since we made our way back home.

'That was no easy squabble,' he remarked and looked at me as if what he really meant to say is he had fucked up. 'We walked on the edge of death tonight. We're lucky to be alive.'

'Hey, sour puss, don't look now but we fucking *won*.' That vodka had me feeling it was true. 'We cut off the head of the snake.'

'Pfft,' he made known his derision. 'You really think that, Jare-bear?'

'Top Cop was boss man.' I made my case but knew it was trash. 'You read that checker board on his face. You know the story it told. You know as well as I do. That's police pageantry. That's the hottest of heat. And we snuffed out that flame.'

Bee set down his drink. Leaned forward. Just looked at me. Long and deliberate. 'You *really* think that?'

I thought of She Beast. Mammoth Maiden. The rozzer queen. I thought of those fingers on my shoulders, the bone-crushing strength in each one of them. I thought of her thighs, the ones that looked like building foundations, her sexy curves and her steel muscles. I thought of her delicious lips and freaky eyes that swam with something inhu-man, something enhanced, malevolent. I thought of how I wanted her naked in my bed, but no bed I've ever know would be big enough. I thought of how utterly scared I was of her superhuman skills, her ab-solute power. I thought of her stature, that of a rhino construct or the tapir that she saddled. I thought of all those things and then I placed her next to Top Cop. Boss man. Head Honcho. Pen pusher. Guy who has unlimited bullets and still can't hit a couple Squidged-up kids on the run. The comparison was a joke. Truth be told, there was no com-parison at all.

'No,' I downed my bevvy. 'No, I fucking don't.'

Bee sat back, relaxed a little. Glad I wasn't going to be the stubborn optimistic. The guy pulling silver linings out of smelly assholes, dirty gutters, and dead rats. Sometimes there ain't no lining. Silver or gold or any other shade of pretty. Sometimes the only thing around to be pulled is that grotty, slime-slick string of black hair clogging the drain at your feet. Sometimes there was just the bad situation staring you in the face. And She Beast being out there, alive and angry and somewhere around an ugly corner, just waiting, desperate to educate you on the meaning of pain; well… there's that bad situation. And no doubt we'd be staring it in the face. Sometime soon, I reckon.

'Another drink?'

My head was swimming. 'Hit me.' Whatever, I'd eat my hangover in the morning with my over-fried syntho eggs and pseudo bacon. I'd deal with it then. With that and the memory of brains and bones on the pavement, the hundreds of fevered rats that rejoiced to sniff them out. For now, I'll take my drink and erase it all away. I'll trade in a morning without brain damage for a passable evening. I gladly accepted that drink.

But before I sipped myself into oblivion I had something to voice. There was an itch I had been aching to scratch. A niggling little thing that I just knew would keep me up, no matter how much vodka I drank. It was something Bee had mentioned in passing. Here in this very same room, me on this very same couch. When me and him and Azalea and Sis were discussing how to rid us of those rozzers. Something about a 'bigger picture.' A 'main objective.' It was his motivation for squashing the cops. Who were like pesky insects to him otherwise, but as a threat to his *bigger picture main objective* they became a serious problem. So what the hell is that all about?

'Hey, Honey Bee?'

'Yeah, Jare-Bear?'

'Something's on my mind.'

'Shoot to kill.'

So I did. 'Look, I know you don't owe me an explanation for all the juicy deets in your life. Hell, I don't even know what *we* are. Like, friends with bennies? Boyfriend squared? Or just strangers having a weird weekend? But I guess it sort of bothers me. You know, after being so intimate so soon, after risking our lives side by side, after sharing a quart of Squidge, having benders and bullets and big bad lawmen run us around town… whatever we are, I feel like we've shared a lot.'

'So you want to know what we are?' He was being a little too sly. Too cool. The way he was looking at me, all relaxed now that I was a little worked up. Or maybe he was just projecting all that confidence and sex appeal. Either way, it made me feel small. Made me feel like he was some rogue millionaire with a black-magic blade and a half corpse, half computerized brindled steed. A heroic knight with bionic bits, a sleek prosthetic. A handsome prince with never-ending coffers of cash and Squidge. And me, little old me. I most definitely by now had lost the one thing I did have. Employment at Taco Nirvana.

So the way he was all calm and cool, enjoying my exasperation, my infatuation, my newb naivety; it got under my skin. Pissed me off plenty. Or maybe this was all on me. All of my insecurities crashing down around me, smothering me in a great big heap of overanalysis.

'Well?' I guess he got tired of waiting while I sat there overanalyzing.

'Yes!' I basically shouted, annoyed at Bee's indifference. 'Yes, I do. I mean, seriously, what *are* we? I don't know what kind of life you live, but I'm guessing not everyone just moves in overnight, gets spoon-fed fine narcotics, fucks and kills cops. I mean, am I right? But that's not even what I want to ask you about. That's just the obvious question lingering in the air. What has been bothering me, the question I needed to ask you, was what all that "bigger picture," "master plan" or "main objective" shit was about.'

'Earlier tonight you'd been talking about it to the others like I wasn't even there. Wasn't sitting on this same fucking couch right in front of you. Scratching my head thinking *huh? Whosawhatsit?* You know, just before we go and risk our lives, facing slugs on ice and flying fire hydrants? I was there too, you know? Risking my ass just like everyone else. Throwing bricks. Remember? The little bitty thing that "may have made the difference.""

'So if I'm not risking my life for my man, but just some guy who hands out drugs like candy, which means I guess I must have been risking my life for some "big picture main objective," then I best fucking know what that objective is. Paint me a picture, Bee. The *bigger picture*. It doesn't have to be a pretty one. I just want it to be true.' There. I said it. I took a breath and took a sip. It was only then that I remembered this is the same guy who dismembers people who rub him the wrong way. But Bee was calm. Unprovoked.

He got up and stretched. Walked over to the bookshelf and reached to retrieve Doc Argyle's memoirs. He tossed it across the coffee table to land in my lap. I spilled a bit of my drink, but it's not like I'd be missing it. Bee approached me, reached down into my lap and opened the pages to the section he was looking for. I could feel his hand on my cock through the pages. I took another sip of my drink just to do something.

'There,' he tapped at the open page. I certainly felt *that*. 'Read it.'

'I'm not really in the mood to -'

'Read it.' His glance wasn't venomous, but it wasn't fuzzy bunnies either. 'It will help you understand all about the "bigger picture." Read it,' he repeated. 'Then we will talk.'

12
FROM THE DIARIES OF
AVID ARGYLE (III)

In retrospect, I realize my onward march to unveil the mysteries of Squidge was far from a cautious endeavor. My gung ho, fly by the seat of my pants approach to it all. A fervent quest to satiate an intrigue that bubbled over the rim of my abilities to moderate my obsession. To seek the potential of that wiggle-worm caterpillar that created life from bare rock... it led me down a path that skirted cliff faces, bogs, and pitfalls that I was blind to. The way I ran down that path, like sprinting in a dark wood, was an approach that lacked all prudent forethought, any patience that most certainly would have been wise. Looking back on those early days of discovery, still cramped in that spaceship amid the uncouth fellows of a prospecting outfit... it's no wonder I went mad with the discovery of Squidge, driven to peel back every single layer until the nakedness of its riddle was an open-faced book that read each and every one of its secrets.

Still... looking back on it all, despite the good fortune that would become my future, my many successes, still... the way I went about things, the chances I had taken... I do believe at the time I was really rather mad. Perhaps I remain mad even today. Perhaps I will become more and more mad as the weeks and months and years tally by. Perhaps this madness is a result, a symptom, a consequence of how I handled things in those early days. Plowed forward, heedless of the obstacles before me. Why swerve or stop? I reasoned. When you can mow things over. But whether I was mad back then, mad today, or becoming crazier with each rise and fall of the sun, whatever the case, I have no regrets. None. For if I have become mad, so what? After all, I have become a god.

It began with that virgin application of first instar Squidge. Fresh from the carefully planted, cleverly placed eggs of the squidge wing butterfly, its newborn brood, a team of a larvae, wriggled forth upon the switchgrass I had uprooted and potted. Such tiny, little things! Voracious eaters, like all caterpillars, they do not pause to take in the world around them. They open their formidable mouths — formidable in relation to their overall size — and gorge away without reserve. It is all that occupies their time. Eating. What little rest they take is segued by more eating.

It is the voracious nature of the larvae, their constant appetite, that results in their rapid growth; prompts the quick transition from their first instar to the second. In some cases this transition takes as little as a single day to begin, sometimes three or four. It is a process of digesting, reabsorbing one's outgrown skin, an economic molting or shedding of sorts with little waste; the worm comes through the process a startlingly larger creature. In some cases, double the size.

Great! Double the size, double the Squidge. Not so. I now know better. And it was this discovery, that each subsequent instar weakens the potency of the biotic narcotic juices within the larva, that led me to take action in the incredibly hasty and hazardous way that I did. But one cannot blame a certain eagerness, surely. For here I was with a crop of newly hatched first instar larvae before me. Living parcels of liquid miracle. Within as little as a day, the caterpillars and the minuscule volume, but oh-so-powerful drug that was their guts, may degenerate, transform, into a larger supply of watered down product. The window to harvest was a narrow one. To dawdle was to cast away a richness, profound and potent. To mull things over, utterly wasteful.

So I took the plunge. And I was rewarded for it.

I plucked the closest caterpillar. I held it intimately close to my face. Between my thumb and forefinger, great leviathans gently sandwiching a minnow, the wiggling thing looked on the edge of microscopic. So small as to hardly be seen at all. But then again, my vision has always been second rate. There has never been a time I haven't had to rely on the aid of devices, glasses or contacts or holographic lenses, to provide my eyes with quality sight. My glasses were elsewhere. Perhaps left in my locker. I did not pause to consider the risks. I did not think to go fetch my glasses. I just acted, no hesitation, total impulse, when I plucked a second larva, a third, a fourth, and crushed them all between my digits to form the quantity of a single drop. A liquid green jewel, like pureed kale and cabbage, clung to the tip of my finger. I held it over my opened eye, let it fall, then used the remaining residue still staining my fingers to rub as well as I could into my other eye.

I blinked a mild sting away. I licked my fingers clean and tasted an astringent tang. Then suddenly, euphorically, supernaturally, I could see as no glasses or holographic lens had ever had me seeing before. I was seeing in ultra, extra vision. I could zoom inward, see micro textures in the metalwork as if blatant scars, deep violent gouges. Colors were brighter than I knew could ever be. What is that color? And that one too? There is no name for that shade. That alien hue. It cannot be seen by human eyes. I'll call it the color of divinity, of sublimity.

The beauty of the world was striking in all of its immeasurable flaws, the ones I didn't know were there at all. So very many flaws. So many marring grooves and nicks and dents and smears among pockmarked surfaces. Yet utterly stunning, a jaw-dropping vista of picturesque magnificence, this collection of radically refined detail.

This condition of superhuman sight, of otherworldly, enhanced ability faded within ten, perhaps fifteen minutes. But while my eyes no longer saw details as if under a microscope, revealing unknown dimensions, any and all truths to be seen, neither did my eyes return to their original humdrum, deprived state of subpar sight. Since the incident, that ill-advised experiment that ended a complete and total success, I have never again needed the aid of devices. Glasses, contacts, holographic lenses... these are crude contraptions, half-baked inventions of man, with abilities that pale next to the interior juices of the squidge wing's first instar larvae.

I see in one eye perhaps as well as any man or computer could. In the other, the one that received the full drop, I see details undreamed of. These details overwhelm the rest of me, for the rest of me...is merely human. All of my other parts, inside and out, none of them exposed to a miracle. None enhanced by god. For this reason I wear a patch over my right optic. It helps the rest of me function as I cannot process the grand vision of the divine eye.

It was upon that very moment... the one that taught me divinity, its experience, its power...it was precisely that moment that I knew what I must do. What I absolutely, devoutly, without an ounce of faltering, must accomplish. That I must complete my transition. My metamorphosis. As if an egg into a worm into a beautiful butterfly. I must transcend the limits of humanity. Its claustrophobic limits. I must cast them off like an unwanted cloak. A molting. A shedding of the outgrown skin.

I will become baptized. Bathed. Drowned in Squidge. I will be the first born child of the first instar worm. Such was my internal babbling.

And now, looking back on it all, I have, indeed, become what I knew that I must.

This world has a god. This god is me.

'He's mad,' I declared.

'He said so himself,' Bee agreed. 'But read one more passage. Just see how mad Avid Argyle really is. See how evil. How selfish. Go on,' he urged. 'Then we will talk.'

I had had my fill of the mad doc's ravings. I sighed. I sipped my vodka. And picked up the manuscript once more.

And like a god, yet before I became one, I had a chance to employ a rather different sort of miracle. The miracle of life.

I had deduced rather early on after the initial discovery of the squidge wing larvae that it was entirely possible the little worms could create life from practically nothing. From little more than the basest of elements; ash and bare rock, scorched landscapes of impoverished fields, barren hills. On a planet bereft of life, I witnessed it; an impossible oasis. That anomaly of switch grass and heather, that tiny patch of micro environment on the otherwise wholly dead planet of Eight Ball. Its presence, a small viridescent dot on a large canvas of fiery basalt, in my estimation, was well outside the realm of possibility. Yet unless I accept hallucination or holographic infringement, delusion of the mind or the cunning craft of a master illusionist, it was, irrefutably, before me in that hot skillet of endless rock. There, yet impossible to be there. And thus, miraculous.

It would not prove long for me to adopt the idea. Not long at all. For after I brushed those verdant shoots with outstretched fingers, amazed and perplexed, how could I doubt it? That the small, solitary arena of life was the product of the squidge wing and its curious larvae. That the highly localized life-bearing zone was of their own making.

After the incident with my avian construct, the accidental rupture of a cocoon that led to its improved flight, temperament and overall functionality, I began to wonder. After the removal of that stubborn stuttering from Bee's crippled oration, like a scalpel to a malignant carbuncle, beautifying his speech and gifting him with eloquence — and all with but the merest touch of residue from the pulverized chrysalis — my intrigue peaked, my conviction grew.

Many times over a thought crossed my mind; these creatures are miracles incarnate. And I, their founder... needless to say I became giddy. And I guarded my discovery as if it were an innocent baby, a child of prophecy heralded to become the future king, he who is hunted by a jealous tyrant who does not wish to be later on overthrown. But I will see this prophecy through. The child shall grow into manhood. My idea, like a seed, would grow to its maximum fruition. My hypotheses would become the reality of the future. My inkling, my intuition, would in time overthrow all notion of today's concept of knowing. These worms, they are life. They are all that is missing in today's tainted reality.

I tested my hypothesis. I took a caterpillar of moderate size, likely fourth or perhaps fifth instar. I applied the excreted juices from the little worm's innards onto a bare, black rock I had brought in from the outside environs. I had but to wait a minute, perhaps less, when a dry, mint colored moss or lichen suddenly crystallized onto the rock, spreading from the epicentre of applied Squidge. The growth slowed and then halted, leaving one face of the rock a radius of simplistic vegetation.

To the outside observer, someone detached from a scientific outlook, this may have seemed a neat or clever trick, something to applaud once but be bored to witness again. For me, a devout follower of all things fascinating, a man of science and virtue, it was the first chapter in a holy book of miracles. God's work, and I his profit.

I dropped more Squidge onto the same rock. A gentle rain of chlorophyll green, the guts of god's fat little cherubs. His angels. The rock, about the size of a grapefruit, now split and cracked with burrowing roots. Grasses and small shrubs shot forth as if watching a time-lapse holographic nature documentary. The rock from which the plants had grown rolled over against the weight of their outward and vertical growth. After seven applications of Squidge I could no longer go on. The small section of garden in the room was no longer something I could conceal from the crew. So I hefted up what must have been something about half my own weight in grass clumps, small hedges, and young saplings. I tossed them down the incinerator and walked back to my room hardly capable of holding in the rapture that was bursting at the seams of my soul.

I had in my grasp the power to create life. To form worlds. To turn bare, black rock, volcanic sputum, ash and waste, into pastures of rich green fields, tree-laden forests, edible, aromatic, oxygenating. Such was the potency of Squidge. One could localize a sight, concentrate the growth and form a copse in a day over a small section. One modest patch at a time, turning futile acreage of infertility into fruitful segments of flourishing, liveable land. Over a handful of decades this slow spread of rich life would create regions capable of sustaining small cities. Where once a single, bereft cactus may have clung to life in yesteryears, tomorrow we shall walk among the amassed biodiversity of a young, ecologically rich, vibrant civilization.

This was one idea. Another may be more effective yet. Rather than concentrate the application of Squidge to a small segment, getting results fast but in highly limited sections, Squidge could be significantly watered down, diluted into a base mixture, making its potency very much diminished but its application global. By vaporizing the greatly weakened potency of Squidge, dispersing it over continents in its mildest of form instead of an acre or so in its high level concentration, one could achieve a widespread effect, a worldwide effect, but without the same immediate result.

It was this particular strategy that would likely appeal to the off-world colonies. Those roughneck pioneers toughing it out in the harsh and limited terraforming worlds. By using the atmospheric dispersers they could feed to their impoverished worlds diluted Squidge, a mild but miraculous vapor. It would enrich the atmosphere, cleanse the air, fall with the rain to spank the land and drown in waters, gently, hardly, but effectively over time, purifying all and everything. In fifty years it would be as if one hundred or more had passed under the normal routine. This was terraforming in fast motion. It was the abridged version to a very long, arduous read with a glorious ending. The ending was the goal.

In terms of prospecting planets for future terraforming, just apply this method of slow Squidge release and return to a lush world three or four generations later. Why do all the work, waste all those lives? It was in more than one way revolutionary, my little wiggling worms.

There were many options. Many ways to consider how best to employ the miraculous gift of Squidge. But were there options? Were there, really? For if one option gleams gold, a twinkling beacon of unfiltered radiance, among all others that merely reflect its great light off of their dull, unremarkable surfaces, then surely, unequivocally, the idea of options becomes moot, even absurd. One does not pick up the dull rocks that lay beside nuggets of gold.

I recognized this gleaming gold among the lesser pebbles. I fixed my gaze upon its sheen and never looked further afield, never yonder. I locked in and marched straight into that fire. The beacon that seized me. And I, in turn, seized it. The best option. The only option.

To condense Squidge, to localize its application, but not by the square mile or acreage. My focus would be narrower, would delve deeper. Its intensive application would elevate each square inch. Square inch of what? Of me! Me! A blank canvas of inadequacy; the human form, the mind of man.

Bah! Wretched and third rate. I'd paint with the sublime colors of Squidge a pretty picture over that drab, taut sheet of nothing. That irksome insufficiency that is the fiber of mortal man. And like a work of art, a masterpiece, the Squidge-infused subject will emulate the gods. Me. A model of perfection. Me. The new definition of it.

My soft flesh and membrane, the bones and gristle beneath, my elastic ligaments, network of nerves, and the slowly failing organs that keep me alive. The same organs that come with collapse as a cost of living. No longer! No expiration. No countdown to the end. From the minuscule hairs upon my knuckles to the ever important beating heart encased within my center, no longer would I be a man. None of me. No longer would I be crude flesh, but divine contraption. Internal. External. Each cell a new being.

It sounds good on my tongue so I tend to wax repetitive. But like with sweet candy, one always wishes for one more lick. So I'll say it again. I, Avid Argyle, will become a god. That was then. This is now. So with a shift of tense I'll say it one last time for the sake of indulgence; I, Avid Argyle, have become a god. Third time's a charm: I Avid Argyle am God.

I was relieved to be finished with the passage. I threw down the papers and threw back my bevvy. It was a small comfort after all of that madhouse drivel. 'Well, I ain't exactly up to my ears in the warm and fuzzies,' I gave my critique. 'Doc Argyle seems about as tame as a rabid wolverine with a hot chilli up its ass.'

'He is far less gentle than any wolverine, construct or natural.'

'Yeah, well, if he and I ever go clothes shopping together I'll be taking him over to the straightjacket aisle. Fifty percent off if you're foaming at the mouth. Great bargain.'

'Funny,' Bee said without laughter, without a hint of amusement. 'But it's far from a joke. Argyle, whether I like it or not, *is* what he says he is. If not a god by religious definition, then a god by the definition that says gods are superhuman, elevated from man, all powerful, destructive and untouchable. I fear he is mankind's greatest threat.'

'I'll sift out his name from the rest of the party invitations.' I was drunk.

'You do realize this is serious, Jarred?'

'Yeah,' I swallowed a hiccup. 'I do.' And I did, I just didn't care. Not then. Not in the moment. Not while my head was swimming with way too much alcohol. A few days ago I was working the beef skillet at Taco Nirvana. This threat to mankind stuff, business with gods and all-powerful ex-lovers, it was sort of off the charts for little old me.

'You do realize the evil of his actions? The selfishness of his choice? The egotistical, criminal use of Squidge that he employed in lieu of methods that would better mankind?'

'You mean how he pimped up his body? Gave himself the deluxe? How he put all his eggs into one basket. That basket, himself. How he neglected the needy, the desperate, the societal struggle of expansion into terraforming worlds. All that shit?'

'Yes,' Bee wasn't downplaying it. Wasn't watering it down. "All that shit." He was downright livid. All passion and fire sitting right beneath that semblance of calm. I shook myself and sat up straight. I willed myself a fraction more sober. I put on my game face for the Bee.

'Sounds pretty bad,' I admitted. 'Straight up icky vibes.'

'And then some,' Bee amended. 'Avid is evil. He is a vile enemy to all humanity. His self-obsessed, egotistical and malign acts have betrayed us all. His misuse of Squidge is a grotesque affront to man. For using Squidge to turn himself into a god, a superhuman, but also for withholding Squidge from impoverished planets, terraforming worlds, and lifeless landscapes that have been tarnished by man. Squidge could beautify cities, environments. Squidge could stave off extinctions, reinvigorate ecosystems, save worlds or give birth to them from bare rock. Squidge is the miracle drug…not because it can make a man into a god. But because, as if a god, it can shower down benevolence and good tidings upon the many worlds of mankind, upon *any* world. It could wash away the sins of man. Purify them. Leave them so clean and sparkling that even Nyvyn, little saint, would shine bright, a proper home to house the happy masses. Wouldn't you like that, Jarred? To walk out your door and not smell the shit. To look around and see something that makes you feel glad to be where you are. To breath healthy air. To eat genuine proteins. To feel sunlight, unfiltered by smog, on your skin. To say with pride, "Nyvyn is my home."'

The notion of pride linked to anything regarding Nyvyn, unless, of course, it was in reference to leaving it behind, was completely paradoxical. Utterly perverse. Yet still, I hadn't thought of it in this way. That Squidge could better our world. Our entire existence.

To me, less than a week ago, Squidge was a way to have a little fun. To enhance your evening with a buzz like no other. A narcotic to boost the icky vibes into something kind of nice. This whole business of creating gods, creating worlds, of 'miracles' referring to anything beyond a euphemism for getting high, tripping out, well, that's all shit completely new to me.

'That would be nice,' I lamely said. But in my estimation I was being generous. Me and the Drome are like slugs and salt. Oil and water. We don't mix.

Bee sighed. Tousled up his lovely, long locks and pinched the bridge of his finely shaped nose. 'Just think about it. Give it a good ponder. Life doesn't have to be one big, bad joke. We can do something about it. We can mop up all the shit.'

He turned to go. Retreated towards the bed for some long overdue shuteye. 'The bigger picture,' I called out to him from the couch. 'We stop Doc Argyle.'

Bee didn't turn to face me. Just stopped in his tracks and said with his back and broad shoulders staring me down. 'That's the gist of it.' He kicked off his sneakers, threw his clothes to the floor, stretched like a tomcat, and plopped down onto the mattress like a heavy sow keeling over for a hearty snooze. 'Kill Argyle. Reclaim the Squidge. Save the world.' Then Bee went quiet. I figured he was already in Z-town. Dreaming of this and that. Killing villains and saving the day.

At the end of the long night I felt I knew a little bit more about where Bee stood. Where his mind was at. Where he might soon be headed. The wool was a little less over my eyes where the bigger picture was concerned. The main objective.

But sitting there alone, late into the night on that couch, well buzzed and a little overwhelmed by it all, I suddenly realized with a little ironic chuckle that I still didn't know where Bee and I stood. I had no better notion of *us*. What I was to him. What we were to each other.

I never did get the answer to that other question.

13
PILLOW TALK

I was lying in bed. Me and the Bee. I knew he was awake. All that fidgeting. Dead men couldn't be more tired than I was. But I was also more wired than a malfunctioned fuck bot gone haywire. Thrust and shriek and repeat. I wasn't anywhere near Z-town. And without sleeping pills I wasn't about to find a cab to get me there. Probably a good idea not to. All that booze... pills might get me to Z-town. But it might end up a one way trip. Last time I checked, Bee didn't have a defibrillator on standby.

Despite a day spent running from madhouse rozzers, a night ambushing them, battling with them, despite too many drinks, a boatload of adrenaline, and far too many applications of Squidge... despite the many untamed wiles of twenty-four hour batshit antics, here we were, me and the Bee. And neither one of us could salvage a wink of much-needed sleep.

'You awake?' I asked but didn't need to. I could tell by the tossing and turning, the outward breaths of exasperation. Bee was wide awake.

'I'm wide awake.'

'Yeah, me too.'

'Just too raucous a day. Even for me.'

'It breaks records in that department.'

'Not quite.'

'Well, it does by a country fucking mile for *me*.' I thought about asking what day could've possibly been wilder than this one. But then I remembered. Of course... this is the guy that lost an eye and a leg, the conclusion of a lovers' spat. And that sort of drew the line between what sort of action a guy like Bee saw on a daily basis versus a guy like me. My lovers' spats ended with a slammed door. A slap across the cheek. A few "fuck yous" thrown out of open windows as I walked down the street half naked, my clothes in bundles in my arms. Once a girl threw my records out the window. That was the peak level of tragedy in my life. Broken records, missed opportunities. Not broken bones, missing limbs and one half of my optical organs. I once burned my wrist real bad on the beef skillet at the Taco Nirvana. To this day, I›ve got a little red scar. Doesn›t measure up though, does it?

'Is now a good time, you know, since the two of us can't find a ride to Z-town...' I began.

'I'm not in the mood for fucking.'

'No, no. That's not what I meant.'

'Well?'

'You've shed some pretty good light on a lot of things tonight. I'm feeling a lot less left in the dark. But, you know, I'm still sort of waiting for you to open up about one thing.'

'My falling out with Avid.'

The lovers' quarrel. It had become something of a myth for me in recent days, an epic tale shrouded in mystery. 'Yeah,' I tentatively urged. 'I feel like it's important. For the bigger picture stuff, my involvement in it and all that.' I swallowed in the dark. A big nervous gulp. 'But... but also important... for, you know, *us*. For moving forward and for going a little deeper. A bit beyond guzzling fine spirits and rare narcotics, running from cops and killing them. Bee.' And in that small pause that hung heavy in the dark I realized my sincerity was in every way genuine, 'I want to scratch beyond the surface. I want to go deeper. I want to know you.'

Bee turned over to face me. Our heads rested on our pillows as we faced inward towards each other. His gaze and mine were locked, one unto the other, a breadth of mere inches. His green bionic eye cascaded emerald streaks of mute light on the bed between us, code falling like a gentle rain. My own eye, luminescent only for its wet reflection of Bee's in front of me, drank in that pretty creature, that lovely face framed in dark curls and a sturdy, sculpted jawline.

'He had been abusive for a while at the time it had happened,' he began, and I could smell the sweet stink of a Killer Bee cocktail on his words. 'When I tried to intervene. When our differences escalated to more than a heated exchange of words, slammed doors and a day or two of ghosting each other.'

'Really, we had been falling out of love for months. Had *already* fallen out of love. It happens slowly, so it creeps up on you; a failing relationship. But looking back on it I see my partnership with Avid in transparent clarity. Crystal clear. We had been out of love since the moment Argyle found Squidge. Since the moment his obsession for a young man with a lisp swapped to one for caterpillars with innards that got you drunk on miracles.'

'He liked my lisp. It gave him power, authority. Made me a good listener. What else could I do? I could hardly speak without the shame that came with it. Avid, he liked to talk. To hear the oration of his own soliloquy. I was a youthful body and a young face. But most of all, I was an ear for listening with a mouth not so great for rebuttal but excellent for kissing. When I lost that lisp I also lost half of what made Avid attracted to me. But more than that, I could not compete with those wiggling worms found in that patch of grass. The ones that bore into Avid's soul. Claimed him, completely. Possessed him. Turned him into the man, or as he would call himself, god, that he is today.'

He reached over and stroked my hair. Played with it between his fingers. Zeros and ones stared me in the face, a whole slew of them. He smiled and sighed, tender for a change. 'Avid had been collecting first instar larvae for months. He bred the squidge wing, kept the little critters coming, eggs and worm and butterfly, collecting what he could of the littlest worms without damaging the cycle, stashing them, storing them, amassing them. He kept them fresh with a magic of deep, kelp-forest green. Rejuvenation magic. But more than that it merged and twisted into threads of bruised-flesh blue and ripe-plum purple. It was expensive magic. Rare magic. But Argyle had Squidge to trade and he got what he wanted. It kept the first instar worms in stasis. Alive and well and completely frozen in time. In this way he had all the time in the world to gather what he needed for the perverse baptism of ascending to the divine.'

'I knew about his eye. The one that drank in the insect gore and could see in colors and detail only eagles and androids could dream of. He couldn't exactly hide the fact, what, with that cumbersome eyepatch. I knew that it wouldn't stop with his eye. I knew it wouldn't conclude with that, the be-all end-all. I knew Avid would douse something else, something more. That he'd gradually chip away at his body and make himself "better." I knew from my days on board the prospecting ship, sharing his bed, that he was partial to lathering up his penis, making himself rather epic beneath the sheets. I can attest to that… it *was* epic. So it didn't come as a surprise when I found out he'd been exploring the effects of further self-application.'

'But I had no real notion of how far he would go. Not by a long shot. What was more evident to me at the time than his advancements of physicality, of ability, of steroid-like boosts of bodily capacity, was his rapid decline of personality, of charm, his downward plunge from casual, easy-going guy to the quick-to-anger, mean-spirited bastard he was becoming more and more with each passing day.'

'Then came the day when all was revealed. The day it became all too obvious how batshit, crap bananas Avid really had become. How far he'd go. Like, to the fucking moon far. Yonder, man. Way off. No holding back on the loony juice. It was a sight to behold. It scared me, Jarred. And as it turned out,' He fondled his bionic eye, his prosthetic leg from beneath the sheets, 'it scarred me too.'

He came in for a little cuddle and I nuzzled into his neck. I kissed his collarbone and he patted my head, traced my ear with a light caress. 'He was unloading the caterpillars. The tiny, first instar worms. He had awoken them from their magic stasis, the thousands of them, tens of thousands, and poured them from large canvas sacks into the two-person bathtub of our bathroom. He stripped naked, eyepatch and all, and stepped into the tub with the wiggling swarm. One leg came over the rim and down to crush a hundred or more insects. Then the other leg. A massacre. Then a go-get-em, army march of up and down, legs as if working a bellows, two fleshy pistons, squelching, squishing, mashing and mushing, a nightmare of oozing insect innards. He was ecstatic, overjoyed, off-kilter. His hair was up, wild in a wave of disarray as his knees shot upward, downward, crushing the tiny worms by the masses like an old winemaker would pulverize his harvested grapes. Bare feet stamping, crushing, liquefying the vast hoard of larvae into a semblance of some insta-dins split pea soup.'

'I confess I was frozen in fear. Or revulsion, more like. The delight on Avid's face, so complete and focused to the task. I couldn't have been

104

ten or fifteen feet from him, watching it all in plain sight, yet I swear my presence had gone unnoticed until the very end. It was then, you see, that I intervened.'

'When Avid had sufficiently extruded the slime and liquid guts from each and every caterpillar, when the bathtub was sloshing with his erratic movements like an emerald sea in a gale, he stopped all motion, went rigid, and let himself slump and sink and submerge into the viridescent goop.'

Bee shuddered, pressed his eyes closed, took a long inward breath and a exhaled slow and steady. I put a hand on his shoulder. I rubbed his flank. Tugged him closer.

'It's alright,' I told him. 'You're okay, Bee. You're okay.'

He turned over onto his back and stared upward at the ceiling, green light rippling over the white paint with the glow of his bionic optic. 'It was horrible, Jarred.'

'It sounds like a fucked up, horror holo-film. The kind that they don't show in most cinemas. Real niche, gag-worthy shit. The kind of stuff roborgs watch to remind themselves they can still feel revulsion. To dredge up that tiny fraction of themselves that may yet be decent.'

'Something like that,' Bee agreed. 'Except it was real. Except it was my life, my lover.'

'That's nasty times nasty. Icky Vibes, XL.'

'He was drowning himself, Jarred.'

'Sorry, what?'

'Avid, he was drowning himself. He took the plunge. Slipped down and dipped under the liquefied gore, the bathtub of max potency Squidge. He was breathing it in from beneath the surface. Gulping it down into his tummy, inhaling it like lines of nose candy, like snow through a rolled dollar, except he was in it, under it, submerged in it. He was dying from drowning in first instar Squidge. He was dying in the best way any man might hope for. He was choking on one big miracle. He was dying, and he was smiling.'

'Madhouse on fire.'

'Don't I know it.'

'So, like… did he die?'

'He did,' Bee told me. 'But then he didn't. He went still, went rigid, went all corpse on my ass. He was in the next realm. Beyond the veil. A body in the bath under some thick, snotty water. There I was, looking down at a man as dead as could be. Green from beneath a murky pool, unmoving, cold, and without a pulse. Then he shudders. Quakes. Shakes. Hands gripping the rims of the bath and suddenly he's standing, knee deep and dripping globs of lime green.'

'I was just taking it in, horror-struck. But when Avid bent downward and started lapping it all up; all that wretched spinach and sewage syrup, slurp after slurp from his cupped hands, I couldn't watch any longer. I took quick strides to halt his madness. To stop him. Save him, if I could. As if he wasn't already damned. And he was. Very much damned. Doomed and demonic.'

'I grabbed his wrist, nice and firm. No nonsense. Now, let me express this much, I was much stronger than Avid. I was twice, if not thrice as strong, several inches taller, ten years younger, and more active, fit, and battle tested than Avid. Yet when I took hold of his wrist he simply flicked me off with a lightning quick, whiplash slap that sent me flying.'

'I got up, abashed and not yet aware of my plight. I charged Avid. I thought, okay tough guy, no more fucking around. I was going to punch him out, pin him down, pump his stomach and call the ambulance. Whatever the case, I was going to pull the plug on the hideous charade the night had become. But Avid's eyes opened and a golden light spilled forth to blind me. I was in mid-punch and the next thing I know my eye was across the room, dotting the carpet with deep crimson as it rolled to hit the wall. I blinked. Blinked with my one eye. And in that infinitesimal space of time my leg was flying like a tossed stick for Rover in some green, city park. 'Go fetch,' Avid sneered.

'And I did. That's exactly what I did. I crawled in agony on the floor and found my leg, tucked it under one arm, scrambled to the far side of the room and cradled my pulverized eye. I thought for sure I would bleed out. And I may have if I hadn't moved the way I did. My mad scramble out the door, a hurried, frantic, breakneck escape. I descended the stairs, fell down the stairs, a truly bone-chilling diabolical laughter emanating from behind that closed door up the stairwell.'

'I collapsed in the street and woke up in some dingy, back alley hospital. The nurses were borgs and bots with low AIs. No personality chip. Just the standard medical program. Monotone voice. No one to talk to. Bedridden and forlorn. I was distraught in the face of my piteous plight, but more than that, much more than that, I was enraged. I was livid beneath the skin. A molten current roiled within. Bubbled, burped and nearly burst in eruption. And I think it was that red hot rage. That furnace of hatred. I think it was that, and only that, that kept me alive. Saw me through.'

'And then the vats, the magic, the prosthetics. You know the rest, more or less.' Bee sighed and suddenly I felt his tense form relax, unwind, unravel. He went soft and pliant, a warm band of putty, and molded to me, his stomach to my back. We rocked back and forth. We spooned. We cuddled. We necked each other and suddenly it was pash, pash, pash.

'You know something, Jare-Bare?'

'What's that, Honey Bee?'

'I think I've found that I'm now in the mood for fucking after all.'

'Don't waste your breath telling me twice.'

And he didn't. We just got busy. Frisky and fun under the sheets in the late, late hours of the night. And the way that it felt, how it was different from the other times before, how it was lovely, like a flower, yet exuberant and wild like fireworks, it spoke volumes about what exactly Bee and I had become. What we were to each other. It revealed a great deal about *us*.

And when the hazy sun, shrouded by a thick layer of smog rose to herald a new day upon Palindrome, Nyvyn, "little saint," through the muted opacity filters of Bee's bedroom, I knew the answer to that *other* question.

I smiled in the gloom. And at last, fell asleep.

14
WHAT NOW?

We woke and ate breakfast with gusto. A real mean appetite. Bee had a killer bee and fried eggs. A dab of ketchup. I had a beer and a sausage.

Azalea Ren walked through the room and looked a picture of health. All smiles. No flying fire hydrants on his mind. He was all about the raisin bran, the glass of cold OJ. Lily came next, clad in skin and tatts and piercings. I saw her you-know-what but she saw me looking and tossed on an XL tee-shirt. She had hash-browns with a splash of vinegar. A Bloody Mary and a drop of Squidge.

It was AM-amazing. Morning time niceties. We were feeling alright. It was almost as if we hadn't been dodging those bullies left and right. Those cryo slugs and fire hydrants. All in all, we woke up on the right side of the bedsies.

'Some night,' Ren said, big grin on his face. He had eaten all the bran flakes and now it was just raisins and milk. The good stuff. He transmogrified into Top Cop, blue and red plaid across his ugly mug, and munched away at those sugar-coated syntho-nuggets that passed for dried grapes.

'Bad taste, Ren.' Lily shovelled in the dregs of her plate. Licked her lips. Burped. Everything she did turned me on. Even the gross stuff. 'Change back, or even better, do that girl you were doing last night.' Ren wobbled and melted at the edges, reconstituted into something much prettier. A dark-skinned lady with cherry red lips and a short pixie hairdo. Her perfect body was artistry. I thought about those moans, that shrieking, from behind Lily's closed door last night. I pictured the two of them, Lily and the dusky sprite, and I found myself trying to will back a big league chubby.

'So anyways…' I began. 'Where do we go from here?'

'Well, one thing's for certain,' Lily threw down a holo-projector onto the counter. 'I won't be running the Bee and the Lily anytime soon. No B and L to run. Check this out.' She punched a button and the holo-feed played a ten second loop. 'Batty did a bit of flying this morning. He recorded this little slice of not-so-nice.' The holo-vid showed us the outside of the Bee and the Lilly. Elegant neon lights and steps leading down beneath the streets. Police tape was barring the entrance, the out-side area. And right in the center of the picture, iron arms crossed and coliseum pillared legs planted wide among the asphalt, a hard-edged, no-nonsense, titan-sized bombshell bobby with a look that said "fuck with me and I'll stomp you to the ground with the rest of the flattened bubblegum and the run-over rats."

'It's a damned shame, that,' Bee nodded towards the holo-feed, started making a second killer bee. 'A real cock-up, last night. Not kill-ing big girl when we had her cornered.'

'Not exactly easy to do, cornered or not,' I said. 'You see that fire hydrant flying horizontal? Biggest bullet I've ever seen. And that great hulking ox pulled the fucker right from the foundations of the street. She Cop is a meat flower of muscle. A jacked up diesel machine. Crikey, that bitch scares the pants off my ass.'

'You'd get spooked by your own fart, shit brains.'

'Hey, Lily, spin on this, slag!'

'Spin on what? I don't see anything.'

'Why don't you lift that XL parachute your wearing for a shirt, give us a show. You'll see something soon enough.'

'Eat me.'

'Yes, please.'

'Enough!' Bee was frazzled. Real down about letting She Beast give us the slip. And it *was* trouble, her being alive. Her being out there. I didn't blame him a certain measure of vexation. 'So the Bee and the Lily is out of commission. We'll have to live with that. We'll take out that size twelve gumshoe later. But right now, lets just put her on the back burner. Let her stand outside the BL thinking we might show up. That's a fine waste of her time because we won't.' He shot a meaningful look at his little sis, 'Will we, Lily?'

'No, Bee. We won't.'

'Good.' His second killer bee was ready to go. He took a sip. Nodded. 'Okay, then. Come gather.'

So we huddled on the couches, our seat of council, and shared some heavy glances, chewed our lips and studied our nails.

'No more diversions,' Bee announced. 'No more side quests. No distractions. We've got to move forward, not sideways. And for fuck's sake, please, not backwards. We have to work together. All four of us.'

Lily looked over to me. Ren was studying me with his peripherals, I was sure of it, but he was tact enough to look straight on.

'Jarred knows,' Bee said. 'I told him everything. He's with us. And just so it's out in the open, he's with me.' He put his well-muscled arm over my shoulder and held me close. Ecstatic, I turned to smile at him and my eyes went wide when my mouth was full of tongue and my lips were wet against Bee's. I kissed him back and just sort of withered away. In a good way. And when he pulled away, cut things short, I was left breathless, heady, a half mast in my trousers and a stupid grin on my face.

'Gross,' Lily said.

'Good show,' Ren gave his blessing.

'So... Jarred knows about Argyle?' Lily squinted.

'Yeah.'

'And how he's a...'

'God. Indeed.'

'And how we mean to...'

'Kill him. Of course. Like I said, I told him everything.'

'So now what?' Lily was hot to get things going. To make amends on behalf of her brother. To sort out all the bad shit and get her bar back.

'Well, we all know we can't just march into Argyle HQ.'

'Why?' I asked.

'It's loaded with security,' Ren chimed in. 'And not the slip-past-the-guard-whose-reading-a-magazine kind of security.'

'Not even close,' Lily edged forward.

And Bee gave me the spooky deets. The ins and outs of Argyle HQ defenses. How holographic Crimson Mages use red magic, pure offensive output. We're talking fire, electricity, beams or balls of pure energy, lasers, poisonous gasses or vacuous pockets of antimatter. An arsenal of death. Because they are holograms they cannot be harmed without special technology or obscure forms of magic. It's bad fucking juju. Icky Vibes, special edition.

'Yeah, and that's just the front door,' Ren tells me, then notifies me that once inside there's a squad of chimpanzee ninjas, high-tech, top-of-the-line constructs of jungle simian and chrome. They wield venom-coated slender wires so thin as to seem invisible, so sharp as to seem like death carried on the wind. They throw sticky fruit all over you, banana mash and pineapple, they make those paper cuts sting like no beef skillet at Taco Nirvana ever could. They pick up your fingers off the ground, chew them like jerky and do the whole oo-oo-ah-ah-ah ape thing, real loud and off-putting.

'And let's not mention the cyborg assassins near the top levels,' Lily stated. 'Their eyes see through walls, attuned to heat signatures and micro-movements. They can see you three floors beneath them just by listening to your beating heart.' She went on to let me know they have voracious sexual appetites, so they don't just kill you, they maim you, do what they want with you, then more often than not throw you to the next cyborg in the queue or throw you from the nearest window.

'Right,' I said, sold on the whole "security is tight" thing. 'So we don't go through the front door. How about riding batty to the top. Start at the end, rather than climb the mountain from the base.'

'Remember that avian construct, Jarred? The one you read about in Argyle's diaries?' Bee asked me.

'Uh huh.'

'Well, birdy got the first instar treatment same as Avid. That construct is a veritable dragon. Where once it chugged and labored on its own ragged breath, diseased, malformed, pitiful... now it is like a pick-of-the-litter gryphon. Pure bread and pure killer. It roosts among the tall spires of Argyle HQ. It is said that it breathes blue fire. Its shrieking screams will steal your hearing, burst your ears. Its talons and beak will make short work of metal plating, reinforced armor. Big Bird will snack on us all. Flying to the top is as surefire a way to die as knocking on the front door. Both deaths would be gruesome. I'd sooner avoid either.'

'So where the fuck does that leave us?' I asked. 'What options do we have? 'Cause I'm adding up all the figures and it sums up to a big mounting tally of jack-shit-fuck-all. It sounds to me like the fat lady is singing real loud. Vibrato. Echoing her sentiment with each jiggle of her bucksome bosom. I mean, roosting dragons, red hot mages, ninja chimps and cyborg fanny assassins... it's over, am I right?' They all stared at me. What? Judging me? Was I missing something here? I didn't want to throw away my life for nothing. I didn't want to lose Bee on a suicide mission. I'd take some heat, take some risks, but I wasn't about to just plunge off a cliff and hope to bounce back up to the ledge.

'So, like, what options do we fucking have?' I repeated.

It was Ren who stepped forward. Calm and cool, Azalea Ren. His guise was normal Ren, but he still had that pixie haircut. Presently, it returned to his normal do.

'We thrust ourselves deep into Nyvyn's manhole. We wade the cancerous bowels of the little saint. We traverse his labyrinthine sewers.'

...

'And we commune with the rats.'

15
GROTTO

We were well doused in Confusion Brew. Head, shoulders, knees, and toes. We weren't stinting. Until we got ourselves down into that subterranean cesspit of Drome, the great toilet maze, we weren't going to take our chances getting spotted by She Beast, the new Top Cop. So we were playing it safe. Strolling down Ribald Row. Whistling like we weren't wanted by the law. Smiling like the world around us wasn't a heap of utter garbage, a sputum-slick scrap of shit-stained tissue.

Even the roborgs were smiling. Playing with themselves where two scales of metal parted for some pink-red flesh. Mangy dogs buried their heads in refuse. Cats, fat on rats, sprawled in the pseudo-sun that shown anaemically through the blanket of smog overhead. There wouldn't be any sunshine, weak or otherwise, where we were headed. Palindrome's great cloaca. Little nephew's festering rump hole. The sewer systems of Nyvyn.

Here we come.

We hung a left down some drab alleyway and pulled the cork on a manhole. Steam billowed up like a geyser. The underworld burped a wafting vapor that stank like old underwear, hot dogs, shit, and last week's insta-dins.

'Ladies first,' I offered to Lily.

'In that case, after you.' She sneered.

Bee saved us the squabble, climbed down the metal rail, one rusted rung at a time. From below, in the basement gloom, he called up to us. 'Come on,' he beckoned. 'It's not that bad.'

Not that bad? Fuck's sake. Those are either some low standards Bee has or he has a champion tolerance for bad smells and fecal streams. As soon as I found my footing on the narrow ledge that bordered a slow flowing brown current of Drome's collective ass shrapnel I grabbed the ladder to head straight back up. 'Oh, no you don't' Bee pulled me down by my shirt. 'Come on,' he cuffed my shoulder. 'Don't be a baby, baby.'

Lily snickered. Ren smiled amicably. He carried a rose in his breast pocket, brought it to his nose and sniffed heartily. A nosegay. Good prep. Trust Azalea Ren. That guy is tops. He passed them around, for each of us a rose. Mine was yellow. Bee's was pink. Lily and Ren's of pure white snow. Other than those fresh, bright petals the world was brown. Brown and black and gray. But mostly brown. The color of poo. And man-oh-man was there plenty of *that*.

The plan was simple. But how simple would it be to pull it off? That was the real question. We were to strike a deal with the rat prince, Agouti. He lorded over the rats of Drome, specifically the sewer clans. He was a cross betwixt man and rodent. What he began as, what species he was born into this world, is shrouded in mystery. No one knows. Not even Agouti. But through mutation, a steady diet of irradiated cheese and trash, living in a sunless underworld of warm flowing excrement, he had become what he is today; a hunched over, hairy, orange toothed, pink-tailed small man (or large rat). He could climb walls like a spider. Squeeze through crannies like a bad smell. His beady eyes penetrated the dark and the motherfucker *loved* his cheese.

Agouti was master of the gongpit. Sewer sultan. King of shit slick brick and subterranean tunnels. If we could meet his price, we'd leave with a detailed map of the Palindrome sewer network. We could travel the city from beneath her skirts. We could come and go, almost like teleportation, exit and entrance via manhole or culvert. We could enter establishments, buildings, towers, HQs... we could do this from the inside, like a bacterial infection, like parasites. We could come up through the pipes, like rats. And *this* was how we would get to the Squidge vaults in Argyle HQ.

It all came down to Agouti. Rat man. *Rattus sapiens*. His seat of power was in Flotsam Prime. It was there where we were headed. Where our careful footsteps carried us.

And careful, indeed, we most certainly needed to be. The narrow ledge was perhaps two feet wide. Large enough to walk on, but not comfortably. Not with that nasty bog lapping over the outside edge. The walkway hugged the fringe of the tunnel and was slick with slime. One misplaced step and you'd be flat on your back, or worse, you'd be doing the doggy paddle in a stinky poo pool. On one side, a fetid, murky bayou, on the other, a wall, which curved inward, dripping with warm moisture. The turbid, slow flow at the edge of our thin byway was of unknown depth. But judging by the half-pipe that was the tunnel before us, a height of ten, perhaps twelve feet, the downward depth of the polluted water was almost certain to be the same.

Presently, we took three blessed upward steps. That much further from the nasty water gave a me a good measure more of comfort. The squish and squelch beneath my plastic sneakers was giving me the willies, a mean case of the shivers. The dry bricks, by comparison, seemed a luxury. Five star sewer lodgings.

Unfortunately, my high times came crashing down in a hurry. We came to a duct that belched hot, sour air, like sweaty feet and overcooked beans. Our course demanded that we cross the lazy flow of the diseased latrine oozing beneath us. Our means to do so? The duct.

So, overcooked beans and sweaty feet it was. Hot in the face. Like a yeti's breath. Tooth decay. Grandpa's laundry after that bad case of the squirts. It wasn't nice. But I held my tongue. I needed my hands for all that crawling, otherwise I would have held my nose, too.

Out of the ducts, safely deposited on the other side, we found ourselves in a wider, gloomier grotto. Brick and raw rock interchanged at irregular intervals. Engineering of man meets natural cave system. It was a bit of both. The water here was rank, like elsewhere, but perhaps only half as badly. There was a slight, clear quality to the water. Whereas the last liquid avenue was split pea and brown lentil soup, this waterway, by comparison, was consommé, or watered down chocolate milk.

Little caiman constructs slithered in the still water. Their snouts penetrated the surface and they smiled razor sharp grins, beady, orange eyes staring us down with vertically slit pupils. A larger lizard from the other side of the grotto made a splash that told us "I'm pretty fucking big." Komodo dragons or maybe Top Cop's monitor lizard coming back for revenge. Note to self: stay out of the fucking water.

Bloated goldfish the size of puppy dogs bobbed in the murky water. A malformed, possibly mutated variety, with protruding, balloon eyes. Like toddler's flotation devices growing from their faces. Water wings with a center black dot, a weeping pupil. Demented and obscene, tortured, hideous things. They were the denizen descendants of their forbears, flushed down the dunny, a pet fish's funeral. The pollutants and filth of the sewer canals was a substance so strong that the castaway, dead goldfish had been roused to a semi-animate, undead state. Their mouths puckered with wet noises. Oily bubbles on their fish lips. One was torn to ribbons by a greedy caiman. I looked away. Stared at my feet taking each ginger, deliberate step.

'You ever hear about the rumor of Shit Shell?' Ren cheerfully asked us.

'Huh?' Lily made a face. 'What's that? The ugliest seashell on the beach?'

'It's an urban legend of sorts,' he explained.

'The giant turtle?' Bee inquired.

'That's the one,' Ren nodded.

'Can't be true. A story to tell children to keep them from the sewers.'

Ren smiled. 'Never be so sure, Bee. The world is a fine arena for the weird.'

'Yeah,' I agreed. 'You seen these nasty-ass goldfish floating on their sides? I'll be off seafood for weeks.'

Lily took out her guns and extended her arms out over the water. *Bang! Bang!* Like two pin-pricked beach balls, a goldfish's inflated eyes popped and sagged in the water, a ruin of scaly flesh and membrane. The caimans smelled the blood on the water. They came like cockroaches to a long forgotten insta-din going moldy behind the couch. They savaged the maimed goldfish, a gang of thrashing, splashing tails and gnashing teeth. First the gunfire and now the feeding frenzy, the grotto was alive with a cacophonous din.

Then, as if one, like how flocks of tiny birds turn on a dime as a collective unit, how shoals of sardines jackknife, lightning quick, as if one mind, so too did the caimans react. In an instant, blink and you'll miss it, they shot forth, away from their meal and off to deeper, darker, unseen waters. Whatever large lizard had made that splash earlier from the far end of the grotto crawled back out of the water and scurried into a fissure in the brick. The dim tunnel went still, utterly silent. We held our breaths and slowed our steps. And then, from deep beneath the murky water, a low, resounding thud.

Next came the low-toned, bemoaning chorus of what may have been a whale, a leviathan beneath the deep. The water trembled, bubbled, and we all clung to the wall, clung to each other. We whimpered our own pitiful moans to mingle with the groaning sounds of whatever mythic beast lurked within the depths of the sewer. Then, in an almost biblical moment of horror, the patchwork pattern of a terrapin shell the size of a city park broke the surface of the water. A pug nose and wide set black eyes, a downward turned mouth, a wrinkled head extending on an old man's neck, a turtle face the size of a convenience store. It looked at us, it blinked, and then, absurdly cute, adorable and terrifying all at once, it yawned. Then it returned to the depths of the grotto and was seen no more.

'Shit Shell,' Ren announced.

'So it *does* exist.' And as if we had just seen a passing alley cat or a holo-kid on a skateboard, we carried on, not another word. We walked the slime-slick brick ledges, one careful step at a time. Ever closer, ever deeper, into a weird world of filth, zeroing in on Flotsam Prime.

16
AGOUTI

While the bad smells stuck around, the Confusion Brew had run its course. We were all looking like our usual selves. Well, all of us apart from Ren. He was wearing the guise of that fat little cutie he slipped into the other night. The one who weaved the throng of Ribald Row, dodging cop gazes and cryo bullets. I was watching her juicy thighs, her round buns cinched tight in blue denim. I was connecting the dots of her lovely cellulite, wishing I could practice a little braille with a poking finger. Ren must have known I was getting lost in his jiggle because he turned around and I got the fright of my life. Like two giant skin tags pouring outward from his temples, heavy, sagging water balloons or bloated scrota, alien appendages. The sick bastard did the transmogrify boogie. The plump cutie with a nice set of grab-ems turned to reveal a dire looking, nasty-ass goldfish face. His fish lips puckered noisily.

'Definitely off seafood,' I gagged.

Ren slipped back into himself and giggled.

'Not funny,' I whined. 'Will I ever look at sushi in the same loving way?'

'Try a caterpillar roll,' Bee offered.

What's this? Packed lunch? 'You have sushi?'

'Squidge,' he corrected.

'Oh.' I was getting spoiled... shrugging off fine narcotics in favor for rice wrapped in seaweed. I took the Squidge and gave my nostrils a jolt. I could smell the sewers like a bloodhound might. Not the collective slop, but the sum of it parts. In this way I zeroed in on the rose sticking out of my shirt pocket. Made it my olfactory mantra. *Nothing but the rose. Nothing but the rose.* It was working. Sort of. Not really.

The grotto was well behind us. We'd been going at it for a few hours. Hanging rights and lefts, creeping ever downward, sliding down sloped ramps slick with shit, wading knee-deep in putrid scum. The caimans were gone. The goldfish too. Now it was pale salamanders with skin growing over their eyes. Blind as bats. They climbed walls with suction toes and flicked their purple tongues to snatch whatever tiny morsel was on the wing.

Above us — *way* above us — a rectangle of gray light illuminated the ceiling. We looked upward at the open aperture of a curbside sewage grate. The city streets, so far above us. Shooting downward, a beam of soft radiance hit the sordid waters beside us. Like a solid square pillar, the shaft of light stretched from ceiling to floor. Two feet echoed on the grate far above. Two black, sneaker-shaped silhouettes. They assumed a stance, planted firm, and a trickle of amber liquid fell like salty rain.

'Charming,' said Lily. Took out her guns, sent two quick bangs close enough to discourage the peeing man from finishing what he had started. We heard his startled curses, witnessed his retreat, smiled, and carried onward.

It wasn't much later on when we spotted the first rat. A big, greasy old thing. Then we saw another. And another. And soon it was wasn't worth mentioning. All those rats. Like stars in the sky. You know, if you could see them through all the smog. So many rats. So very many rats. Some scurried, some swam, some squeaked or slept or ate or fucked or defecated. So many damned rats it was dizzying. It was like the pathway before us was moving. Alive. A carpet of matted, brown fur and beady eyes.

Lily kicked one into the brown water and Bee went all shame-on-you on her ass. 'We got dealings with Agouti. His rat majesty. These are his subjects,' he gestured with a sweeping wave. 'Leave them be,' he warned. 'Treat the rats well.'

'At least until we get what we want out of Agouti,' I whispered to Lily.

'Yeah,' she winked. 'Then it's anything goes. Rats be damned.'

The waterway opened up after we walked through a lantern-lit archway. We now stood on the edge of a small lake, a gymnasium sized cavern with stalactites that dangled from the ceiling like an old crone's dried up titties. Bats deposited a steady rain of guano and the formidable shadows of opportunistic fish rippled the water with large gaping mouths jonesing for an easy snack. There, before us, tied to a mooring upon which sat an impressively plump rat, a wooden boat and a paddle.

At the far end of the lake was another archway. It glowed with a flickering dim lit yellow. Another lantern to mark the way.

'That's it,' said Ren, pointing across the water. 'I'm certain of it. Flotsam Prime.'

'Into the boat.' We heeded the Bee. He took up the paddle and with strong arms made broad strokes in the water that had us going at a good pace. About halfway across the lake, closing in on the archway that would lead us to Agouti and his stinking rat palace, I noticed a piteous whimper and soft, blue glow of light from down in the depths.

'Do you hear that?' Lily asked.

And we all went quiet. Bee stopped paddling. And we held our breaths, zeroed in on that tiny noise.

Help! Help! Help me, please!

Squinting into the depths you could just make it out. The small child in the water. He was made of light, a holo-kid. He must've wandered into the sewers or got swept up by the Flow and sent down a dingy culvert. Maybe he fell into an open manhole, got lost and drowned in this watery dungeon. Not that holo-kids could drown. Not really. But they could sink. And there he was, that poor little kid made of light, just whimpering in the cold, dirty water with fish and eels and countless dribbles of bat guano. Holographic batteries can last a lifetime. Who knows how many months, how many years, the child trudged the bottom of that tarnished well.

Bee paddled onward. None of us protested to do otherwise. Maybe the next passerby will stop to fish out the tike. Just don't hold your breath.

We moored the boat and jumped to dry land. Well, sort of dry land. It was sullied with bat shit and moist with rat piss. Through the arch we followed Bee, our esteemed leader. Proudly, we stood beside his majestic form, poised between the walls of the archway and looking down upon the vastness of Flotsam Prime.

We had left a gymnasium for a lofty cathedral. While the bad smell remained, as always, and a certain grotty, grotesque element clung to the black rock and mildewed brick around us, the sight of Flotsam Prime, nonetheless, made a mighty impression. Vast, imposing, and harsh, the jagged landscape in all of its immensity stole my very breath. Or was that the ammonia from all that sticky urine?

In any case, we were here. And we descended the trail into a valley of refuse and rats. The countless rodents, black and brown, parted for us as we advanced. Now a throne of piled-up brimming garbage sacks loomed ahead. Atop its many well-stuffed shimmering bags of black plastic sat a rat (or a man?) that was the largest rat (or smallest man?)

I had ever seen.

'Agouti,' Ren announced. 'High Lord of vermin. Emperor of the pink tail. Prince of plague. Domineer over the mighty mischief of rats. King of Flotsam Prime.'

At the base of Agouti's throne the million rats around us scurried inward to flank us, encircling us on all sides. They remained docile, yet looked ready to pounce. At a moment's notice, a signal from the Big Cheese, and we'd be rat scraps. Morsels for voracious orange-toothed mouths. So we'd be playing it nice. As if we had any choice.

'Agouti,' Bee addressed the rat man. 'We come seeking council and trade. We wish for you to impart your great wisdom, bestow us with your famed sewer lore.'

Agouti chewed on a stringy piece of meat. Caiman, maybe. Or salamander. He studied the meat held in his scrawny fingers and tossed it, unceremoniously, into the throng. A handful of rats screamed and squealed in dispute. The lucky winner came out of the fray with a bite of low-grade protein.

'Well met, sons of Nyvyn.' His amber teeth gleamed in the lantern light. 'What offerings have you for my many wisdoms?'

Bee unharnessed a large satchel that had been strapped to his back. He unzipped the parcel and proceeded to unload its contents, would-be gifts for the rat man, bargaining chips for his "many wisdoms."

'We are given to understand you have a liking for cheese,' Bee said to the rat, who upon hearing that last word, "cheese," perked with decipherable interest.

'Cheese, you say?' He leaned forward, beady black eyes greedy for the sharpness of yellow-hued coagulation of mammary juice. 'Cheese is friend.'

'Then friends, you have many.' Then Bee unloaded great wheels of

Havarti, massive blocks of Cheddar, packets of pre-sliced syntho-Swiss and big balls of mozzarella. Next, he shoveled out dozens of packets of insta-dins, mac-n-cheese or cheese quesadilla or four-cheese pizza. He got out a grater and snowed some Parmesan on top.

'And Squidge,' Bee added, 'for the tongue, if you like. To enhance your palate for maximized enjoyment of cheese.' He threw down four or five packets of the stuff we had been drinking like water.

Agouti was sold. He was creaming in his trousers. You know, if he had been wearing any. He fondled his pale pink tail with jittery little fingers and gnashed his candy-corn incisors in apparent glee. 'This is goodness. This is cheese. Sons of Nyvyn bestow many fine friends. Cheese is friends.'

Cheese is friends. There was something to the simplicity of that unquestionable truth I found both honorable and amicable. I decided I liked Agouti. Though I had doubts for the merits of his supposed "many wisdoms."

'It is all yours, Lord Agouti,' Bee conferred. 'And indeed, we have more to offer.'

'More?' His eagerness was rife. His excitement palpable.

'Yes,' Bee assured the rat man up on his towering sacks of rubbish. 'We are prepared to give to you all of this cheese, these *friends,* the Squidge as well. And in addition, we will return at a later time, with an offering constructed from parts filched from playgrounds and city parks… we will construct a rat wheel large and beautiful, one befitting even the most lordly of rodents.'

'Wheels of cheese and wheels for running,' Agouti sang like a child. 'All is joy. Cheese is keen.'

'Cheese is keen,' we echoed his sentiments.

'And now I would ask a small favor of you, O king of rats.'

'Speak and ye shall have, man friend, son of Drome.'

'A detailed map of the sewers, a full blueprint of all passageways, ducts, pipes, and manholes.'

'You wish to obtain rat secrecy?' For the first time Agouti looked like he might not be digging the deal. 'You seek the sacred knowledge? You dare ask so high a price.'

Bee leaned over to Lily, whispered something. Lily grinned, rested her hands on those guns that were itching for things to get hairy. Holstered as they were, their personality magic was well stifled. They'd be getting impatient for some target practice. I just *know* Lily felt the same.

But it never came to that. Bee held his ground and repeated those sagacious words of rat wisdom, 'Cheese is friends.'

Agouti's cheeks spread wide and his face was all orange incisors, a big, fat happy rodent grin on his gormless mug. 'We have a deal, son of Nyvyn.'

And that's how we left the great stinking sewers of Palindrome, the little saint's diseased intestine, his moldering bowels, with about thirty pounds less of cheese than we had entered it. It's how we left the subterranean cesspools and the rat empire of Flotsam Prime behind... with a complete copy of the complexities of the underground world. We had the key to travel, unseen and protected, free from obstruction, from giant cop ladies with seven feet of sex-appeal. We had a map to every secret backdoor that led to just about anywhere. The city was ours. Every drab inch of the Drome. In exchange for some curd and a few packets of Squidge we had our ticket into Argyle HQ.

When times are good you can't help but tell it like it is. Say it with a smile.

Cheese is friends.

17
HAPPY BIRTHDAY TO ME

When we got back home we did the whole shower bonanza. Soap suds worked up into a lather. Rub-a-dub-dub, nooks and and crannies, foam and froth and squeaky clean. When we stepped out of the shower we were freshy-fresh-fresh. No residual slime. No sewer sludge dripping at the elbows. Just coconut and vanilla, suds and bubs of goodly scent. Worthy aroma.

When I went to the kitchen, towel round my waist, I saw the calendar pinned up by magnets to the fridge. Oddtober 13th, today, my birthday. Happy oh-my-God-I'm-getting-old. Thirty-three. A third of a century.

Bee came right behind me. No need for a towel. Naked as a jaybird. *You are endowed, son. Well endowed.* An anaconda hung from below his navel and came alive with rigidity. Either I was a snake charmer or Bee was happy to see me. When I took him in my mouth I knew which one it was. Both. And I smiled, despite the encumbrance.

'It's my birthday,' I said in passing, almost wistfully.

'No shit?'

I'd had enough of shit for one day. 'None whatsoever.'

'How old?'

'Twenty-eight.' Okay, so maybe there was still a little room for more.

'Spring chicken, Jare-Bear.'

'cluck-cluck-cluck.'

Then it was all eggs and hash browns and killer bees. The breakfast boogie. Lily and Ren emerged from their cave, hair all disheveled, rubbing eyes and letting loose frequent wide-mouthed yawns. We got home around sunrise and those two had managed a two hour snooze after their shower and shag. 'Hit me with some HB, extra crisp and a dab of vinnie.' Lily got her fix of fried potato, a splash of vinegar. Ren whipped her up a fine looking bloody mary then poured the raisin bran. Soon it was all milk and sugar-coated syntho nuggets. Then, when breakfast was sitting well in our tummies we studied the elaborate blueprints of Palindrome's underworld.

That's when we got the bad news.

'It's hopeless,' Bee lamented. 'Look.' He pointed at what appeared to me an intricate mess of lines and arrows. I had no aptitude for blueprints. In short, I had no idea what was hopeless about it. No idea what *it* was at all.

'Oh yes,' Ren squinted, 'I see what you mean.'

'Shit,' said Lilly. 'Dead end.'

I squirmed in my seat and stopped trying to decipher what I was looking at. 'What's the problem?' I asked.

'A toilet,' Bee told me. 'The only way into Argyle HQ, apart from the traditional means; the front door with its many and diverse ways to die.'

'You mean, we have to go in through the dunny?' I asked.

'That's just it,' Ren explained. 'We can't fit through. These blueprints were made for rats, not people.'

'So turn into one,' I suggested. 'Do the transmogrify twist.'

'There are limits to my abilities, Jarred. I can turn into a rat, but I'd be the biggest rat you'd ever seen. I can make myself small, to a degree.

But I can't shrink down to nothing. I can't make myself so small that I could wade through the U-bend.'

'Then how do we make ourselves small enough?' I innocently asked.

Lily shook her head. Bee sighed. Ren patted my shoulder, kind as ever. 'Sorry to say, it just isn't…' He trailed off, looked upward and propped up his chin in one hand. The universal gesture of ponderous thought.

'Possible?' I asked.

He nodded slowly. 'In fact, it *is*.'

Then Bee and Lily were all questions. Hows and whats and wheres. And Ren gave it to them. The juicy deets. The nitty gritty.

'Amber magic,' he informed. 'A cousin to yellow. Manipulation voodoo. It could miniaturize us if prepared in the right way.'

'Small enough to slip through the john?'

'Small enough to slip through arteries, to hug tight to blood cells like flotation devices, to make love to an amoeba. But we won't go that far,' Ren advised. 'We'll stop when we're just the right size to slide up through the loo.'

'So where do we get the amber juju?'

'Ah… well… here's the rub.' And the deets came pouring out like an overturned tin of shit. Azalea Ren was a man about town. His lore of the Drome was a veritable tome of street-smart names and places and know-how. He rattled it off. All the to-dos. The shopping list. The shit we needed to hear but didn't want to.

To obtain the amber magic we had to seek out another weirdo. Another bigwig among their own, niche little corner of hell. We required an audience with the roborg sorceress, Repugna, in the heart of the junkyard district. We would have to traverse a vast region of crushed cars and cardboard, splintered wood, jettisoned knick-knacks, forsaken appliances and old, discarded allsorts. It would not, as it turns out, be a cakewalk. The city of junk is the active battleground of a turf war between two android factions, those who worship Motherboard, the computer queen, and those who worship Hard Drive, the sultan of circuitry.

We'd have to dodge confrontation as well as track down the borg. The saving grace of it all is her palace shouldn't be too difficult to find. Rumor has it she dwells in a gutted out freight carrier. A rusted, hollow, hulking ship that hasn't set sail for centuries. It should be big. Real fucking big. So there's that. A nice big target beats a needle in a haystack.

Then there would be negotiations. We could probably bully the amber from Repugna, flat out wrestle it from her grasp. But that's bad biz. So we'd prep some downloadable drugs for trade. Bring the usual packets of Squidge. And hope that unlike most roborgs, Repugna was the exception to wanting a good romp on the mattress, a hearty shag and some sexual favors. If it came to that we'd be drawing straws and I'd be breaking a sweat when the short one was revealed. I shivered while mulling it over.

'Okay then,' Bee announced. 'We've got ourselves a plan.'

'Shall we hit the road?' Lily, always so eager.

'Not today, sis.'

'No?'

'Today's a day of rest,' he decreed. 'Fresh from the sewers, we've earned it. And besides...' he threw an arm around my waist and squeezed me tight. 'It's Jarred's birthday.'

'And there's that excuse I was waiting for,' Lily said. 'I'll fix us all some drinks.'

'Allow me,' said Ren. And the rest of the day was a blur of booze and birthday cake. Cocktails and drugs and brouhaha.

◆ ◆ ◆

'Wake up,' Bee roused me from my sleep. He touched me, all sensual, and though I smiled in the dark I pushed his hand away.

'Too tired.'

'Not for *this*,' he urged and pulled me out of bed.

He led me across the dark room to where the holo-projector lay. 'Really, Bee, I'm not in the mood for videos.'

'Trust me, Jare-Bear. You're in the mood for *this*.'

I could hear Lily and Ren through their closed door. Those two, they were always going at it. I'd pay to be a fly on the wall in that room. Well, turns out I'd not need to.

'Check it out,' and Bee punched a button that filled the room with the oh, sweet sight of the delicious holo-feed. There in front of me, real as the real thing, a three dimensional projection of Ren and Lily getting nasty and exotic. They took turns doing the oo-la-la and tickle-your-fancy.

'What is this?' I asked.

Bee whispered how he had placed his spare bionic eye in the bedroom where Lily and Ren had been spending their nights. Embedded in a cranny, a fissure in the mortar, Bee's computerized eye was trained on the mattress. Presently, it was the occupied stage for impassioned eroticism. Drinking in that holo-feed, eyes wide and greedy, I watched a live performance of Lily and Ren getting hot and wild.

I was well roused. The prospect of sleep a bygone pastime long forgotten. Bee cradled me from behind and worked the joystick. I watched his little sister doing all sorts of nasty with a partner that was shifting shapes, swapping sexes, juggling body types and skin tones, pulling out all the stops. From within the other room, but projected directly before me, little sister moaned and reared and arched those fine shapes, slick with sweat, into the air. Meanwhile, here in the flesh, big brother worked his magic on my hot rod and the sheer kink of the brother-sister thing had me finishing sooner than I'd like to have.

'Happy birthday,' Bee whispered and killed the feed.

And reflecting on the day, the headache and haze and rot in my gut, the evening of drinks and drugs and now one hell of a show... it really was. It really was a very happy birthday.

18
SKIRMISH

The Drizzleway led us down the esplanade along the Flow. The brown and gray brick spires of the central business district stood stark in the distance, sombre figures casting long, drab shadows. It was good to get away from the weight and webbing of all that overhead metal grating, that mishmash of zigzagging gridiron. It was nice to see the open sky, even it was all smog. Even if the seagulls were filling the sky with their squabbles over castaway insta-dins or those dead catfish that washed up along the riverside.

I was pleased to be on the fringes of the Dome. Pleased to be out of the hustle and bustle and roborg-laden alleyways. I was pleased to no end to be done with that miserable job working the beef skillet at Taco Nirvana. I was pleased to be loaded up to the gills on Squidge. To have a warm hand to hold. To lean into Bee, steal a kiss and a cuddle. To be looking at Lily's fine backside as it did that flick back and forth that it does when she walks. I was grateful for the goodness that had been my weird and wild week. And it struck me, a fine thought indeed, how it had been a while since I'd felt those familiar, icky vibes.

'Nosegay?' Ren did the rounds with his roses. Blood red, zinfandel pink, pale peach and midnight sky. We'd sniff the soft petals when the rubbish got up to our elbows, when it became all too stifling.

'I think we're far enough,' Bee announced. 'There'd be little risk now if we go by construct.' And out came his purple piccolo. A flick of his fingers and a puff from his lips, a haunting melody carried on the wind and next there was clipping and clopping of horse hooves on the pavement. Bee's brindled mare. Neighing and whinnying. Ragged flesh and metal, digger bucket ribcage and rubber ligaments.

Next, parting the smog in a series of widespread leathern whooshes, a giant chiropteran construct came onto the scene. Cute and hideous by turns, Batty, Lily's trusted familiar.

'Now we can travel in style, with speed.'

And so Bee mounted his mare and I mounted Bee. Lily and Ren each clung to a rubber-coated ankle tipped in talons of wrought iron and took to the air. Wind in our hair, Squidge in our eyes and noses, we were feeling alright. We were in good spirits about the little visit to trash land. About our dealings with Repugna, the roborg sorceress.

The speed with which we were moving, it wouldn't be long. We'd be sifting through the heaps of rubbish for signs of our quarry. We'd be on the lookout for a hollowed out, overturned freight carrier and the mad witch who lives within. We'd be playing neutral party to a turf war or avoiding it altogether. And at the end of the day we'd be coming home with a nice slice of amber magic up our sleeves. Or so the plan was supposed to go.

The Drizzleway ended where the garbage began. The road was simply lost to the ground coverage of shit and refuse. Buried, completely, the path became useless. We now waded through sun bleached aluminum cans, grotty diapers, wet cardboard and all manner of this and that and every other useless, discarded object in between. The unwanted castaways of Palindrome. Little saint's vast waste disposal.

Bee's mare was struggling to make good ground, impeded by the layers of filth, the odd, jagged rust shard or protruding spoke that savaged its legs and ankles. Bee shook his head, unmounted, Squidged up the various tears and ailments suffered by his equine construct and sent it home. 'We'll have to go by foot,' he told me, then called out to the others. 'Lily, take Batty up into the air. Get a good lay of the landfill. Scout and report.'

'Aye aye.' She was up and away. Ren in tow. The two of them disappeared over a slope of old automobiles and sofas. The Bee and I trudged on. Grunting with each step of poor footing. I cringed as I stepped onto something that whined beneath my foot, squirmed away. At one point we came across a holo-kid buried in tractor tires and sodden rolls of carpet. 'Help me!' And this time we did. What is it with holo-kids getting run over by buses and trapped in precarious places? In any case, we watched him skip back towards the city. With our track record we'll likely catch him on the way back, floating face downward in the meandering dark waters of the wretched Flow.

It was then that we heard the gunfire. It came from over that rise of mangled appliances, splintered cabinets and soiled stuffed animals. I thought I heard a scream, a woman's perhaps. And then I knew I heard a scream, a giant chiropteran shriek to be certain.

'Lily!' I raced after Bee up the lofty mound of detritus. The gunfire didn't let up and I was just praying that it was Lily doing all the trigger finger fun. Her and those pretty pistols with a penchant for boring holes in flesh and taking lives. I was banking on the notion that those firearms, bad personality and all, were the ones making all that noise. But as we raised over the crest of debris and looked downward into a valley of shit and waste I took in a sorry sight that said otherwise.

Lily was alright, wedged between a hollowed out bus and a hard place, dishing out as many slugs as were dealt to her. Ren seemed okay too, flush against a metal container. Bullets bounced off the opposite side, a steady rain. Batty, in the crossfire, was a dishevelled heap of torn leather, matted fur, and blood. If he was still alive he wouldn't be much longer. Lily was livid, anger plain on her face. But beneath the rage was something far more painful. Even from here, high up atop the mound of garbage, I could see she was distraught with woe. Her eye makeup tallied downward in dark smears to her jawline. So she had a heart after all. I felt a pang of sorrow. For her and for Batty.

I looked at the assailants. Android roughnecks. All matte black and gunmetal gray. Big angry yellow 'H' over their foreheads and chests. Disciples of Hard Drive, the sultan of circuitry. They must have seen Lily and Ren and taken them for the enemy, supporters of Mother-board, the computer queen.

Automatic rifles rained incendiary and armor piercing rounds that ricocheted off of hubcaps and car doors. Laser beams singed splintered planks of wood, broken televisions, and moldering scraps of who-knows-what. Lily broke her cover, dove, shot, and one less android stood as her opposition. It malfunctioned in a sizzle of live wires and system alarms, then it coughed and sputtered and was no more.

Ren transformed into a sack of filth, or maybe he was just con-cealed beneath one, and didn't move a muscle. Smart move.

Bee was gripping his femur. The one unattached to his body. White knuckles around the bone hilt of his black magic seeing-sword. He was gritting his teeth and I could tell he was about to make his move. Make a mad dash to aid his sister. Take out those androids. Slice them to rib-bons, nuts and bolts, metal plating and shattered circuit boards.

But he didn't have to. Someone else did the dirty work. And *man*, did they make that dirty work look pretty. She came out of nowhere, like a magenta motion trail of high speed savagery. It was hard to tell, so fast did she move, but I think she took the first android out with a kick to the knee. Its leg bent in the wrong direction, a brutal ninety-degree angle of pain that excreted lubricants and grease and a hydra's head of colored wires, frayed and on fire. Bullets came flying at a pink blur that ducked and bobbed and weaved. Unscathed, she ate up the distance between her and her next victim. Strong hands wrapped around a metal head and just plum and straightforward ripped it clean off its shoulders. System warnings echoed among the commotion as flashing red lights warned the computer man of his plight. Don't need the extra warning, thanks. The torn off head was enough indication.

Soon, I myself was confused. I couldn't make out all the details of that brutal ballet, those super sleek, hyper-fast martial arts moves of fatal precision. We just watched it unfold. And it didn't take long. The last android standing dropped his laser gun and ran. He didn't make it far. The bubblegum warrior took up the nearest piece of rubbish, a sturdy scrap of jagged metal pylon, and hurled it like an ancient soldier with a javelin. As if a well-practiced routine, the spear flew through the air with grace and good speed and landed to penetrate through the back of a shiny chrome skull. So much for the opposition.

This strange and alluring, fuchsia stranger turned towards us, who like paralytic fools watched in a stupor, spellbound and frozen in place. 'Hiya guys,' she called out, all smiles and cheer. She let go of the metal spinal column she absentmindedly clutched on to. The same one she ripped out of one of her android victims.

'My name's Aurora Storm,' she grinned and giggled, flashed us a peace sign and a thumbs up. 'But everyone just calls me Baby.'

19
BABY

I wasn't really the type to look twice at a syntho-girl. The robo-boys didn't exactly turn my head either. What can I say? Droids just weren't my thing. I like a little squish, warmth beneath the skin. I like little hairs that catch the sunlight. Salt and sweat. Pores and imperfections. I like cute little toes that clam up. Chipped nail polish and chewed cuticles. I like mouths wet with saliva and imperfect teeth. I like a girl, a boy, who needs to eat. Needs to sleep. I just like my lads and lasses living. Running on caloric intake and proper shut-eye, no battery packs or plugs.

But saying all that, how I prefer those flesh and blood bodies, how the robo-gals and syntho-guys weren't my flavor du jour, I found myself eyeing up this sassy little scrap of sizzling circuitry that wasn't half bad. In fact, I think I was crushing on her. And as soon as the notion entered my mind I knew it to be true. I wanted her. Every inch of stainless steel, of molded plastic, of foam and silicone. I wanted to finger her grooves, her hard edges. Pink chrome and state-of-the-art processors. Her high-tech tits and RAM-packed ass… I wanted it all!

Flirtatious, cheeky AI and a voice box that crooned in low, sultry notes of honey-coated kitty purring. Her eyes lit up, yellow orbs of neon, and my heart skipped a beat. I was lost in their beauty. Fuck me, I didn't see this coming. I was in love with an appliance.

'Well met, Baby,' said Bee. 'You just got us out of a hard spot.'

'Nothing like a little cleanup,' she winked. I took a look at the city-wide trash heap all around us. Cleanup? I think you missed a spot.

'You sure made short work of those droids,' Bee relaxed a bit. Sheathed his sword.

'Hard Drive's lot. Misguided fools. They brand themselves with the 'H' in his name. Of course, those of us who are not corrupted, we read the 'H' differently. For us, it simply means heretic.'

'And who exactly, if I may inquire, are the uncorrupted?'

'Those like me,' Baby smiled, a flash of pearlescent dental implants, porcelain polish, sheer white veneer and varnish. 'Those who adhere to the rightful rule of Motherboard.'

'Long may she reign,' Bee shot me a look. Kept me silent. I guess that whole neutrality thing is out the window. But then again, that wasn't on us. Hard Drive's rabble shoot first, ask questions later. They just open fire. They didn't give us a chance to tell them we just didn't care. Hard Drive, Motherboard, it's just different names to the same damn thing. Like chicken or beef at Taco Nirvana. It's all just syntho-meat, pseudo protein.

Back behind us, Lily was down on her knees. She was stifling those tears. Doing her best to uphold that tough-girl act. Bent over Batty, who now was unquestionably dead, she caressed his upturned snout, his pointed ears. Ren put a hand on her shoulder and that was all she wrote. The waterworks came pouring out. Eye makeup a ruinous smear of harlequin horror.

Bee went over to console his sister. Then it was just me and Baby, side by side. I took her hand and she let me. AIs are like that; they don't really have many social filters. They're lax when it comes to faux pas. I was banking on that particularity to her character. Especially when I leaned in and kissed her neck. She just tilted her jaw, obligingly, let me in for a good necking. It was a good, prolonged session of taste the robot before I could will myself to stop. It was all nice to meet you, now let me devour you. If Bee hadn't been glaring my way I would have got busy right there among the rubbish.

'I'm Jarred.'

'Jarred,' Baby smiled. 'Like rose.'

'Funny,' I remarked, 'I always thought it meant descent.'

Then she left my side to offer Lily her condolences. I studied her smooth, ergonomic movements. I watched her factory fresh parts and fittings move with grace, with sex appeal. Call me a technophile if you must, but I was red hot for that pretty pink appliance.

We would have buried Batty. We wanted to. But apart from all that trash there was nothing to cover him over with. It seemed undignified, so we set up a funeral pyre. Baby's hand unhinged at the wrist, a polished chrome cylinder. She extended her arm, took aim, and then came a deluge of liquid flame shooting out from its open aperture. When the deed was done she used her arm canon to deploy a waft of extinguisher to douse the flame, stop the endless dunes of rubbish from burning up like the cane fields. Then she flipped her hand back into place. Gave it a twist. And that was that. It was back to being just a hand. So I took it again. Held it lovingly. 'I love a versatile girl,' I leaned into her.

'Come with me,' she urged and led me onward. I didn't want to leave her side so we carried on over the next crest of rubbish.

'Where to?' Ren called out.

'To become indoctrinated,' her voice filled the valley of trash, deep and lulling, a tasteful, electronic purr. 'To take audience with her majesty. To be humbled in the presence of Motherboard, computer queen, matron machine.'

I didn't see their faces. I couldn't read how they had reacted. Me and Baby, we were already over the lip of the ridge of refuse. But their intention — Bee's and Ren's and Lily's — was made clear enough when a minute later, one by one, they too raised over the high ridge to descend all that rubbish to follow in Baby's wake. For lack of any better ideas, they'd check out Motherboard. They'd say their vows, pledge their allegiance, then as soon as they were out the door they'd wipe their asses with them. If it lent some insight, gave a scent on the trail for our Squidged up noses to follow, then kissing a little computer ass would be well worth it. I, for one, was all about kissing some computer ass.

Baby slowed her pace to let the others catch up. Now, led by a sexy pink death machine, we awaited the computer queen, Motherboard herself. I guess we'd take our chances getting her favor. Getting her approval to seek out Repugna. As things stood, we hadn't a clue where to find the roborg sorceress. Baby was keeping hush-hush about it when we asked her. Just told us to ask Motherboard. Earn her favor. Receive her blessing.

We exchanged glances and rolled our eyes. The smog, for once, finally parted and the bright sun shone hot on all that garbage, making it smell even worse. Blue sky... I was beginning to think it was a myth. Now all I wanted was the return of that cooling pollutant haze.

Hot and smelly, we trudged on. One hand interlocking fingers with a fuchsia femme bot, the other playing thumb-war with my man, I took each step in stride. Ren was rubbing Lily's back, comforting her as best one could while amid all that knee-deep trash. A motley collection of souls, flesh and digital, amid an unsavory expanse of filth. There we were, like nomads in search of something better. Like a small party of fish swimming in a vast sea of shit. Step by arduous step, we trudged on.

20
MOTHERBOARD

We were taking a rest. Lathering our gums in Squidge. Crunching on uncooked insta-din noodles. Pressing our nosegays right up under our nozzies so we didn't have to smell... what even *is* that? Just look away. Smell that rose. And look at Baby. Aurora Storm. Get lost in those LED forget-me-not eyes.

'I think I love you,' I told her.

'Thank you.'

'Do you love me too?'

'Mmmhmm.' Her smile came easy. All those pretty little porcelain pegs. Did you hear that? She loves me! But something seemed too automatic. Just trying to please. Tell me what I wanted to hear.

'There's a tarp over there...' I nodded in the direction of a soiled and badly torn plastic sheet. 'We could...'

'Fuck, it's hot!' Bee suddenly bemoaned.

'Yeah, and it's not getting any cooler,' Ren looked up to the anomaly of blue sky. He did the transmogrify boogie. Suddenly he was green skinned and well spiked with thorns. A cactus man. Then he gave up on the joke, turned back into Ren.

'Let's get going,' Lily moaned.

And then my dreams of intimacy were dashed to the hot wind. Baby got up, smiled at me, and led on towards an endless horizon of debris. As the hours went by, as the sun crawled across the sky, a piti-less bastard of unrelenting heat, I watched Baby with a growing need. A fount of desire. But then I considered, quite sudden and abrupt, as if the notion hit me like something falling from the sky; one day, she too, will be parts strewn about in a junkyard. Nuts and bolts and bits of plastic. It didn't exactly wholesale remove my hard on for her sexy circuitry, but it made me stop and pause.

Then I looked over to Bee. My sweet, damaged, Honey Bee. There was a warmth to my smile, a fuzzy in my gut, as I looked upon him struggling through the vast fields of detritus. Baby was the new, hot commodity. But Bee… Bee was Bee. I considered love and lust and friendship. Infatuation with its heady intoxication, its unrelenting gravity, its demand to be deeply submerged within, drowned within. And I thought of how infatuation often leaves as quick as it comes. But genuine love, perhaps not as loudly dressed, continues to catch our eye, month after month, year after year. In its mellow state, it becomes compatible in the long term. It's a lifelong habit. And looking at Bee, that silly sword on his back with its blinking eye, I knew he was my life-long habit. One I didn't want to quit. And Baby, well, I'd partake in any sexual fantasy, you name it and I'd get in line, but she was more like that silly sword, its blinking eye. Because what I felt for Aurora Storm… it was fleeting. Strong, but fleeting. It was a blink of an eye.

My thoughts were interrupted by the sudden arrival of two sleek, chrome fellows glinting in the sunlight. 'Baby,' they greeted, then looked to the rest of us. 'These are your companions?' The voice was like tin. Lifeless, but friendly enough.

'Greetings, brethren,' she smiled at the metal men and turned back to face us. 'These are children of Nyvyn. Flesh folk from the gray spires. I found them in conflict with the heretics. They wish to be indoctrinated at once.' Yeah… we were just *itching* for some computer mama to brand us with her logo. We'd play nice if it meant we came out winners.

'Then they are most welcome. Come, Motherboard awaits.'

As we walked on, wading through yet further stretches of landfill, Baby turned to assure us of the androids' good intentions. 'These are sons of Motherboard. Friends and brothers. This is CPU and GPU, high ranking components. They've come to take us the final leg of the journey.'

And then, at last something to break up the endless wastes, far in the distance… a stark, featureless, monolithic slab. I took it for some sort of strange lodgings, a crude castle, the exterior of a cubed fortress. I didn't know as I looked on from the swell of a high-crested rubbish dune; that what I gazed upon was no dwelling or structure of any kind.

What I looked upon, I was soon to find, was Motherboard herself.

It was the size of a city block. *She?* Motherboard, a mammoth black box. Computer people groveled at the base of her immensity. Dozens, hundreds, *thousands?* Countless models, various complexities, high-end, low-end, mid-grade machines. Androids and cyborgs, borgs and bots, high tech, state-of-the-art men and women shaped computers. AI's off the charts. Brainiacs without a brain. Processor units sizzling with hot circuits, solving problems, smashing equations, eating up input after input, chewing up all that data, grinding it into wads of processed information, spitting it back out, a perfect output, then opening wide for more.

There were simpler, rudimentary models as well. Appliances with limited, low-level AIs. Machines designed for simple tasks. Debrissensing vacuum cleaners (boy you're in the right fucking place!). Holographic carolers that looped any one of ten or twelve preset songs. Toasters or coffee machines with personality chips, ones that can ask you how you'd like your crumpet, whether you take milk or sugar.

From top-of-the-line, smartypants AI processors encased in can't-tell-them-from-the-real-thing bodies, down to those soft titties or snake in their trousers, to automated drink-stirrers that whistle your favorite tunes to help pass the time of their ten-second task... they were all abound. The silicone and plastic horde. The metallic throng.

They lovingly suckled computer juice from Motherboard. Sockets and plugs and cables binding child to mother. They leached off of her incredible power. Or perhaps gave their own in offering. Either way, no one was complaining. On the contrary, they all seemed blissed out. Drooling grease or excreting lubricants, synthetic eyeballs way in the back of chrome-rimmed sockets. What was I even looking at? A computer orgy? Next question: how do I get involved?

When she spoke the world rumbled. 'Children of flesh. Organ carriers. What business brings you before Motherboard?'

CPU and GPU got down on their knees. Bowing reverently, their posteriors gleamed a respective silver and gold. Baby followed suit, bubblegum ass looking good up in the air and together the three of them spoke as if one mind. 'O Matron, Mother of machines, we come to you humbled and in awe. Long may you reign, computer supreme. We bask in your digital glory. We revel in the shadow of your prodigious processor.'

Baby rose to her feet and gestured to the four of us "flesh folk." We were minding our Ps and Qs, just standing aloof. Not one of us knew what the hell we had walked into. I think the each of us was just processing it. You know, with our brains. Not processors. We were just

146

waiting out this weird moment hoping it would end well.

'These are my friends. Skin children of the Saint. They did battle with the heretics and smote them with strong conviction.'

Well that's one way of putting it. We mostly just ducked behind cover, tried not to piss in our pants. But hey, the embellishment couldn't hurt our case.

'Jarred is their leader,' she pointed to me and I paled. I looked to Bee, who just nodded, straight-faced and stoic. Lily looked constipated. Ren was stifling a grin. 'He is a brave man and has expressed romantic interest in this model. I would like to honor his sentiments and bond with him. Transfer ownership to his name.' *Ownership?* Oh, how a vast catalogue of kinky notions entered into my mind. 'I would like to do so with your blessing,' Baby continued. 'As such, I have brought him here. It is Jarred's wish and mine, his companions also, that all the skin children be indoctrinated.'

Again, I looked to Bee. I offered an expression that said "is this really happening?" And also "Are you okay with this?" He was, by all appearances, as cool as a cucumber. I guess his thoughts were for the mission. And maybe he's just not the jealous type. Or in any case, maybe he just couldn't find it in him to be jealous of a machine. Me? I was sort of buzzing. I felt like I was about to have my cake and eat it too. Stay with Bee but also — what was it? — be *bonded* to Baby. Obtain *ownership?* Whatever the case, Bee was downplaying it all. Shirking any dramas, any icky vibes.

Motherboard didn't lend any expression to hint upon her sentiments. Need I remind? We were engaged in discourse with a giant black cube. By all appearances, it was not at all unlike conversing with some monument of modern art. A giant shoebox or a geometric sculpture of minimalist taste. Baby had her say and the "skin kids" swallowed it, part and parcel. Now it was the cube's turn to process it all. The ball was in Motherboard's court.

Some euphoric cyborg was gyrating and humming in all of his bliss. A fevered loop of electronic ecstasy. Clinging to a massive wall that was one of Motherboard's six sides, the computer man opened his mouth impossibly wide to let a network of cables extending from power nodes travel down his mouth to feed him warm fuzzy currents of information. His synthesized vocals gurgled a hypnotic and somewhat repulsive moaning of pure joy. This sound, loud in the comparative silence, made Motherboard's delayed response seem half a lifetime.

And at last, she spoke. 'The bond between blood and circuit, flesh and metal... it shall be honored. Ownership has been transferred to Jarred, leader of the skin men. Congratulations, Baby. You are decreed, bride and bond. And Jarred...'

I looked up at the broad black face of a featureless chalkboard the size of an apartment complex. 'Yes, Matron Motherboard?'

'Congratulations to you, too. Decreed, husband and bond. And to all of your train, ye children of flesh, souls of the city of gray spires. A hearty congratulations, indeed, for now we begin your digital indoctrination. I shall bestow you with your implements.'

Implements?

'Please,' Motherboard directed, 'kneel and bow your heads.'

I, for one, was nervous. The only implements I had need of were already attached to me. Those two words coupled together... implement and indoctrination... it had me sweating with more than just the heat. But once again, a searching glance at Bee was met with calm poise and acceptance. So we knelt in the rubbish. We bowed our heads.

Long, tentacle-like appendages, cables or thick wires, extended like snakes in water from orifices in Motherboard, wiggling and slithering across the hot air to rest upon the nape of our bared necks. For a horrific instant I thought perhaps this was an elaborate, deranged computer ritual of execution. But the moment passed. And a very minor, hardly noticeable prick behind the ear was the gist of it.

'Welcome to the fold, sons of skin,' Motherboard's deep voice shook the earth, but more than that, it penetrated deep within our minds. Fully indoctrinated, members of whatever strange computer cult we were up to our asses in, we now bore the "implement." Tucked behind our ears, beneath our skulls and into our brains, a tiny microchip. It was the little bit of machine that made us brethren. What deemed us true children of the Matron. Through the device that was now a shared part of us all, we were connected to all others indoctrinated, with Motherboard herself. We were, in effect, a part of the greater computer network.

I fingered the little plug of metal behind my ear. I heard in my mind Motherboard's assurances. I heard Baby whispering in my brain. I heard Bee and Ren and Lily conversing in excitement. I heard all, and gained much from the conglomerate shared mind. Yet I was able to silence it. Mute it. Keep it separate and at bay. It dawned on me in that moment. This wasn't just us playing nice. Pretending to kiss someone's ass and then taking advantage when we turned the corner. This was a genuine, invaluable gift. This was an upgrade. A trade in for the deluxe model. We'd just pimped up our bodies. Got a new paint job and a tune up.

I told Baby through digital brainwaves 'I love you, wifey.' And then I heard her say it back. 'Right back at you, hubbie dub-dub.' I whispered to Bee on the currents of some invisible pathway that would always connect us, 'I love you more, sweet Honey Bee.' And he turned to smile at me, a glint in his gelatin peeper and a cascade of code in the other. 'I love you too, Jare-Bear.'

And then Motherboard…

No longer imposing. No longer this grand, mysterious cube that dominates and dictates all. No longer an expressionless, monotone paperweight of astronomical dimension. She spoke in our minds so sweet and soft and wise. I could see her, somehow, as I heard her comforting praises, her melodic words. And what I saw was a beautiful woman. Matronly, intelligent, strong. She was, in all aspect, motherly. And her words sent us on our way.

'Go forth, sons of skin. Rejoice in your marriage to machine. Go seek Repugna. You have my good graces. Baby will guide you. And take comfort; should you ever need me, know I am always there for you. I am always with you.'

And just as the hot sun relented, sinking low behind the far-off spires of Palindrome, the cool air came in and swept away the smell of rubbish. In good spirits, despite a hard day, we walked on, feeling light on our feet and well rewarded. On my left I held the hand of my computer bride. On my right, the hand of my dearest lover. And me, in the middle, I felt the richest man in all the world.

We walked on. Silhouetted in sunset.

21
CAMP FIRE

The blue sky turned orange, then pink, then purple, a bruised fruit of violet and navy. The moon was new, shy and reserved. I was grateful for her introverted tendency this evening. It meant that the rare clear sky would be peppered with stars. Stars! Those twinkling little gems, shards of cubic zirconium, diamond and quartz embroidered on a sheet of purest of pitch ink. I had not seen them unaided by Squidge. Not in years. I have *never* seen them. Not like *this*. Not away from the bright glare of Palindrome's nocturnal sheen. The myriad of neon lights, of flashing signs, illuminated screens and holographs that fill every sordid corner, the adverts and devices that mask the stars in those ultra-rare evenings where the smog hasn't already done so.

Yet here, among the rubbish, far from the brick spires of Drome that stood like somber sentinels in the distance, the stars were present. More than that, they were abound. Multitudinous. Abundant and bright. I looked up in awe at what I knew were astronomical bodies of raging fire, burning gasses. Many of these stars would have planets in tow, revolving around them even as they revolved themselves, spinning, tirelessly, round and round, and that somewhere up in that sky, among those stars, there was likely a world not unlike our own, and that on that world, maybe, someone not unlike myself, looked up to their own sky, had similar thoughts. Perhaps that someone did so now. Perhaps this very moment we were looking at each other.

This is the magic of a sky full of stars. It turns your imagination wild. You get lost in it. All those many bits of white. Like the scratch of a bearded chin over a black tabletop, a scattering of dandruff. Or more elegant, those embroidered gems. Precious rocks cut and polished, sewn into black velvet.

'Isn't it beautiful?' Lily was softened by the night sky. Her teenage rage was well watered down. She acted her own age, sort of. Ren held her snug as they both stared upward, eyes wet and gleaming. Bee, too. He was taking it in. One optic saw it like we did, a celestial work of art. The natural world in its best nighttime attire. His other eye, the one that glowed green and tinkled down an endless rain of 0s and 1s... I couldn't begin to guess. But my own eyes saw it for what it was; evening at its best. The raw glamour of the infinite cosmos in all of its profound expanse. Even Baby was looking upward. Her golden LED eyes assessing the sky, cataloguing constellations. And then she announced the count total: 4,548... the number of stars discernible to the human eye. Somehow it seemed lacking. Far too small. Doubtless she was right, but I'd go on imagining it was millions.

I noted the bloated rat, one of the more well-known constellations. Ah... and now the deranged roborg. You couldn't miss it. All the obvious ones, twinkling like they do in the holo-film night scenes. I was looking upward so often that I found myself tripping. Stumbling on the garbage we walked on top of or waded through. When I put out my arms to catch my balance and brought my upward gaze back to level ground I was stunned to see a pair of heretics rising the next crest of shit.

My tummy did that whole skydive drop sensation with the sudden nerves. I was ripped out of my stargazing reverie and totally on edge. I was about to sound the alarm when the would-be dicey episode came to a close. It was over. Over before it even started.

Baby had read my reaction from the linked network of our minds. One circuit chip to the next, my message of distress carried on the invisible pathways, the digital ether. Before I could voice my concern in the old-fashioned, traditional, vocal sense, I had communicated via computerized link. And just like that, Baby knew what I knew. Saw what I saw. But then she did what I certainly could not do. She danced across the fields of filth like a jackrabbit farting rocket fuel. Each stride was like the leap of a well-tuned gazelle construct, a polished hot rod with flames coming out the tailpipe.

Kick. Sweep. Smash. Punch. Pry apart some metal plating. Tear out a spaghetti dinner of fried wires and sizzling circuitry. The two heretics lay among the rubbish, rubbish themselves, smoking little camp-fires in the cool night air.

'Hey,' I called out to the others. 'Let's call it a night. Let's light a campfire.' And that was all the convincing that they needed. We'd had a hard day of run-ins with trigger-happy android heretics, the loss of a beloved chiropteran construct, a long hike through five billion pounds of junkyard detritus… some of us tied the knot, wedding vows between man and machine, and then there was that business of a computer cult indoctrination. We'd even each undergone a minor surgical procedure, implanted with new pieces of ourselves we had yet to master. We were beat. And we were ready to plop our asses down on the garbage and have a beer, have a snooze.

We fed pieces of trash to the small fires that smoldered from torn open android chest cavities. The flames took shape, grew tall, and not long later we were sitting round a warm, cozy campfire passing around narcotics and booze. I lathered up Baby in Squidge and she gleamed, well-lubricated, in the orange cast of the fire. I lay on Bee's lap and looked up to the stars, Squidge in my eyes, the sky was on steroids. The dazzling cast of diamond-filtered refracted light was a heady kaleidoscope of woah-that's-wow. Bee ran his fingers through my hair. Baby massaged my legs and feet. Ren and Lily were behind a hollowed-out car. I heard the shift of garbage, the zip of opened up tight denim, the low moans and the climactic squeal. We were all having a moment. Feeling the fuzzies, warm and wonderful. Icky vibes miles off back in the Drome.

I slipped into Ren's mind. Suddenly I was inside Lily. Woah! Now that's real sweet. Ren felt me swimming in his brain, didn't seem to mind. So I had Lily without laying a finger on her. Had her while I lay in Bee's lap on the other side of the camp fire. While Baby worked her magic on my sore calves.

Then I felt Bee slip into *my* mind. Except *my* mind was in Ren's. We were all sort of in each other's business. It was weird. It was exhilarating. I jumped ship, went into the totally different vessel of the electric mind, Baby's computerized brain. It was neat and tidy, clean and efficient. I felt the ninja, kung-fu, gymnastic abilities that I did not have. I solved a complex equation. Figured it out just for the heck of it. Mathematics I'd just stare and blink at while in my own mind. Then I jumped back. Back into me. *Well that was cool.*

And the rest of us must have been thinking the same thing. Because we were conversing without moving our mouths. Without making a sound. We were letting each other in. Blocking each other out. We were playing. Learning. And having a good old merry time.

We were singing bawdy songs. Dancing. Laughing.

Baby engaged in a remote chess game with Motherboard miles away. They completed 131 matches in 90 seconds. Motherboard won them all, but Baby manged to kill her queen twice.

I ate some raw insta-dins and wished I had brought a toothbrush. I drank way too much way too fast and the stars started spinning. My night was coming to a close. I was about to get some much needed shut-eye on a pile of garbage as big a county. I curled against Baby. I nuzzled into Bee. I hiccuped once or twice.

Then I was walking the dream streets of Z-town. Population snooze.

22
REPUGNA

Amber magic. That's what this whole venture through the endless rubbish was all about. An offshoot of yellow voodoo. Something to make
us small. Why? So we could wiggle on up through the U-bend. Come
up through the dunny. Then it'd be all 'Surprise! Here we are!' Argyle
HQ, with all its demonic sentries, its holographic red mages and ninja
chimps, simian constructs of death-wielding horror, assassin droids that
can see through walls, through floors, you know, those metal bastards
with a penchant for hold-you-down-and-do-you... they'd be watching
us from three levels down, up through the floors, cracking the vaults,
collecting all the first instar Squidge.

Amber magic. It was the key. The paramount piece for making
all of these sewer strolls and trash trots worth it. We'd need it. And
we've yet to have it. So when Baby led us down and up another crest of
shit and then we saw it, the overturned, rusted-out husk of an ancient
freight carrier, we knew... knew this was the moment it all boiled down
to. That inside, or somewhere nearby, lurked a strange roborg sorcerer
who had what we needed.

Amber Magic.

The clouds had returned by the time we woke with awful hangovers in the morning. As we made our final approach toward the sorceress' stronghold the familiar tinkle of acid rain dampened our heads and

all the garbage strewn about us.

'So what's the skinny?' Lily looked over to Bee. 'How do we make the roborg witch put out?'

Poor choice of words. All roborgs are happy to put out. Seems to go with their nature. And the number one thing I was fearing right now was that Repugna would settle her eye on me. That she might withhold the amber juju unless I too put out. I shivered. We'll cross that rickety bridge over a bed of spikes when we come to it.

Bee jiggled the pack on his shoulders. 'This here isn't for exercise,' he told Lily. 'Think I like the sore back this thing gives me at the end of the day? I'm not lugging around a change of clothes either. This pack is loaded with downloadable drugs. The latest. Hardest. Ones that will corrupt hardware real good, leave a machine feeling high as a kite on all the best programs and updates. Nasty malware that feels oh-so-good. Cartridges and discs and chips, I've got em all.'

'And you think that will be enough?'

'She's roborg, ain't she?' Bee was being Bee. Calm and collected. No worries whatsoever. It annoyed me a bit. Me, here, sweating it like cold beer on a hot day. And him, just… chilling. No icky vibes on his mind. It was commendable. Cool. Or was it just foolish?

'So what are you saying?' Lily wasn't letting up. 'That because she's roborg it guarantees she wants to fry her circuits? Fuck her head?'

'That's what I'm saying, Lily. Kudos to you for working it out like a gumshoe sleuth.'

'Hey, fuck you, Bro.'

'Look,' he eased up a bit, probably on account of Batty related condolences. 'I don't think we have to worry, Sis. I've got some primo circuit breakers and some edgy wire fryers. If the malware doesn't tickle her GPU spot then I've got Squidge for the human bits of her. I've bottled up a bit of confusion brew… it might be her thing to trick someone into thinking she's a good lay… who knows? If it's the bargaining chip that wins us the amber shrink juice I'll hand it over. If she wants a romp in the hay then that's probably what she'll get.' *Gulp.* 'But don't worry… it won't come to that.'

But what if it does?

'Well, *I'm* not fucking her.'

'Hopefully none of us will.'

Then Baby said something only a computer ever would. 'In my brief time spent with you four, I was given to understand that you like "fucking," as you seem to favor calling sexual intercourse.'

I laughed. 'Yeah, well… you ain't wrong, Baby. But it's not just any hole in the wall or any old bent over ass that fits the bill. I like pizza but I wouldn't eat one that was three weeks sitting in the bin. Roborgs… they ain't exactly za fresh after the knock at your door.'

She cocked her pink head, blinked her yellow LEDs. 'I was talking about sexual intercourse. I didn't know we were talking about pizza. I'll replay the conversation if you like?'

'Never mind, Baby.' And then I thought about that little chip in my noggin. 'Wait… *here.*' And I sent her my thoughts, electric direct.

'Metaphor. Of course.' Baby flashed those tidy little pegs of snow-white china. 'I think I would also prefer fresh pizza. But as you know, I do not eat.'

Were we still talking in metaphors?

The rain picked up just as we reached the freight carrier. We huddled inside the great, wide maw that was its opening. No door or gate, it was accessible to the outside world of garbage, a metal cave. It was overturned and hollowed out, so the hull was the roof. The hard rain made a pleasant sound on the outside surface. Deep within, an orange flicker danced on the corroded metal. Little flashes of timid light. A fire?

Wet as we were from all the acid rain, the squelching puddles of garbage water, a warm fire seemed a welcome little slice of pleasant. But fires don't just flicker up on their own. A fire meant company. And just as likely as anything else, it could mean bad company. But we weren't here for making friends. For singing songs round the fire and merrymaking. We were here to make a deal. And we'd need that company, bad or worse, if the deal was to be made. So let's make it. Let's make nice with whatever company awaited in the gloom of this cold, dead ship.

Repugna, here we come.

But before we took two steps, the ground beneath us trembled and moved. A section detached altogether. A piece of the floor just in front of us. It scurried and hissed. What the fuck is that? It moved like lightning, erratic and ultra-fast. It circled us and turned away, turned back, circled us again. Whatever it was, it was keeping us from making a move. We were just sitting ducks in the face of all that speed.

Then Baby decided she had had enough. Yeah, she's fast too. Little rocket jets propelled her to and fro, back and forth, she met erratic with erratic, every step of the way. Then she pounced like a cougar and the wild dance came to a close. Held firm, pinned under super strong bionic arms of magenta chrome over titanium skeleton, a flat-bodied construct wiggled in a futile effort to dislodge itself from beneath a hydraulic-pumped stranglehold.

'It's incredibly strong,' Baby said with a smile.

'Yeah, but what is it?' I asked.

Then I saw for myself. An insect. Long jagged legs and brown scaled carapace. Searching, feeling antennae shifting back and forth. As big as a pig. A nasty-ass cockroach.

'Ugh!' Lily turned away. 'Kill it. Quick.'

'I wouldn't,' advised Ren.

'No...' Bee agreed. 'Baby, let it go.'

And the moment she let up it wiggled free and zipped back into the shadows. It scurried almost faster than my eyes could follow it. Way back into the deep dark confines of the freight carrier. Back to where the orange flicker of fire played against the cold walls.

'I hate cockroaches,' Lily complained.

I wasn't exactly against her on this one. 'Why did you let it go?' I asked Bee.

'That was a construct,' Bee told us. 'Which means it belongs to someone.' He turned to Lily. 'Would you have been willing to make a deal with those androids after they had put Batty on ice?' He asked her. 'You think you could've been civil with them?'

'Fuck no,' she spat. 'My guns would do all the dealing. And they aren't one bit of civil.'

'Exactly. So that's why we let it go.'

'Because it's Repugna's pet,' Ren told her. 'It's the sorceress' familiar. Just like your Batty was to you, like Bee's brindled mare is to him.'

Lily kicked a piece of rubbish that had made its way inside. The aluminum can echoed through the hollowed-out ship. 'I hate cockroaches.'

'Yeah, well, I hate deals that don't go my way. Let's not fuck this one up before it begins, okay?'

'Okay...'

'Good. Now let's get this shit over.'

We turned to face the long dark hall that ended in that faint, dancing light. The shadows moved and swayed, hypnotic and haunting. Each step had me more and more nervous. More afraid. All those shadows... all those undulating shapes... I felt as if we walked down an accursed crypt of a thousand ghosts.

One tentative step at a time.

◆ ◆ ◆

When darkness gave way to light, when we entered the orange-cast glow of the warm fire, we came upon a scene that we had not at all expected. What I assumed would be a shrouded figured hunched over a bubbling cauldron, sprinkling pinches of herbs or scraps of flesh into the boiling brew of some ungodly potion; instead I found a slob, a total slouch, ear to ear grin and wide eyes of interest drinking in the glow of a holo-show, some light-hearted roborg romcom or equivalent drivel. One arm dipped into a bucket of unsavory snacks, the other wrapped lovingly around a cockroach construct the size of a mattress.

She burst into laughter at some halfhearted attempt at humor emitting from the holo-feed. 'Go on girl!' She shouted at the picture. 'He's in for the kiss, baby. Go on and give it to him!' I heard sucking, smacking noises. 'Thata girl!'

'Excuse me,' Bee interrupted as we came so near as to no longer be ignored.

'Huh?' The roborg grunted. 'What do you want?'

Bee looked to the rest of us, gave us the this-is-one-wackjob-weirdo look and we all agreed, nodding our heads. 'Repugna, is it?'

She burst into laughter again. The holo-show was a hit in this oh-so-strange household. 'Oh, that is rich! That is good going girl. I knew she had it in her.' She turned to the rest of us. 'I knew she had it in her.'

'As did we all,' Bee submitted. 'May we join you for the show?' He was plucking the right strings, playing the right tune. He was giving the roborg couch potato exactly what she wanted. Romcom enthusiasm. Soap opera esteem.

'Join Repugna,' she took the bait. 'Come, watch and see. No one thought it would work out… the babysitter and the business man. He's so cold, they'd say. She's so flighty, so hopeless. But Repugna knew. Look! See how they hold hands. A walk in the park. It's always the walk in the park right before the scene with the kiss. The part where two bare feet entwine and poke out from the bed sheets.' She looked directly over at me. 'That's the best part. The part I'd like to try.'

The insta-dins I had eaten raw were coming up to my mouth from my stomach. I took the far, far edge of the couch and watched the holo-program with trepidation. The giant cockroach nuzzled against Lily. She visibly squirmed. Bee was Bee. Always Bee. He was already playing the game. Sewing the seeds for a good deal. Ren, he was smiling. Actually watching the roborg cinema. Ren was special. A shifting enigma.

When the babysitter and the businessman had their wedding a cheery pop-song started to play and the credits rolled. Thank god that's over. Even the Squidge hadn't salvaged the godawful film.

'Encore?' Repugna suggested, and even Bee couldn't stifle a flinch.

'Perhaps another time,' Bee warily ventured. 'I would like to discuss a proposition.'

Repugna opened up her large thighs and the room took on a new dimension of unpleasant odor. She sprawled on the couch and spilled over onto Bee's lap, playing with her stringy hair and looking dreamily up into his eyes. 'You have pretty eyes.'

Bee looked down into hers. Opaque, pale glass with expanding, contracting digital lens pupils. 'You too,' he lied like an artist. 'Eyes that would see fine opportunities. Especially if they looked you right in the face.'

The roborg giggled. Had sex on the mind. 'Are you my opportunity?'

'No,' Bee was quick not to nurture the notion any further. 'But I bring opportunity.' He jiggled his encumbered pack. 'Tell me, Repugna, have you ever watched rob-romcoms with Squidge in your peepers? How about circuit breakers? Wire fryers? Chip rot or digital fever? I've got them all. All the fun flavors. They'll make those romcoms twice as romantic, three times as funny. They'll turn that bucket of pseudo-chews you were wolfing on into caviar. Crème de la crème. Capiche?'

'Malware?' She perked.

'The best of the bad.'

There was a long pause where all we could hear was the pattering of the rain on the upturned metal hull of the freight carrier cave, the little rasp of cockroach chitin rubbing up against mildewed sofa. Then the relative quiet ended in an eruption of operatic laughter. And man, have I yet to mention? I *hate* opera. Regugna was overjoyed or deranged or both and I just sort of slowly walked backwards. Bee and Lilly, Ren and Baby, they were made of sterner stuff. They just took it in stride. Smiled, hands in pockets, all casual. Meanwhile, Repugna was dancing a jig, farting with each step. She ran to a corner and squatted, relieved herself and stepped in the puddle on her happy prance back towards the rest of us.

'Drugs for my plugs,' the chant went on. 'Spiked electrodes to wack all my diodes, cathodes, anodes. Sizzle my pizzle and tickle my bingo pad.' Evidently — maybe? — Repugna was pleased.

'Of course, all good things come with a price,' Bee added at the opportune time. He took advantage of the roborg's overeager reverie. He had hooked her in, established an expectation, then doused a little water on what was becoming a wild fire. He reigned in the untamed stallion. He had brandished the carrot. Now it was time for the stick.

'Price. Price. Price.' Repugna paced and pulled at her wispy hair.

'Fair price, to be sure? Lodgings and a meal?'

I took a look around. *Some* lodgings. Shit and refuse from the junk-yard blew in with every wind. Giant cockroaches with beady black eyes. And as to any meal that this deranged sorceress may prepare… I'd stick with my raw insta-dins. I'd seen what she snacked on. Little hard chews that looked like congealed phlegm. Sour apple confectionery and dust bunnies? The shit found beneath the seats in cinemas.

'Repugna can give clean, handsome man a home,' she upped the ante. 'His friends are welcome too. We can share a bed. Share a kiss or a cuddle. Entwine our bare feet as they pop out from beneath the sheets.'

I looked at her feet. Raw and red and plump with gout. Hard, yellow nails and visible fungus beneath each toe. I looked away. I searched for my nosegay for something pleasant. Anything but Repugna. I must have dropped it. My pretty petals of zinfandel pink, lost among the rubbish.

'Tempting,' Bee said with tact. 'But what you offer is not what I seek. Lodgings, for an evening, perhaps. But we are monks on a no-madic journey. We are amidst a trial of stern fasting. No meals for us. We are thrust deep into a steadfast vow, a pledge of celibacy. No footsie beneath the sheets for me and my companions. No sexy time or shared beds.' Not a bad story. He'd say anything to get us out of a corner.

Repugna slumped. 'You cannot have my cockroach,' she said defensively. She clung to the insect like a mother would an infant.

'I wouldn't dream of it,' Bee assured her.

'So, what do you want? What can I offer? I'll start by saying my collection of holo-films, my romcoms and roborg soaps… I will not part with them.'

'I am not a cruel man,' Bee appeased. 'Take solace. All that I require is something small. In fact, that's the whole notion… to make myself small. Me and my companions. We wish to shrink. About yay big,' he spread his hands six inches apart. 'We've been told you can do it, Repugna. Your name is a legend on the lips of every magic enthusiast. We've come to you through garbage and gunfire. We've come to seek your craft. Specifically, what we require...'

'Amber magic.' She said and smiled. Something about that smile made me weak in the knees. Her fevered, frantic need for the malware was suddenly well in check. She was poised. In control. It was my deepest fear that she now knew she held the bargaining chip of greater power.

'For the drugs,' Bee reiterated the deal. Tried to bring back the attention to the good he had to offer. 'The best of the worst for your systems.'

'It is a good start,' Repugna quipped.

'It is a good start, middle, and end. Take the deal.'

'For enough amber magic to make you all yay big?' She held out her hands, ten inches apart.

'Yay big,' Bee corrected. Hands six inches apart.

Long pause. Uncomfortable pause. Repugna smiling throughout. 'Not enough,' she said. 'Need more from you.'

Lily put her hands on her pistols, Bee motioned to her, told his sister to cool her jets.

'I've got Squidge,' Bee offered.

'Bah. You offer gold when you offer computer drugs. What need have I for silver? No caterpillar juice for me.'

'Well then,' Bee crossed his arms. 'Name your terms. What do you require?'

She arched her back and gave us a second round of that operatic laughter. Long and diabolical, like a holo-film villain. Her rolls and flesh between the plated metal jiggled with each convulsing bob of her laughter.

I took her in. Repugna, the roborg sorceress. I just stared, open mouthed, in revulsion. What an absolute nut-job. What an off-kilter, off-putting piece of ick. She was quirky as fuck. Man, did this borg bitch have a glitch. She was all about the downloadable drugs. It was her die-hard schtick. She wasn't having any of the Squidge. Just wanted the latest techno viruses and corrupted programs. She also wanted sex. And *that* was a problem.

She looked half yeti. Like a chimpanzee with too much flesh. But that wasn't even flesh, it was just slabs of pseudo skin. Fake implants. And it fucking *smelled*. It was greasy to the touch and the only reason I had the misfortune of knowing is because she begged me to tickle her under the arm. It was during that romcom we had watched. Said she had an itch. Please scratch it for me, she begged. I obliged, but never again. My fingers still smell like I stuck them in the guts of something dead. Like I'd reached into a bucket of yesterday's catch. Bloated pilchards or the dead remains of those godawful goldfish we saw back in the sewers.

I just watched her, still laughing. Sort of hoping Lily would lose her cool and just unleash those angry guns that had a hankering for spilled blood and casualties. I looked on, as did we all, while the seconds went by, then the minutes. And she just kept cackling. This fruitcake, madhouse, roborg freak with her batshit antics, her weird ways. When all the jiggling and wiggling of synthetic skin, mottled, fetid epidermal slabs and loose-fitting metal plating came to a halt with the last of that overdone, long laughter, I felt as if I had come back from a journey to hell. I felt scarred and ruined but a little grateful to come out only emotionally and physiologically damaged. So long as it didn't turn into anything physical I'd leave this place considering myself lucky. I'd cash in my chips with all the nightmares and bad memories. I'd take that way sooner than the ouch and degradation that came with a romp with a roborg.

'The drugs,' Repugna repeated. 'I'll need all of those. You keep the Squidge, but apply a bit to my cockroach construct first. His legs are arthritic, that may help.'

'Done,' Bee agreed. 'Is that all?'

Repugna got sly. Got shifty. Lord save me, I knew what was fucking coming. I have a sixth sense for things I really badly don't need. 'There is *one* more thing I'll require to officialize our deal.'

In the silence that filled the next seconds the rain had eased and the roof was no longer loud with white noise. Even the cockroach remained quiet, his chitin no longer abrasive with the couch where he lay. All was tense in that eternal ten seconds.

'I have not made love in years,' Repugna told us. 'And I can't get by on romcoms alone. I cannot live vicariously forever. Those lighthearted holo-films staunch the blood, but my wounds are deep. I need love. I need deep, physical love.'

More silence. Then the roborg looked my way. I went ashen. White as pure parchment. I felt myself dying like a fish out of water. A flower uprooted.

'We are monks,' Bee reminded. 'Sworn to celibacy.'

'Your vows are your own problem.'

And again, those pale, fish-eye, camera lens eyes rested on my shaking figure.

'I'll do it,' Baby stepped forward. What a champ. It sicked me to share my bride, but better her than me.

Repugna shook her head. 'No good.'

'Because I am machine?'

'Machine is fine,' she told us. 'But I want man. Flesh or metal or a bit of both. Man for me. Man in the sack, one night.'

Ren did the transmogrify tango. Where a moment ago he was man, now she was woman. Unfair! So now it was down to me and Bee.

'Thumb war?' Bee looked at me and suggested.

I was all clammed up. Cold sweat and loose stool. 'How about a renegotiation?'

'Drugs and man,' Repugna was firm. 'Then enough amber juju to make you all yay big.'

'Yay big,' Bee amended. Then he walked over to me, not an ounce of fear in his eye, living or computer. He extended his hand for a round of thumb war. Like I had a chance against his practiced hand. I sent out a plea. Some of that digital telepathy. From my chip to his, brain to brain, I relayed the message. 'How about heft up that sword, chummy? Do your Jare-Bear a real solid. Just cut this roborg bitch and make her give us the pixie juice. What do ya say? Do it for me?'

Then my own head filled with his response as I stared at his apologetic smile, his sorry-for-me eyes. 'Can't tarnish the legit biz. Karma has a way of hunting us down, for the good and the bad both. I've got to go through with this. *You've* got to go through with this. Don't worry, we'll Squidge you up real good. You may even like it.'

'Fuck you, Bee.'

And our electronic discourse was at an end.

Again he extended his hand, and this time I took it. Bee smiled, nodded. 'One, two, three, four...' Then we said it together. 'I declare a thumb war.'

And his thumb promptly squashed down upon my own. I sagged to my knees. I paled. And I wept.

◆ ◆ ◆

I had dodged plenty of bullets over the past week. But none like this…

It had been Baby's idea. 'Come with me,' she called, and led me back to the entrance of the hollowed-out freight carrier. I had been given a grace period of three hours. To calm my nerves. To gather my mettle. Before… you know… I had to *appease* Repugna.

'It's just for one night,' Bee had tried to console me.

'The scars will last a lifetime,' I had told him. And since then, I hadn't said a word. I just huddled up in the corner and hugged my knees. Until Baby came around. She took my hand and breathed a little life into my dying soul.

We stood, hand in hand, looking across the vast ocean of garbage. 'I deployed some nanobots,' she told me.

'Some nano-whats?'

'Nanobots. Tiny drones. No larger than a nanometer, one billionth of a meter.'

'Okay…' I had no idea where the hell this was leading. 'So some small robots are running around, so what?'

'Flying around, actually,' Baby corrected.

'Running, flying, swimming, fucking… who gives a shit, Baby? I got a gorilla roborg witch counting down the minutes until she has her way with me. You ever heard of dubcon?'

She cocked her fuchsia head, blinked her golden LEDs.

'Dubcon,' I repeated. 'Dubious consent. I don't mind it so much when I'm not on the wrong end of it. But what I've got waiting for me… I'm on the wrong fucking end, you get me?'

'Dubcon,' she tried out the word. 'Actually, now that you mention it.

The nanobots I've deployed are performing a task that adequately fits this description.'

I looked at her like her head was her ass and her ass was a traffic cone. I just stared, nonplussed. 'What the fuck are you on about, Baby? You bust a plug? Pop a circuit? You been taking some of that malware from Bee?'

'Of course not,' she assured me. 'But the nanobots… they've scouted the area. They've located some heretic droids. Hard Drive's minions.'

'Okay…'

'And they've infiltrated one. A male model. They've entered his circuitry and corrupted his programming.' She pointed out into the endless dunes of shit. 'Look, here it comes now. Right in time.'

'I don't get it,' I confessed. 'Why is he coming?'

'Dubious consent,' she smiled. 'My nanobots have rewritten the android's programming. Its personality chip has been stripped, reconstituted. Its drive of devotion has been redirected. No longer will it obediently serve the heretic prince, the false leader, Hard Drive. The droid's focus will now rest solely on worshiping Repugna, attending her every need.'

'You mind raped him?'

'It had no mind to rape, by strict definition. But as a machine, I appreciate your way of looking at it. And yes, that is an adequate way of putting it.'

'And now he'll *want* to get frisky with Repuggo the ape?'

'The programming I have installed within the android will tell it that it is enjoying itself. It will be eager to please. And I have upped its sexual know-how. The ins and outs of how to pleasure a woman, or in this case, a female roborg.' Baby flashed me those pearly white dentures and winked a playful LED. 'The droid will keep the sorceress happy.'

It all translated to one thing: I was off the fucking hook! I leapt into Baby's arms and cried into her smooth, sleek, silicone breasts.

When we left with the amber magic that we required and walked backed out into the trash, we did so with smiles on our faces, a skip in our step, and the sound of joyful moans, wild and predatory, echoing in our ears from the hollowed-out freight carrier at our backs. I still wasn't talking to Bee. I was still pissed off about it all. But I was smiling with the rest of the group. When it comes to brushing oh-so-close with an oncoming bus packed full of hideous and revolting horrors, relief goes a long fucking way.

So I dodged that bus. I dodged the bullet. But most importantly, Repugna was happy. And with amber magic in our mitts, we hadn't long to wait before we made our big move. The sunset lit the smog an amber hue like the magic we now carried. I looked around at the marmalade glow of a desert of detritus. I grinned from ear to ear. Never before had trash looked so lovely.

23
CHROME AND MUSCLE

I had gotten so used to all the rubbish I was beginning to think I would miss it. After all, it was among the endless trash where I had met Baby. And she... well... she was a steal.

My wedded wife. Can you imagine? I can't. And I'm me! But now that these few days have passed, I can't imagine it elsewise either. It's funny, that. Like all the rubbish. The crazy things we get used to so fast when it's around. Like herpes or that bad smell or the crisscross grating above our heads. So prevalent, it just becomes a part of life. It becomes us.

Our perception of the world. Our reality. It's what's around us. And for days it's been countless pieces of junk and a beautiful, pink, robot mistress. My, how things were about to change. But that's just another thing we get used to real fast. Like the sores and lesions and regrets we collect along the way. That's a part of life too. Those sudden, dramatic changes.

'Are you going to miss Repugna, Jarred?'

Too soon. I didn't even dignify him with a retort. And I was beginning to think that Bee *was*, in fact, a little jealous. He was being *too* cool. Too blasé. The way he left me to the wolves. Sealed my fate with a thumb war I couldn't win. Just threw me to the roborg witch, like a scrap of meat to the rats.

I looked at Baby. Pretty in pink. My metal bride. The one who saved me from the same fate Bee had nonchalantly ordained. Right about now I know which one of those two I'd sooner call a friend. Baby had my back. Bee... well, he certainly had *his*. As to mine? I'm no longer sure. So yeah... maybe he ought to be jealous. Cause Baby, she may be cold to the touch, hard on the exterior, but behind that cool metal plating was a tender warmth and a whole lotta love. Two things Bee was a bit short on.

'Look,' Ren pointed. 'The road.'

There was a perceptible thinning out of rubbish at the bottom of the trash mound we had just scaled. It marked the border of the great junkyard district. Where the bits and bobs of shit, of discarded trinkets, abandoned items, and old, broken appliances tapered down to little or nothing, a road could be found, slithering out from beneath the dunes of crap. Beside it, visible once more, the wide, brown ribbon of lazy current, the murky depths of the river Flow.

Out first steps upon the solid pavement took practice, so used we were to walking on the unsteady piles of filth. 'Terra firma,' Bee said without joy.

'Back in the Drome,' Lily stated, matter of fact.

'It'll be good to make you all a drink,' Ren smiled. But as he looked back to the vast region of landfill now behind us he wore an expression that seemed to touch on sorrow.

'We'll drink to Batty's memory,' And my words found purchase in the hearts of my companions. Lily, watery eyes and genuine smile of gratitude, gave me a nod. I think it was the first honest gesture of decency shared between us. Ren, still a woman, turned back to his natural form, gave my shoulder a squeeze. And Bee, I'd take his stony silence as reserved appreciation.

And then whatever moment we had shared became moot, utterly forgettable. Because what we now looked at on the road looking straight back at us, eyes on fire with a rage that even those bomber shades couldn't hide, was a familiar face that was pretty to look upon but that I never wanted to see again; all seven feet of hot body and rozzer rage... She Beast, the new and improved Top Cop. At her side, two lackey gumshoe sleuths, hands tattooed, one red and one blue. Their well-inked fists held firm to the collar of their hyena constructs. In the background, lumbering and large, a mammoth tapir with jowly slabs of pseudo skin and metal plating.

So now the icky vibes were heavy and thick. Cloying and stagnant. We were up to our ears in it. We were swimming in the ick. Drowning in our rotten luck.

But wait...

And then I smiled. Counted my blessings and tallied more than zero. Stepping up to the plate, someone She Beast hadn't factored into the equation, my bubblegum bride, a sleek, magenta machine. Her beauty was a matter of taste. Her incredible strength and stellar combat abilities, resounding fact. She stepped forward, flashed her yellow LEDs at the rozzer queen, 'Out of our way,' she instructed.

'Or what?' A titan of few words, I'd almost forgotten that booming timbre. The one that belonged to a bear. Trust She Beast to make it sexy. Low rasp, all authoritative, like the warning growl of a lioness, but coated in honey. How she scared me to death yet turned me on.

Baby's face spread wide with an alabaster grin. I smiled myself, admiring those pretty little chompers. Then, all demure and cheery, cute as a bug's fucking ear, she told it like it was. 'Or I'll kill you, of course.'

And then the curtains drew and the shit show began.

The flatfoots dressed in blue sicked their hyenas on Baby. She sidestepped them both, nice and neat, and gave one a swift whack on its breeches. It whined and turned back for round two but a volley of slugs, each with a mean personality, burrowed into its flank and the rest was all sizzles, fire, and blood. Lily blew smoke from two red-hot barrels and winked, watching the last breath of a dying feliform, almost-dog construct.

The other beast, unscathed, came at Ren and things got a little hairy. He did the transmogrify boogie, turning himself into a perfect copy of the construct's cop owner. Visually, the rendition was a flawless double. But the nostrils on that laughing bastard of a cat-dog freak-show quivered and did their smelling thing, getting rich wafts of the real Ren. So after a moment of hesitant confusion the hyena doubled its speed and worked its hard bite into the shapeshifter's wrist.

Ren's image flickered between his normal self and the ink mitt gumshoe. He lost his ability with the pain. Against his will, he reverted back into Ren as we know him. Then came the sad bit. A bit I don't like much telling. But here we are, at that point when it happened. When that rabid, pseudo-dog feline jerked its strong neck to the side and its clamped jaws took Azalea Ren's dominant hand with it. He held up the stump where his digits had just been and watched for a moment as it spurted up regular pulses of blood. Then he screamed and went ashen, fell to the floor.

The hyena rejoiced with a maniac cackle and chomp, chomp, chomped Ren's graceful hand to ragged bits. The animal's glorious moment was not to last long. In fact, it hardly lasted two seconds. Bee had closed the distance between himself and the beast. With Squidged up thighs, hammies and calves all doused in the goo, he did the 16-beat mad dash, fast-as-freak run and sent that black magic seeing-sword arching through the air to come down like vengeance itself. It didn't skip a beat as it clove clean through skull and brain, thick corded neck and hide. Bee bent to fetch Ren's severed hand but it was beyond what the rejuvenation vats could manage. Any semblance of a human hand was gone. Nothing left but bone shrapnel and minced meat.

The hyenas dead, their owners got a taste of the rage. They came as a pair, singling out Bee, but they neglected the pink robot lady that they mistakenly got too close to. Baby grabbed one of the cops by his shirt collar as he ran past her. She yanked him back, whiplash fast, and nutted him one good. That was *some* headbutt. Magenta chrome casing crushed his cranium and made jelly out of his frontal lobe. She still held on to his collar, but then let him drop to plop face-first onto the street. A smear of pink pulp squelched onto the ground to make modern art across the pavement.

The other lackey rozzer didn't have much better luck as he squared off against Bee. He took a bullet in his back, courtesy of little sis, and proceeded to stumble straight into big brother's extended sword. He slid down to the hilt, which penetrated his pulverized heart, and that was that. Two cops and two hyenas dead at our feet. The rest of us not sweating it. Except for Ren, who admittedly, had seen far better days.

I was beginning to measure the odds. So I considered; Bee's sword, Lily's guns, Baby's arsenal of pain that is every inch of her formidable self. I was starting to feel pretty jolly about this run-in with the colossal queen of the cops. The icky vibes were fading with each fallen foe. But one look at that seven foot rozzer, head-to-toe in blue, a pent up bottle of rage... I just wasn't sure. Even with the odds in our favor, I couldn't help but notice that big old stitch in my side, that ulcer in my tummy that told me I was more than a little nervous, that I was scared out of my fucking wits.

Baby made the first move, a motion trail of ultra pink. Officer Hot

Stuff crouched low, poised for the punch. She was all geared up to grapple her adversary in mitts twice as large as my own. But the pretty pink robo gal feigned the attack. Little boosts of jet fuel propelled her to the side in midair and she landed in a twirl, hit the ground running, then took to the air in a gymnast blaze of Kung Fu. Arching, twisting, aerodynamic wonder, Baby angled her flying form to soar speedily up and over the dumbstruck tapir construct. In an artful work of combative grace and precision, her free-flying momentum and jet fuel propulsion angled a punch from titanium spiked knuckles, just so, to come crushing down on the pseudo animal's spinal column. From between a broad and well-muscled set of shoulders, right where the back meets the nape of the neck, sparks flew in a pyrotechnic firework show as blood gurgled to smoke in the fire.

Flip of the wrist, arm canon primed, Baby wasted no time with another assault. Liquid flame erupted from the stump at her wrist and doused the tapir in a wildfire of searing agony. It thrashed and moaned and charged blindly. It was taking bullets like a champ, a dozen or more, as Lily worked the triggers of those mean, angry guns. She was button mashing like a video game enthusiast. It was all bang bang bang and the next thing you know you've got a tapir on fire looking like the biggest piece of melted Swiss cheese anyone has ever seen.

That thing was a goner. No way anything lives through that. But it was still rearing and roaring, bucking spasmodically in an effort to free itself of the flames, the raging torment. The tapir was wild with panic. A zigzagging to-and-fro wrecking ball of erratic dance. In its wailing death throes, it sprawled to the side and momentarily pinned Baby's leg to the asphalt under two tons of flaming synthetic muscle and steel skeleton.

It was the opening that Top Cop had been waiting for. She slipped on her brass knuckles and took out her bobby club. With legs near as long as I am tall she devoured the pavement, supersonic speed, and sent a thundering punch to go cracking and crunching onto Baby's chrome-capped knee.

Baby didn't scream, didn't make a sound. But if she had been human the whole world would have heard her pain. Stoic machine, she just watched in silence as her leg splintered in a disarray of fragmented shrapnel, a wriggling octopus of sizzling live wire.

And those brass knuckles at the end of a muscle-pumped, long arm kept thudding into all that magenta chrome plating. The pretty paint was chipped and scratched in a dozen different places. Here and there and everywhere the plain, silver metal shown like scars. Baby was a polka-dot ruin of nicks and dents.

An iron studded truncheon came crashing down to fizzle out one of those golden LEDs I had grown accustomed to getting lost within. Baby's pretty yellow eye. And next her perfect pearly teeth, shattered, scattered upon the pavement. My android bride was becoming scrap before my eyes.

But she found her second wind, sweet Baby Cakes. She caught the next downward pummel of the bobby baton and wrenched it free. She smashed it down onto She Beast's shoulder, next her chest. The wind knocked out of her, Top Cop stumbled backward and gasped for air.

Then Bee was on her, amped up with Squidge, black magic sword transmitting images from an infused biological eye. Seeing with the blade, the opportunity to slice, Bee sent the wicked instrument flying. And just like that, Top Cop was down to her final arm.

But that final arm was no slouch, as it turns out. In a rage of frustration She Beast rounded on Bee and gave him a hearty knuckle sandwich in the gut. It sent him reeling. Down on hands and knees. Keeled over, coughing bile and blood.

Baby was back on her feet, but one leg dangled like a useless metal skin tag. Still, she had some fuel in the tank. She wrapped Top Cop on the side of the head. She was offering concussion, free of charge, and tore off an ear for good measure. The rozzer queen's bomber sunglasses shattered and her mercurial, techno eyes of augmentation were molten with outrage. Then muscle grappled with chrome. Meat versus machine. And to my horror, I watched Baby come apart, piece by piece, under the prying fingers and terrible strength of a seven foot bombshell blonde.

Then worst of all. Salt in the wound. She Beast hefted up what remained of Baby, a collection of parts, and hurled them far out to splash and sink down into the murky depths of the Flow. Now there would be no hope of reconstructing her. My robot bride was gone. Me, a widower.

Goodbye, Baby. I watched with tears welling up as the brown ripple from where she sank returned to calm, undisturbed water. So long, Aurora Storm.

The time to grieve would come. But it wasn't right now. Right now, there was a blonde behemoth coming my way. She tore open several packs of medi gel between her teeth and rubbed her raw stump into the residue. As the gel bonded with her tissue and the haemorrhaging came to a stop she at once became refocused. She didn't even cry out in pain. Was she even human? Then she glared at me with those uncanny, silver eyes. Scanned me or saw through me, viewing me in whatever way those odd peepers do in addition to just plain seeing me. Those eyes, in the least, could not be human. No way. That was military grade techno optic juju. That was top of the line science spiked with voodoo magic. Hex vision or arcane eyeball.

As those eyes drank in a vision of me holding my breath, nearly pissing in my pants, I was pleased to find that their attention was taken away from me. Steady gunfire coming from Lily kept Top Cop preoccupied. She couldn't waste a moment glaring at me with that volley of slugs raining down on each and every inch of the seven foot target that she offered. She took one in the foot and cringed, hardly grunting, then dove behind the smouldering corpse of her tapir construct. The barrage of bullets thudded against the expired beast, each impact a dull, muted drum, softened by many layers of pseudo flesh and syntho-muscle. A perfect meat shield.

Bee edged around the dead tapir, hoping to catch Blondie off guard. Fat chance. She was waiting for this obvious tactic and jumped Bee first. She knocked his sword from his hand and twisted him around, hugging his back to her belly with an arm that ended at the elbow, holding him by the throat with her remaining hand. She might only have one but it was twice as big as anyone else's, so it counted for a lot. Bee's neck looked a thin, frail thing around that monster grip. Pinning him in this way, she stepped out to face the gunfire that she knew would stop when she revealed that Bee was her new meat shield. She walked slowly towards Lily and let Bee choke a little under her tightened grip. 'Your guns,' she commanded.

'Get fucked, big foot bitch.'

'Your guns, or his life.' And this time she squeezed so hard that Bee's biological eye bulged, his computer eye went static.

And I wondered for a moment why Lily looked like she was trying not to smile. I could see it, that smirk beneath a veil of pretended vexation. Then I remembered… Lily's guns, in the handgrip… how she told me that they injected strong barbiturates if unregistered hands took hold of them. Coma or death. Either way, it would chalk up the same thing. Nothing much easier than a death match with a comatose opponent. But would the toxins be strong enough?

Lily seemed to think so. Pretending to be all sore about it, she relinquished her pistols. She slowly lowered her guns to the pavement, muttered some curses in a fine execution of consummate acting, then kicked the guns over to the XL constable. Copper Queen only had a single hand to pick them up, so she kicked one into the Flow. Here, Lily's curses did not require acting. Her anger was rife, and it was very real. Then picking up the remaining gun, She Beast smiled for a second or two. In that moment she had perceived victory. Oh, darling, you couldn't be any more wrong.

Her brief smile turned to surprise as scores of tiny needles entered the flesh of her palm. The sting was evident, but not in any way unendurable. To someone like Top Cop, who took losing half of an arm and a bullet in the foot like a champ, the pinpricks were utterly unremarkable. The injection of hefty barbiturates, however, which she was not quite yet aware of, would have a far less subtle effect.

The rozzer queen pushed Bee away from her. Pushed him real hard onto the pavement. She held out Lily's pistol and trained it on each of us in turn. 'Which one of you scumbags to do first?'

'You can do me anytime you like,' I said, and gave her the head to toe. Let her know I was undressing her with my eyes. 'Just be gentle, will you? You're an awful big girl. Perhaps to be safe, let me be on top?'

Lily guffawed. Bee smiled. I was being braver than I actually was. Cause in actual fact, I wasn't being that brave at all. Lipping off like that, being bad in the face of a mean cop monster, I was only doing it cause I saw what those barbiturates were doing to her. She was wobbling at the knees. The gun in her hand wavering and off target. Her eyes — those oh-so-freaky eyes — they were rolling from side to side, now up into her head. She opened her mouth to speak but the only thing that came out was a big foaming bubble of froth. She fell forward to her knees. Then completed the fall, face first, scuffed nose and broken teeth slamming hard onto the pavement.

'She's out,' Lily announced. Then she ran to Ren, tended to her lover. Bee walked over to She Beast, knelt by her side, pressed two fingers to a thick neck corded with muscle.

'Still alive,' he told me. Then he raised up his blade, ready to do the deed. But something dawned on me, and I stopped him. 'What is it?' He asked.

I looked down at Top Cop. I took in the immensity of her person. Even torn to pieces, disheveled and broken, she was still beautiful to behold. Even out cold, battered and maimed, she was still one large bundle of sex appeal. She breathed in ragged breathes, the toxins slowing her heart.

I looked back to Bee. 'It's just that I realized something,' I told him. 'Oh yeah? What's that?'

'You got to swing your sword,' I said. 'Lily, she got to fire all those bullets. But me? I never did get to do my whole brick throwing thing.'

'So what are you saying?'

I picked up a brick that was loose in the road and walked towards the dying rozzer queen. 'I'm saying I want to do my bit.' I stood over the big, bad, bobby broad in blue. Lying there, her face at rest, she suddenly didn't seem so scary. For a moment I pitied her. For a moment I hesitated. Then I thought of Baby. I hefted up the heavy cube of rock. And the rest was history.

Nothing much easier than a death match with a comatose opponent.

24
LICKING OUR WOUNDS

We all smelled worse than shit by the time we got back to Bee's apartment. I mean, we *had* been wading in trash for days. Lily stank more than the rest of us. She was also sopping wet. She had swum out into the brown sludge of the Flow and took over an hour to find and retrieve her lost pistol. As wet and disgusting as she had become, she was still smiling, holding that gun that she had thought to have lost forever.

'Will it still work?' I asked.

'Bit of Squidge and she'll fire alright.'

And even though she was all smiles over the gun, much more than happy, she was sad. We all were. We had lost a lot this day. Ren lost his hand. Baby, her existence. Me, my robot bride. Bee had lost a bit of confidence, letting the big bad cop get the better of him while in the thick of the action. Lily lost her gun, but only for a while. And let's not forget Batty. We'd lost him too. I lost the last shred of any remaining innocence someone like me may yet retain. I lost it, for sure, when I bricked in Sleeping Beauty's head. Come to think of it, there were times I thought I had lost my mind. Like when I almost had to pork Repugna against my will. After that, I had lost my appetite. We'd all lost that stride in our step. Our zest for life. And when we got back to Bee's, we found out he had lost his keys as well.

'Fuck it.' He kicked in his own door. We walked in and washed up. Scrubbed and scoured off the week's worth of filth from our epic junkyard journey. Fresh as daisies, we got ready for a volley of copious cocktails and fine narcotics. They'd help. But they wouldn't heal. All that pain. All that sorrow. It wasn't going to go away in a hurry.

I thought about Baby. Scraps and spare parts. Jagged strips of torn metal. Circuit chips and marigold LED's. But most of all, I thought of her soul. That computer soul that I didn't used to believe in. But now I know to be real. Cause Baby, her soul was more pure than any human's that I had ever known.

Yeah… we sure did lose a lot this day.

I sniffed some Squidge and upended my bevvy. I wiped the tears with my sleeve and sighed. Then I stopped wiping my face. I just let them fall. Them, and all of the snot and heaving sobs. Bee put a hand on my shoulder and pulled me close. Then a second drink had me feeling a little better. More pointedly, a little more numb.

And then there was Ren. Poor Ren. Bee had the cash, so he had assured him; told Ren he would be outfitted with a sleek, super strong, state-of-the-art, mechanized hand. It would be equipped with laser fire capabilities at the end of each digit. Azalea Ren could kill with the point of his finger. Pretty cool. Of course, while his shapeshifter abilities remain intact, his right hand, forevermore, will not be included in the transmogrify process. It did not render his skill useless — far from — but it did limit it to a degree, and to Ren, most of all, it was no small loss.

Bee was convinced he would feel better about it after the cyberneticists came in the morning to outfit Ren with his new hand. 'I've learned to love my bionic eye. And I no longer grieve my missing leg,' he told me. 'It was a hard loss for Ren. I do not belittle that loss. But he'll be okay. His loss is not so bad as others.' He looked at me more tenderly than I'd seen him ever before. 'I'm sorry, Jarred. I'm so sorry about Baby.'

And for the next hour he let me cry into his shirt. He patted me and stroked my hair and told me everything will be okay. That grief is a process and I was in the thick of it. The worst of it. That it would get better. But for now, sorrow was everything. Agony was all I could expect, until that one day down the line when I stop and realize I'm no longer feeling it. The weight of all that sorrow. All that loss. But that at some point, without knowing it, I've moved on. And even then there comes that feeling of guilt that fills the space where once there had been pain. Guilt, for no longer feeling the pain. And then I'll likely miss the pain. Wish it back. Why? Because it validated my love for someone who is no longer there. And so we relive our losses. Play them back. Over and over again. Until one day we think back on the person we had loved and lost and smile at their memory, rather than mourn. It's not a matter of moving on. We never do. Not entirely. It's a matter of learning to live with it. And on that day… down the line… I'll know I'd be okay.

But here, now… It was sob city. Population three boxes of tissues and two swollen eyes. A whole lotta snot.

Ren came out from Lily's room. His eyes were near as red and puffed up as my own. The arm that ended in a wrist was wrapped tight with bandages. He saw me looking and smiled. Bless his heart of gold, he made a joke. He did the transmogrify boogie. Turned himself into a mummy.

'Hey look,' he waved his injured arm all wrapped up in linens. 'And they told me I wouldn't be able to shapeshift my right hand anymore!' I looked at his mummified guise, his bandaged arm that blended flaw-lessly with the image. Lily came in and shook her head, rolled her eyes, but the look on her face said just how much she loved Ren. Bee laughed out loud. Even I managed a smile.

Then Ren plopped down, all smiles himself. You know, as if he *didn't* lose a hand earlier that morning. He put one arm around Bee and one around me. We gave each other a big family cuddle and just kept saying 'I love you guys,' 'I love you.'

And then Lily was tearing up, touched by it all. She joined the fray. She kissed me on cheek and wiped away my tears, she sniffed away her own and gave us three boys one big joint embrace. We just kept saying it. Telling each other we loved each other. Some of us were laughing. Others were crying. Then we'd swap and swap back and then I lost track of even my own laughter, my own tears. We were feeling the sorrow. For all of our losses. But we were feeling grateful, too. For making it through a whole hell of a lot. For coming home in one piece (or mostly in one piece). But most of all, we were feeling grateful to have each other.

I can honestly say, despite the heaviness of that deeply sad day, that never before had I felt such warmth as I did in that moment. Never before had I felt a part of a family. Felt a type of love that didn't come from fucking. Or come after it. But a love that felt more, or in any case different, to what I had ever known. Something far more cohesive. Or maybe I was just starting to feel those drinks in my belly. My bloodstream delivering to my brain a bit of release and maybe even a bit of joy. Whatever it was, I think I knew what it meant to feel a part of group. Part of a family. I'd had my share of partners, more fuck buddies than I could count. I'd had some long haul relationships. Some real heart breakers by the end. I'd fallen in love once or twice or thrice, each time redefining the meaning for myself. But I'd never felt *this*.

I clutched on to those who felt to me like brothers and sisters. My friends who had transcended friendship, who had become something more. And even though the pain was there, was hard and harsh and burned like fire. It wasn't the only thing in the room. The only thing within myself. There was love, and light and joy. And that's when I knew it. That I would see that day when smiles came quicker than tears.

I clutched even harder. I was one of four in a tangle of limbs and soft kisses. I smiled. And then I cried.

2 5
INTERIM

I was so used to hangovers that I didn't call them that anymore. I just called them morning. One thing I wasn't yet used to were the communal breakfasts. All that delicious fried food that was actually hot off the skillet. And not near as bad as the beef skillet at Taco Nirvana. No insta-dins or syntho protein, but the real deal, or as close as you'd get in a shit-stack like the Drome.

The smell of hash browns got Lily up out of bed. She was always last to join, a late sleeper. Coming out in panties, a sleeveless shirt, and more tattoos than I could count, near as many piercings, she took a seat and yawned, rubbed her half-closed eyes, and waited for the service. Ren had finished his bran flakes, was taking his time with the little nuggets that passed for raisins. He sipped at his cold OJ and got up to get busy with some of that barkeep magic. Ladies first, he handed Lily her accustomed Bloody Mary. Next was Bee's Killer Bee, companion of choice to those fried eggs and ketchup. Then my beer, which washed down the sausage real nice. It was a hell of a feast. A good way to start a bad day.

The cyberneticists walked right in. They didn't bother to knock. They couldn't, not with the door off its hinges and leaned up flat against the wall. Turns out Bee's keys were in his back pocket. Oops. Oh well. Some of us lost brides. Others a hand. I don't think Bee was sweating it; losing a door.

'Come on in,' Bee said to the techno doctors. You know, as if they weren't already halfway down the hallway.

'Are you Ren?' One of them asked, a man with glasses thicker than the syntho pads of a surgical ass.

Bee showed his hands. Plural.

'It's *this* one,' said the second robo medic, lab coat concealing what look like a whole lotta metal, her head well plated in titanium and shimmering panels slipping below her white collar. She pointed at Ren with a hand that might look like his own by the end of the procedure.

The man with the glasses took out a case with sciencey bits and bobs. Laser implements and gleaming wires as thin as spider silk. 'The procedure is a relatively simple one. There is little risk.' He told us without a smile. 'But it will take some time. It is not a job to be rushed'

'A simple procedure,' the lady cyborg doc concurred. 'But a meticulous one. Each wire must bond and fuse with the severed nerve endings. There are 17,000 touch receptors in the palm alone. I suggest you take a walk. Or busy yourself with something that minimizes interference.'

'How long?' Bee asked.

'Ten hours. Eight, if things go exceedingly smooth.' The man looked like an owl with that blank expression, eyes the size of dinner plates in the magnification of those hefty spectacles.

'That is, of course, the deluxe treatment,' the woman of patchwork flesh and metal explained. 'We could reduce the receptor count to whatever you require. Ten thousand, for instance, would take several hours less than seventeen. It would also knock off a good deal of the bill. Of course, the patient's new hand would not be nearly as sensitive. It would feel, but do so with a numbed sensation. It is entirely up to you.'

Bee did not waste time considering the options. 'I want the best,' he made it clear. 'Only the best for Ren.'

'We should get started then.'

'Take it easy, Ren,' Bee patted his friend on the shoulder. 'Take it from me; bionic augmentation ain't so bad.' He smiled and winked. Winked with that green glow of cascading code. Then Ren gave all the thumbs up he could muster; one.

'We'll get out of your hair,' Bee told the cyberneticists.

So we hit the ugly streets of Drome. We walked its drab byways. We wiled away the hours at one of the only reputable establishments in this godforsaken city. We killed some time at the Bee and the Lily. Ahh… where it all started.

We had the place to ourselves. After all, the bar was closed. It had been shut down since the queen of the cops flushed the Bee and the Lily out, had them on the run. All that yellow police tape keeping would-be regulars at bay… the bar had been dead for over a week. No sense reopening it. Not yet. The checkerboard Top Cop and the seven foot rozzer maiden were on ice. Out of the picture. But that didn't mean some other blue bottle bear wouldn't step up to the plate, fill someone's gumshoes. Better to lie low. Keep the peace. Keep out of sight… for now.

There'd be time to reopen the doors to the public. Tear down the investigation tape and serve the local drunks their evening poison. Actually, when all this batshit, crazy, cock-slap hoo-ha came to a close I was jonesing to get myself a job here. Busboy or doorman. I don't know, maybe learn to swirl cocktails from the best of the barmen, shapeshift wonder, Azalea Ren. Lord knows I ain't going back to Taco Nirvana. I'd

rather eat broken glass. Rather bonk Repugna. Well... maybe not *that*.
Still, I had my eyes set on pulling my weight. You know, apart from
the occasional toss of a brick in a back alley. Yeah, pulling my weight. I
think the Bee and the Lily would be a good place to start.

After a few more wild episodes of madhouse hullabaloo. Like later tonight, when we'd kick back some amber magic and shrink to the
size of a can of cola. Shuffle around like rats, no bigger than the local
vermin, and pipe-slide our way across town and up through high rise
plumbing. Up and out of the john. After that, hell, I don't know what to
expect. A week ago the most interesting thing was whether it would be
insta-dins for dinner or end-the-shift Taco Nirvana takeaway. Now, it
was left, right lunatic who-the-hell-knows-what's-next. I was just taking it all as it comes.

'God, it's good to be back.' Lily leaned over the bar and embraced
its polished veneer.

'Don't get used to it.'

'Just let me have my moment, Bee.'

'Have your moment then. And I'll have a KB. Get on it, will you,
Sis?'

'Roger that.' She whipped up a Killer Bee, down to the nutmeg
spice, and slid it down the bar to her brother.

'Almost as good as Ren's.' He smacked his lips.

'Half as good as Ren's is high praise.'

'Aye-aye.'

I grinned. Watching the two siblings. Big brother and little sis. Bee
and Lily. They really were my personal top-of-the-pops. I took them
in, the bar, and sipped my vodka martini. Scanning the room I noticed
what a week of closing shop had meant. It meant a lot of lost laughter.
Shared stories. Good times. It meant a lot of lost moolah, too. Plenty of

revenue out the window.

Then I noticed the more subtle, sadder things. Like how all the lilies had wilted in their glass bottles. Had gone brown and crispy. How all of the bees, those *real* buzzing bees, had died. How they lay, like little fuzzy husks, littered upon the tabletops. I noticed the table where Bee and I sat the night that we met. And then couldn't believe it; only a week! And that led to thoughts of all our adventures and misadventures. Baby and all the rest.

For eight or nine hours I sat and sipped or slept or slouched or laughed or cried, cooped up and getting drunk, sharing stories, arguments, and laughter with my lover and his little sister. There was a question to that, as to whether Bee was still my lover. There was some doubt when he left me to the wolves. Left me to Repugna. But that question was answered when we ate up thirty minutes of that long day in the bar by getting more than a little sweet in the backroom.

It was good resolution. Good to know where Bee and I stood. And while I didn't know it until after we got frisky, until after he kissed me and told me that he missed me, I missed him too, but more than that, I *needed* him. Maybe I just couldn't face being alone after losing Baby. Or maybe I was genuinely in love. But whatever was going on in my whirlwind, topsy-turvy mind, I was glad to have Bee. Because really, what we had planned, I don't think I could face it. Shrinking down to the size of a shit-biscuit and doing the doggy paddle in the toilet basin… at the end of that I'd want something good to come home to. And Bee, his warm bed and strong arms… knowing that would come at the end of the day, that was what I needed to get me through it.

'Ren's hand should just about be finished,' Lily upended her drink and wiped down the bar.

'Let's do it.'

And we did. We followed Bee out of the bar and back onto the ugly, old streets of Drome. I took a backward glance and soaked it in. The Bee and the Lily. I sure hope we'd all be coming back.

26
UP THE U-BEND

Ren's new hand was tops. Real flash, mint techno specs. The cyberneticists had fitted the alloy skeleton with a plasticized epidermal layer that molded to the syntho muscles beneath. Nylon tendons worked strong and agile digits that capped in tips with tiny inbuilt lasers that could cut like a razor and burn like a red-hot poker. The pseudo skin was realistic, down to the nails, the cuticles, the wrinkled knuckles and almost invisible, little hairs. Even more impressive, and much to Ren's gratitude, the skin cells were in part synthesized from a chameleon. A computerized neuro-link enabled Ren to send signals from his brain to his mechanical prosthetic. While he would not be able to transmogrify it, change its shape in the way he was used to, he would in the least be able to alter its pigmentation at will. Sport any hue, shade, or color.

Bee paid the bill. And when I heard the total figure my eyes went wide with wow and my mouth hit the floor. His own face remained unmoved, unfazed. Always unfazed. Bee, the epitome of cool.

'Check this out,' Ren said and pointed his new hand in the shape of a gun. He brought down his thumb like the hammer of a pistol and a thin, red beam shot forth from his extended finger. Little trails of smoke went up into the air over the kitchen where an empty can of Dr. Lemon had sat. 'Go on,' Ren urged. 'Take a look.'

Seared into the aluminum, a black, smoldering scar, a perfect circle and a smiley face within. 'That's at its low setting,' he grinned. 'I could engrave my name into solid titanium if I amped up the juice. But, you know, I didn't want to burn the place down.'

'Thank you for that,' Bee remarked. 'So, you like it? Your new hand?'

'You know something,' Ren reached for a pencil, twirled it like a brass band baton, and made a fist to crunch it into a thousand splinters. 'I really do.'

Lily took up Ren's hand and gave it a little squeeze, kissed it softly. He reached up and pressed it against her cheek.

'It feels so real,' she marvelled. And with seventeen thousand receptors it wouldn't feel any less real for Ren.

'Alright folks,' Bee got to the point. 'Let's Squidge up and amber down.' I was nervous about being the size of a banana. But it came to that part of the night. So we Squidged up our nooks, our crannies and our cracks, we took the decanter and popped the glass stopper. 'Bottoms up.' And we passed it around, amber juju down the pipes.

Luck have it, I was the first to shrink down to a miniature me. Suddenly I was looking way, way up into the biggest skirt a girl had ever worn, into the dark recess of two creamy, white thighs, each the size of a high rise. No panties, but plenty of tattoos. And what's that metallic shimmer. Holy shit, so she has a piercing *there* too.

Lily bent over and picked me up. She held me in a clammy hand that easily engulfed me. 'Oh my god, so cute! Can we keep him this way?'

I made a protest but stopped. When they all started laughing at my squeaky, mousey voice I realized anything I had to say would just become a joke. With all her laughter Lily accidentally dropped me. I fell between two soft tits pushed up by a black bra and suddenly I was face to face with an ink-on-flesh version of the devil. Some red, raging skull that seemed to laugh along with the heaving chest that it rested on.

Then Lily started to shrink too. And now we were all arms flying, legs akimbo on the floor. We pushed ourselves up and off each other and now it was just Bee and Ren laughing, two titans that made even She Beast look like an extra small in the kid's section.

But all that laughter now came out like chipmunk chatter, high-pitched eek and squeak. Then it stopped, because, you know, it's really not that funny. In actual fact, it's kind of scary. Freaky as shit. When that Dr. Lemon you had been sipping on is suddenly larger than you. Yeah, none of us were laughing now. We were just padding ourselves, making sure we were still there. Looking around. Gawking. Just taking in the immensity of the biggest apartment on the planet.

Bee accessed the download of the sewer blueprints with his bionic eye and worked it all out. 'This way,' he guided us. And then it was into the bathroom and up the curve of the pale porcelain cliff face, a leap of faith off the rim of the toilet seat, a swan-dive into the swimming pool basin, and a sub-aquatic cavern dive through the u-bend, a water slide ride down the pipework, slick with slime, and a sickening splash into the sewer murk, caiman and bloated goldfish aplenty.

Much to my horror, I tasted the water as I thrashed about in a green-hued pool with flotsam of turds as large as actual logs. A steady, strong hand reached up from the brick pathway at the edge of the canal and pulled me free of the sink. I coughed and sputtered. I gagged and spat. 'Thanks, Bee,' I said when at last I caught my breath.

He patted my back and smiled. You guessed it... calm and cool. I shook my head. How in the hell does he do it?

The next several hours lead us through dim-lit corridors wet with filth and filled with the sounds of splashing, denizens of the mire rippling the brown water, warning hisses and piteous moans. All in all, the junkyard district, the endless dunes of discarded, rotten shit... it was charming next to *this*. I hated the sewers. And being five inches tall only made it worse. Every lump of feces, a boulder. Every mangy rat, a demented lion, a greasy grizzly bear with pink feet and a long, scabby tail. This, if nothing else, was icky fucking vibes.

But the hours passed. And with gratitude to have them behind us, those hours would not be missed. After much consulting, scrupulous examination while poring over the underground blueprints, Bee had lead us to where our ascension would begin. And then it was tough going, real hard work. Getting the fishhooks and silver barbs we brought along to claw our way upward. Bellies up against hollow cylinders wet with slime and drain water, tooth and nail, we made our way upward. And by the end of it my arms were jelly. My abs were mincemeat. And my rapid breath was ragged.

Up, up, up, through the substructure plumping of Argyle HQ. Then up some more. Up through pipes that led to sinks and urinals, kitchens and toilets, up, up, up to the top. How many floors, I didn't care. Ninety or one hundred. It all added up to the same thing. It added up to one nice big total figure: exhaustion and pain.

But then, smooth as a porpoise and streamline as a seal, we slid down and up the u-bend, just like how it all started. But now, across town and high up in the sky to infiltrate an evil corporate headquarters, we waded in the porcelain pool not at the beginning, but the end.

Only one problem. We were still the size of a hot dog bun. But perhaps more of an immediate concern; there was a ceiling above our heads while we did the dog paddle in the dunny. And it wasn't the toilet lid either. It was a hairy old ass. And it was about to number two all over my good mood.

'No way,' Lily bemoaned. 'No fucking way.' But it was actually happening. Something I thought I'd never see. I mean, why would I? A giant ass up in the sky about to rain down yesterday's insta-dins on top of my head. Unless it was a nightmare while I slept, how was I ever to experience anything remotely like what was happening. And when the final push was about to make the toilet bowl a bit more crowded, a lot more unsanitary, Lily got wise. She stood on Ren's shoulders and reached up to press both pistol handles against one of those big, bare cheeks. A hundred tiny needles entered the soft flesh and secreted strong barbiturates.

But it wasn't enough. Reduced to toy-size miniature, ambered down to insect-friendly dimensions, the tiny guns with their infinitesimal needles pierced a skin too thick to penetrate, and uselessly dribbled a dosage of sedative-hypnotics that would likely fail to knock out a pygmy shrew. Then Lily threw wisdom out the window. Or more appropriate, tossed it down the toilet, and loaded some incendiary slugs up into the big, old tush that was our pink-skinned roofing.

'Ouch!! Ow! Oh, ouch!' Suddenly there was open sky above us. No ass to be seen. Then an angry face looked down into the toilet and shrieked to find four gnomes splashing about in the basin.

Bee fumbled in his pockets and produced a small vial of orange tinged liquid. More amber magic? No thanks. I'd rather not experience a toilet at the microbial level. But two drops on his tongue and he was two shoes in the toilet, the rest of his body out, six foot two of Bee. The standard issue. He reached into the toilet to give us what in his regular-sized hand was a the teensiest of containers. In our own, it was merely average size. The vial of dark gold that reversed the spell. And we took turns dropping amber, each of us, one by one, exiting the toilet.

The man fainted when he witnessed what had transpired. Four full-sized adults impossibly springing out from the toilet. 'Well, that's convenient,' Ren said, looking at the man who was deep in the heart of Z-town.

'Even if nothing else is.' Lily wrung out the sewer and toilet water from her shirt.

'Saves me from having to hurt him,' Bee sheathed his sword.

'Poor bastard just came to take a shit,' I pitied him. 'He'll never shake a fear of lavatories after this. It's like when I was kid. When I saw that old holo-film about an orca construct gone batshit manic. There was a scene where it burst through the bottom of a building built over the water. Came right up through the bathroom floor while a guy was trying to unload his guts. I was eight or nine when I saw that. I held in my shit for weeks.'

I looked to the others. They just stared at me. The room was so quiet you could hear a spider fart.

'So *anyways…*' Bee filled the silence. 'that was a bit of a snag to our smooth entrance. But I don't think they'll be any others. Look,' he nudged the passed out man with a toe. He was wearing a janitor's getup, mop wringer bucket on wheels at his side. 'Late hours and all alone. I was a custodian once. The only other people around were security guards. And we know all about the security here. A mean, hard lot that's real generous giving out early funerals. Me? I'd rather skip out on what they're offering.'

'Yeah. Thanks, I'll pass.' Lily agreed.

'And that's why we did all this splish splash in the sewers and the plumbing summit up the pipes. That's why we burst out the poop seat like the maniac orca construct in that holo-film,' he grinned. ''Cause we're up here. We slipped right passed them. And they're down there, all those holographic crimson mages, all those ninja chimps and android assassins. They're all unaware the Squidge vault of Argyle HQ is about to go on a real big diet. It's going to be like we doused all those worms in amber magic, baby. Cause stock levels, there about to get real, real small. Ladies and gentlemen, we're here. And we're about to get our raid on.'

We didn't risk a cheer, but we fist pumped in silence. High-fived each other soundlessly. 'Think you know the taste of Squidge?' Bee asked us. 'Not even fucking close. Your about to get the first real notion of what a true miracle is all about.'

I'd just been the size of an action figure and watched a dark eclipse of pale ass blot out the florescent heavens. I have been humbled in the shadow of a computer the size of a city block. I had dealings with a de-ranged rodent emperor, lord of all vermin. I had wed a pretty pink robot and danced the dance of death with a pinup lady cop that could pump more iron than a gorilla on steroids. My friend could transmogrify at will. My boyfriend could see with a living eye infused in his sword. I can communicate via brain chip in my noggin, full access networking, digital telepathy. And *now... now* I was to witness miracles.

Fuck me...

This was going to be fun.

27
THE SQUIDGE VAULT

We stepped into a room that was a cat's cradle of laser tripwire. We all had the same thought; we should have stayed small for a little longer. The spaces between the green beams left apertures far too narrow for any of us to pass through. I wasn't sure if those lasers would cut us into pieces or trigger an alarm. Either way, it meant the same thing. Our deaths. One indication from the boys downstairs that they had company up in the vaults and we'd be goners.

We fucked things up. We failed.

I looked over to the others and winced. Lily had her hands over her eyes, head down. Utterly defeated. Ren was stone faced, which on him was about as morose as it gets. But Bee was calm as he ever was. He wasn't sweating it one little bit. I was beginning to think that maybe he had some sort of mental handicap, some sort of go-to delusional daydream that always kept him from feeling the icky vibes of reality. I mean, come on. If there was ever a time to take a break from playing it cool, this was surely it.

I was about to call him out on it. But then I heard his voice echoing from within the center of my head. 'Motherboard, do you read me?' He asked from across the invisible digital ether.

'Yes, son of skin,' her matronly reply. 'I hear you well.'

'Can you detect where I am?'

'Certainly. Without effort. You are on the ninety-ninth floor of Argyle Tower.'

'It is good to know you watch over us, Motherboard.'

'Always, my children. You are indoctrinated. You are we. We are the network.' Then, after a short pause. 'I do not detect Baby. Is she offline?'

I wasn't expecting any tears of sadness on this mission. Maybe tears of pain. Tears of turmoil. But of sorrow? It was not the time or place. But when Motherboard asked about Baby I could feel them coming. Tears of sadness. And plenty of them. 'Baby is gone.' It was all I could get out. Something about breaking the news to Motherboard, me and Baby's computerized celebrant that helped us tie the knot between man and machine... it made the reality sink in a little deeper. It tore at my guts.

If I wasn't expecting tears of sorrow while on the mission, I certainly wasn't expecting tears of joy. Pure elation. But life... it's full of some whopping surprises. And what came next was just that. One big whopper of a holy-fucking-shit.

'I've scanned your memories,' Motherboard told us. 'And while I cannot experience the grief that you feel in quite the same way, my circuits resonate with your sorrow. Truly, I am sorry that Baby's hardware has been demolished.' I was blowing snot into my sleeve, walking the sad, sad streets of Sob City. 'But take heart, skin kids. All is not lost. It is my custom to backup the AI programming sequences of all my children. Personality chips and computerized souls. I have them stored on file. Baby remains intact within me. I have but to transfer her to a new body.'

My heart stopped (in a good way). It skipped a beat or two or three. Was I hearing things straight? I tried to speak but words just weren't coming out. Just some garbled nonsense. Probably a bit like Bee back in the old days. Ba-ba-ba-bad stutter.

And in the end, it was Bee who asked the question I'd been meaning to speak. 'If we are understanding you, Motherboard, do you mean to tell us Baby is still alive? That she will come back?'

'*Alive* is a term used for skin men,' Motherboard reasoned. 'Baby exists. Her program is undamaged, uncorrupted. She will function again. Is Baby alive? That is a philosophical question for both the minds of man and machine. But the term, from your viewpoint, is adequate. Yes. Baby is alive.'

And those were the words I needed to hear. I felt a wave of every emotion in the book. It washed over me, a tremendous punch in the gut that somehow left me feeling ten times stronger, even in the midst of my emotional exhaustion. It was like the stim-kick of adrenaline and the comedown all at once. The waterworks were running. The tears kept falling. But now they fell to be tasted on the corners of my mouth, two ends to a big, wide smile.

'That's heartening news, Motherboard. You give us the gift of strength in hearing it,' Bee's communicative thoughts continued to play in my mind. He rubbed my shoulder and mussed my hair as his words echoed on. 'One more gift to ask of you, O Mother Matron.'

'Speak, skin man, and I shall assess your request.'

'Can you penetrate the defensive firewall of the Argyle Tower's computer system?'

'Without issue.'

'You could access the Argyle HQ mainframe computer?'

'Without delay.'

'So you could, if you chose to, shut down all security protocols?'

'Without sizzling a single wire.'

'These pesky lasers, for instance? You could make them disappear?'

'Without a second thought.'

'The alarms?'

'A nanosecond of triviality.'

'The Squidge vault? You could, conceivably, unlock it?'

'As easily as uttering "open sesame."'

'Well then,' Bee digitally conveyed. 'There remains just one further question for you, Motherboard.'

'I am all audio receptors.' Bee paused in confusion. Then Ren puzzled it out, filled us in through the brainwave chatter. 'The computer equivalent of "I'm all ears."'

'Would you do all of those things?' Bee asked. 'The lasers, the alarms, the vault. Would you take care of those for us?'

And all of those green lasers criss-crossing the room blinked out of existence. The massive, walk-in safe in the middle of the room hummed with the release of an airtight locking mechanism, its heavy circular door slowly opened outward.

'Without hesitation,' the matron computer goddess answered.

Boy, she wasn't fucking kidding.

I'd taken so much Squidge since meeting Bee that I was beginning to forget that the stuff is actually quite rare. But even as much as I had applied over the weeks, all those 16-beat sneaker slaps against the pavement, those run-for-your-life mad dashes with Squidged-up thighs and hammies, calves and ankles.... all the eye-drop, make it so something's worth seeing in this shit stack hellhole, the down the gully and into the tummy, make me feel oh so good and giddy... whatever the method of taking the drug, that fine narcotic that made the world better, however much I had used over the last seven days — a whole heck of a lot — I hadn't seen Squidge in its natural form. Its insect origin. I hadn't seen it or experienced it quite like *this*.

Along either side of what was sort of like a very long, large walk-in closet were the acrylic glass walls and doors to freezer compartments. Beyond the glass were frosted shelves with trays, a catalogue of caterpillars labelled and stored by their stages of development. The larger worms, like small penises, were marked *Fifth Instar*. The further we walked into the cool compartment the smaller the frozen pupae became. The labels indicated, in descending order, the various stages, or instars. At the end of the room, smallest of all, were the tiny first instar worms. They were hardly the size of a mice turds. Or broken pencil tips.

I recalled Doc Argyle's mad scribbling. His maniac retelling and obsessive fervency with his experiences and studies of the squidge wing butterfly, its miracle worm pupae. I thought about what Bee had told me. About Argyle's "baptism." How he had filled a bathtub with the guts of first instar pupae. How he had *drowned* in their extruded guts. Then I looked to the oh-so-minuscule things from behind the glass. Like grains of rice. And I considered the total figure, the sum of all those worms he must have collected. That he needed to fill an entire tub. 4,548? The number of stars discernible to the human eye on the clearest of moonless nights in one hemisphere. More. So many more. 17,000? The number of nerve receptors in the palm of a human hand. Again, I'd wager more. Whatever the number, however many caterpillars, I think its fair to round off to a ballpark figure of a non-specific "shit-ton-of-worms."

Ren joined my side. Lily too. They pressed their faces against the glass. 'Here they are, Bee.' Ren called out to our leader, who was trailing behind, wary and perhaps a bit forlorn. To him, these pupae came with memories. Bad memories, to boot. He was probably wading in one or two of them right now. Playing back whatever icky vibes came with those times when his lover, Doc Argyle, went mad with a zealous focus for the miracle worms.

'Check it out,' Lily called to her brother. 'First instar. The good stuff. Let's unload em.'

'No.' Bee came rushing over.

'What do you mean, no?' Lily put her hands on her hips, thrust her head out and sneered, that old, familiar, teenage angst.

'Yeah,' Ren smiled, more relaxed. 'This is what we're here for, Bee. To get loaded on the good stuff. To become more than man. To become gods.'

'How the hell else are we going to kill a god?' Lily asked, meaning Avid Argyle, not the proverbial "man upstairs."

'By becoming gods ourselves, of course,' Ren held out his new hand and high-fived Lily's.

'No.' Bee was firm. 'Out of the question,' unyielding.

'Oh shut the fuck up, will ya?' Lily opened one of the freezer compartments and reached in to take up a tray of what must have contained several hundred first instar caterpillars.

Bee's sword was out. It was lightning. The snap of a whip. Its point was an inch or two from his sister's tattooed throat. Where Ren's new hand had shot up to intervene, Bee held it by the wrist and bent it at an angle that had his friend wincing. 'Drop the fucking worms, Sissy. And don't you dare raise your hand to me again, Ren. I'll cut the thing off and shove it up your ass. I swear I will. Right after I set off the lasers. You get me?'

I just blinked, off to the side. Took it all in. This was the version of

Bee when I met him for the first time. The man who skewered strangers' eyeballs, detached their limbs if they looked at him the wrong way. He traded death for nasty looks. Maiming for minor insults. Blindness for rude behavior. This was the Bee that peaked my interest. And perhaps the one that in the end might turn me away.

'What is your fucking glitch, bro?' Lily set down the tray. Her eyes were wet with fear. Ren was still holding a face of pain. Until the freezer door was closed and Bee let up on his grip, let his friend go.

'Leave the first instar worms alone,' Bee ordered. 'Haven't you heard the stories I've been telling you over the years? Haven't you read the ravings in Argyle's diaries? The ones which I've shown you? First instar Squidge is not meant for man. Not in that way. Its power needs to be diluted. Spread wide. It can turn dead worlds into an oasis of life. For that, it is the miracle we know it to be. But abusing its power, trying to contain that miracle within the vessel of a single soul, a single body... I've seen what it does to men. It's an unholy aberration. It turns man into monster.'

There was a prolonged silence. The hum of the freezer units filled the narrow room. I think Lily was still getting over the fact that her brother pulled out his black magic sword and held the blade a mere caterpillar length from her pretty little neck. I think Ren was still nursing the pain in his wrist, maybe feeling hurt in more ways than the physical pain. Me? I didn't need to think about how I was feeling. I knew. I was just trying to get over the awkwardness of it all. That, and also considering the unsettling notion of that supreme fury that was always laying dormant right beneath Bee's calm, cool demeanor. Honestly, that shit was a match to a gas tank. Doesn't take more than a blink of an eye to go boom. Like an instinctual reaction. Like a wild animal. Yeah... I was just glad I wasn't the one who reached into the freezer.

Then the silence went away. And when Bee spoke he was back to the man he usually was, the cool-as-a-cucumber, easy-going big brother. But I was sort of now thinking; is that just the mask to the real man beneath?

'But you're right,' he said to both Lily and Ren. 'We have to kill a god, or a demon with god-like strength and abilities. And no, we cannot do that as we are. And what I have in mind… I'm not saying it's a surefire way to work. Nor am I saying it won't tear us into shreds, or that it will leave our mortal souls in good nick. But if we augment ourselves enough, outnumbering Avid four to one… if we pump up our innate abilities, our mechanical and magical parts, our swords with eyes or our hands with lasers, our guns with their mean, sadistic tendencies or our timely brick throwing…' and here he offered me a wink. 'If we douse ourselves, just enough, in *second instar* Squidge, then who is to say? Maybe we have a shot. We would be as if four demigods, a gang of pseudo gods. Maybe together we could oust one big bad god, the head honcho himself. I'll take the plunge. Even if it's not quite a full bathtub. But I'll drip this and that into the goo. But we do it with second instar grade. We leave out the first.'

And what else could we do? No one was going to go against Bee and insist on using max potency Squidge. Not if it meant a sword at our throats, a face of rage on the man who wields it. But one by one we all started smiling. Nodding our heads. And even if there was a tinge of bad blood after Bee's violent outburst, some hurt feelings that still remained, I don't think those smiles were forced or fabricated. I think Bee's idea struck a positive chord. I think the plan sounded halfway legit and maybe some of us were glad not to have to spin the roulette wheel, play our hand and hope the odds were in our favor, that the first instar Squidge didn't tear us in two and leave us dead. Second instar

Squidge was plenty powerful. It was a good compromise. And like Bee had said, there were four of us. Maybe it was all we would need to do Argyle dead. Put him on ice just like all of these hundreds of thousands of pupae.

'So let's get to it,' Lily said with energy.

And we did. We did with a gusto. We opened wide the freezer doors to the collection of second instar worms. We removed tray after tray of the hundreds, then thousands, then perhaps tens of thousands of pupae. We took them out of the room to a decorative marble bathtub, one that had been made for Doc Argyle's "baptisms." Into the marble basin we poured the many worms. And just as Avid had, though I warrant with a degree or two less of devout enthusiasm applied to the task, we smashed the little, thawing caterpillars. We used large, marble mortars that were made from the same polished rock as the bathtub. We worked them to grind the worms into a squelching pulp of gore. We did this for many minutes, for perhaps as long as half an hour or longer.

Then, when it got to the point that our arms were tired from all the heavy work, when we were just stirring weighty implements into a soup of guts, when the amassed contents nearly sloshed over the edge, then, we had completed the task. We had prepared the second instar Squidge.

We set down our heavy mortars. We leaned over the tub that was two-thirds full of goo. We watched our own reflections gaze up at us in the bright green shimmer of the liquid sludge. Then we looked to each other, nodded, grinned, and took the plunge.

Bee unsheathed his sword and dipped its blade, hilt and all, the hand and arm that wielded it, down beneath the surface of the snotty slurp of split pea soup. He wailed with the power that took him, *became* him, that clung to his black magic seeing-sword and infused biological eyeball. A deadly tool to begin with, the blade was now an apocalyptic instrument for all foes to fear. Lastly, Bee dunked his head under the green slime as if he were bobbing for apples. His head was fully submerged to the shoulders in caterpillar mincemeat. And when he flung back his hair and took a gasping breath his face was even more beautiful than before. His hair was a shimmer of perfection. Coal black locks that gleamed like camera flashes off of pools of ink.

Lily unholstered her guns. She dunked both pieces beneath the grass-green murk. She was up to her elbows in slime. She held her guns and the hands that held them, the arms that extended them, down beneath that sick drink. She did so for fully a minute. Maybe two. And when she pulled those pistols free from the emerald mire her guns were left shining like bedazzling starlight. They glittered like sun-kissed platinum gold, polished like jewels in a display case at some upmarket jeweler. No doubt, the anger within them was amped a hefty margin. The personality magic within boiling with a mean itch to maim and kill. Where once her black and red tattoos decorated her fingers, hands, and arms, they now glowed in a bright rainbow sheen. It was as if the designs had been inked in bioluminescence, or oil-slick water, or moonlight itself.

Ren dunked in his new, prosthetic hand. He cupped the water with his other hand and anointed himself. On the face and eyes, on patches of his neck and chest, here and there and everywhere. He even put a wet hand down his pants and performed a hastened whore's bath. Genitals slick with goo, that was for the benefit of Lily. For anyone else in his future that may share his bed. He held his mechanical appendage for the self-ordained length of time and took it out, held it high, and felt its mechanics and computer programming advanced to the wazoo. Those lasers that could already pack a hot punch would now be like condensed fire whips of dragon's breath. They'd be molten threads of destruction.

Me? Well, I couldn't resist. I put my hands into the dark green ick. But just a little. I wasn't like these other guys. I didn't have what it takes to augment my body. Transform my soul. Not all the way. Not entirely. So I dipped my fingers and I brought them to my lips. I tasted the slime and I felt its heady improvements. I wanted to do more, but I also was just too afraid to. Last week I was flipping tortillas at Taco Nirvana. Scratching the burned, black bits of grit off of the beef skillet with a spatula. Now I was dabbling with ritual acts that would turn me into a demigod. It seemed a little too fast. Like fucking before kissing, losing your virginity before you've ever tasted someone else's tongue (which, by the way, happened to me in high school).

But I guess in the end fate took hold of my timid ways and threw them out the window. And from the ninety-ninth floor, that's a long fucking drop. Lily came up behind me and tickled my sides. I snorted with wild laughter but soon was shouting out in horror. She wedged me upward, pushed me forward, and the next thing I know I was swimming in caterpillar guts, gulping them in and gasping for my life.

My three companions laughed at my protests as I lay sopping wet, splishing and splashing a dozen gallons of insect gore, all within that fancy, marble tub. So I grabbed the edges, propelled myself out. And holy fucking shit. Someone give me a brick to throw. Because the way I was feeling, I could throw that fucker a country mile.

Then all the laughing stopped. A door opened inward. And four demigods looked into the irksome glance of the one true god. There he stood. In the very same room. The mad doc, Avid Argyle.

28

AVID ARGYLE

I had seen Doc Argyle several dozens of times before. In newscast holo-
feeds, newspapers or magazines, publicized interviews and paparazzi
shots. His face was well known. But from where he stood now, before
my eyes and in the flesh, I hardly recognized him.

He was never a remarkable man. Plain of face and skinny. His
gaunt features and neat goatee lent a certain quality of distinguished
handsomeness to his visage. But any allure was mild, set off by badly
thinning hair and deep-set eyes that bulged a little too fish-like for my
taste. If it weren't for his name, his legacy that linked him to the discovery and product of Squidge, I'd consider him utterly forgettable. Just a
normal man. An average passerby.

But now... now he was anything but. What was I even looking at? I
could tell it was him. I was looking at Avid Argyle just as he was looking
at me, then over to Bee. But was it really him? Was the man at the end
of the room a man at all? And then I remembered. No, he's a god. Yet
somehow I wasn't convinced. Was *this* what a god looks like? It is not
what I would have imagined.

'Sweet Bee,' he intoned, melodic and weird. His voice carried like
strange music from a woodwind instrument rather than a human voice
box. He smiled and his teeth hurt my eyes, bright lights in the face. Red
lips, like raw meat, came down like curtains and blotted out the white

light. I looked at a man whose flesh and coloring was as if the contrast on a photo had been turned up, turned up again, and again, until his image became a disfigured, luminescent monster, all red and orange and bright yellowy white.

'My little honey Bee. My silly, stuttering baby.' The four of us were frozen by Avid's unexpected arrival. We were caught off guard, a little nonplussed. So we just watched that freak of nature and listened to him rattle off cutesy pet names in the direction of his past lover.

'What's this I see?' He indicated the marble tub halfway full with green juice, the splotches of it here and there from our dripping bodies. 'Don't tell me, Bee. Don't you dare tell me that you've used up my first instar worms.' His face went impossibly red. A crimson balloon with a candle held behind it. His eyes went wide and white. I squinted in their glaring light, like two police torches... you know, the ones the rozzers point in your face when they ask you questions. When they get up in your grill.

'I've seen that stuff ruin a man,' Bee spat. 'I wouldn't touch it with a ten foot pole.'

Argyle eased, relaxed. And when he did, those lighthouse eyes dimmed to show something far less freakish, far more natural. But something still wasn't right. Something was dead fucking wrong. I could sense it. A big shit sandwich being served for lunch and daddy ain't gonna let you leave the table till you clear your plate. I could feel it coming. Some wicked, icky vibes.

'Good, good,' Avid said, relieved and appeased. 'Second instar, was it?'

Bee nodded, gripped his sword.

Avid shrugged. 'Bad baby Bee.' He *tsk, tsk, tsked.* 'Naughty little, stuttering simpleton.'

'Hey, fuck you, wack-job, nutter butter bitch!' It was always poetry with Lily.

'You are looking as demure as ever,' the mad doc laughed at her. 'You are a tigress in a cage. A mighty roar, but no claws to show for it. No fangs to bite.' He gave her the head-to-toe, a disparaging expression. 'You are nothing but an uncouth, wild whore. You always have been. And seeing as today will be the day you die, it seems that's the sum of your story.'

It was the first direct threat. And that's all it took. Bee's sword was out, sparkling with second instar juju. That blade was sharp as the kid who wins the spelling bee. Sharp as the smell of blue cheese. It was head and shoulders sharper than any other, like the guillotine that separates head from shoulders. And the arm that wielded it was solid rock. Iron. A chiselled work of sculpted muscle. His eyes were fire, his stance, murderous.

It never did take much with Lily. Even when people aren't calling her names like "uncouth whore." She was provoked real easy. And those gleaming guns were out, polished platinum; bling, ready to bang.

Ren, by her side, primed his newly-amped, five-fingered laser prosthetic and grabbed the side of the marble tub. He gritted his teeth and squeezed oh-so-tight and a fist full of marble cookie crumbs littered the floor like a handful of gravel. Someone ought to tell Ren to give Bee a go in a thumb war. I'd pay to see *that*.

And then there was me. Head to toe doused in insect dribble. I could feel the power within me. I could feel it bursting out, ready to make mischief, make mayhem. I looked around for a brick but settled on two marble mortars, each the length of a forearm. They'd crush a skull, a kneecap easy enough. I was ready to go. I was ready to play hit the piñata with the mad doc Argyle. Something tells me when I burst him open at the seams it wouldn't be sweets and candy spilling out. Now *that* would be a miracle.

The four of us demigods were speaking with our body language. Weapons out, poised for the pounce, mean faces and muscles flexed. Our message was clear enough. But Avid seemed blind to it all. And I don't think it's because his eyes were two beacons of fiery light. I think he saw well enough that we were about to jump him and do our best to hurt more than just his feelings. I think he knew the sitch. Saw it plain as day. It wasn't ignorance or misinterpretation that kept him in a relaxed state of unconcerned blasé. It was just that he didn't see the four of us as a threat. And *that*… that made me nervous as hell.

But there was nothing for it. If we'd bitten off more than we could chew then that was that. Because it was off our plates and in our mouths. Soon it would be down our gullies, come hell or high water. Either way, this wouldn't be easy to swallow.

Then Avid finally made a move. Though his move, I must say, left me wrinkling my brow. He started unbuttoning his shirt, and not just at the collar. We went all the way down, past the navel and then removed his top and threw it to the floor. Next he went for the belt, then the zipper, then those trousers were down at his ankles and he was taking off his socks. I was gobsmacked. Asking the others through digital networking telepathy, 'what the hell is he doing?'

But it wasn't just that he was getting right down to the bare bones of his birthday suit. That was odd enough. Totally peculiar. And it did cross my mind, is this really the time for an exposure? A game of I'll-show-you-mine-if-you-show-me-yours? It wasn't just that. It was his body. All tweaked up on the contrast, a yellow lantern or a lit up tallow candle. And here and there over his flesh and form were great veins and cracks of raw red and fiery illumination. Moving, shifting, flicking, like orange flames, flashing, like scarlet lightning.

Fully nude, he stretched and flexed to pose his power, his deranged, freakish strength that seemed unstable beneath his flesh. He cringed in — what? — fury? Or was it pain? And then I gasped. We all did. When Argyle's breast tore open in a great rent, a horrific gash that spread vertically all the way to his navel. He arched his back and neck and howled in an emotion I could not decipher, I wouldn't begin to guess. But I imagine whatever he was expressing in that demonic moan, whatever sentiment or release of power, there was a great deal of pain included in that bestial shriek. And how could there not be? What, with that deep vermilion slash tallying down his torso.

And just as the wound tore open, so too did it cinch neat and tidily back together, for all appearances healed. Then another tear, smaller but still grim. That too now healed. Then one along the neck and shoulders, a jagged, awful lesion. Lacerations left and right. Suddenly there. Suddenly gone. Avid Argyle's skin was cracking and tearing apart. Ruptures and fissures surfaced from built-up pressure down in the depths of his body where his barely-contained power seeped up and pushed through the skin. His body, too weak a vessel for the first instar Squidge that it carried within. His physical form, too fragile a container. Yet the power he bore from the same source that ate him alive and ripped him apart, that same volatile concoction of max potency Squidge, it also healed him.

His torment was insurmountable. His relief from healing instant. An ongoing torturous routine that fed fuel into what was already a raging, wild fire, the red hot furnace of Avid Argyle's madness. A miserable wretch and a diehard zealot, a Squidge king and a veritable god. He smiled through the pain and flaunted the rude horror of his nudity. And with prodigious strength that knew no bounds, he outstretched his arms, a patchwork of wounds that tore open and healed in sequence, and awaited our attack.

Lily was first. Always first to attack. Just as she was the last to rise out of bed. She did the impossible 32-beat mad dash. A motion blur of silver light where her augmented tattoos shimmered like moonlight on mercury.

Guns out, chrome caps at the ends of sleek, slender arms. Her aim was true. A barrage of perfectly placed projectiles. Bullets with attitude exploded from the barrel and whipped across the space between her and mad Doc Avid. But a 64-beat, I-didn't-even-see-it, lunatic stride to the side had those many bullets sailing passed him into the wall. Where once some fine art decorated the wall, an expensive well-known master-piece, now there was shattered glass, broken frame and tattered canvas. Well… at least the bullets didn't go completely to waste.

The ruined painting got under Argyle's skin. Or maybe that was just molten lava and first instar Squidge bubbling up, seeping through. The worst indigestion anyone has ever had the misfortune to endure. He bent down and took up a flap of torn canvas. He took up the edges of a shattered, ornate frame. He set them back down, lovingly, tender. Then he picked up a shard of glass and flung it like a Frisbee disc without even looking at where he knew it would land.

Six inches into tattooed flesh. Into Lily's breast, and beneath, her heart. She looked down, disbelieving. Then back up. And with the last bit of consciousness left to her she raised her guns once more and fired pointlessly at a target that easily evaded the would-be deadly slugs.

Bee flinched and raised up his sword but it was Ren who moved first. He screamed and wailed in a more emotive way than I knew he was capable of. All other times it was sly smiles and easy-going assurances that it will be okay. Now, he was a raging devil, dial set to full blast. A boiling pot of fuck-that's-scary.

He extended his arm, its prosthetic end deep-red with fury, chameleonic expression coming out with his passion. His face flickered, shifted, melded, molded into various caricatures of anguish and anger. His outstretched mechanical appendage, with all five lasers primed, shot forth red ribbons of hot, eruptive beams that smoked and sizzled, lighting fires wherever they touched. Everywhere, it seemed, except their target.

Just as Lily had missed with her many bullets, now Ren was failing with those red hot threads of condensed energy. Try as he might, he could not connect a single one to his evasive target. He wiggled his fingers like an old crone would creepily do to a small child in a gesture of "Im-going-get-you." Each digit like the twitching legs of a dying spider. The lasers filled the room. They moved inward and out and back and forth. They were not unlike the cat's cradle of security lasers that initially greeted us within this room. Except those were green. But color aside, so too did Ren's lasers fill the entire room.

Yet Avid danced and bent and twirled like a spasmodic ballerina on bad crack. Like an android tripping on the glitch of the best of the worst malware on the market. Even when Ren condensed the lasers into one, a thick, sturdy beam like a cherry-red pillar of doom, still the mad doc dashed and darted, dipped and dived. And then he was right up in Ren's personal space. He smiled that over-saturated, blinding white veneer and I squinted in the glare as he halfheartedly swatted Ren to the side to collide roughly, head first, upon the side of the marble bathtub.

Okay. No more messing around. Now Bee stepped up to the plate.

Calm as a cucumber? Not this time. Not with little sis in the corner bleeding out from her ticker that has ticked its last tick. Not while Avid Argyle, former lover and enemy number one, arch nemesis and kooky fucker to boot stood breathing right before him. No, Bee wasn't calm and collected this time. He was a red hot chilli pepper dipped in molten rock. An atomic bomb with a blast radius of you're-fucking-dead.

Looking at him from where I trembled in the corner, his statuesque, athletic form pumped up in seething rage and well juiced in second instar Squidge, I nodded in confidence to myself. Assured of the outcome of Bee's triumph over Avid. Sword hoisted up, held outward, naked blade emitting a cloud of black magic and ill intent; to be on the wrong end of that was a surefire way to die. Bionic eye a beacon of ghostly green, legs primed and set for the swooping kill. The predatory pounce, the countdown, just waiting, well balanced, on a pair of pristine white sneakers all shiny with caterpillar guts. Bee was a different sort of animal. This was a whole new ballgame. And baby, man-alive! Let the games begin!

Bee did the fuck-knows-beat, the real McCoy mad dash, and his sword swung in a thin whistle first through air and then through the tips of outstretched fingers held forth to guard against his attack. The first half of Avid's fingers fell like baby carrots to the floor. He studied the eight stubs extending from his palms, each a little pulsing fountain of spurting crimson.

'You hurt me,' he marvelled.

'Encore.' Bee swung again. And this time Argyle danced the erratic dance of bob and weave dodging. And like a boxer he feigned and baited, backed up and moved forward. But Bee's sword was seeing from a third eye, and the stalemate was drawn out. Avid got a piece of Bee with a bludgeoning blow to the shoulder. But Bee used the momentum from the punch to continue to spin a full circle and sent his seeing-sword down in an overarching would-be-death slice.

And here, Avid showed his true colors. He flicked closed the fairy tale with the storybook ending. He sidestepped Bee's attack and giggled a bit. He comically stuck his thumb into his mouth and blew out his cheeks, a clown-like expression on his face as each finger, one by one, popped back from nothing. And just like all of those gashes on his chest and neck and back, instantly healed by the Squidge that caused them in the first place, now his maimed hands, too, were perfectly cured of ailment.

As Bee paused to watch in stupefied wonder Avid gave him a good sucker punch in the face. I heard an audible crack from the other side of the room and watched my boyfriend fly half the length between us to thud heavily upon the hard, marble floor.

'And then there was one,' mad Doc Avid smiled my way. My tummy went wobbly with fear and my stool suddenly wanted very much to soil my trousers. 'The others, I know. Sweet, baby Bee. Delicious, like honey. His foul sister, Lily. That little whore got what she deserved. Ren, the barkeep with a thousand faces, the genetic mutant. But you… you seem out of place.'

Maybe that's because I'm the guy that works the beef skillet at Taco Nirvana. Maybe because I'm just another guy trying not to die of boredom or depression in this gray, shit-stack town. Maybe that's because I am not a magic-clad, mechanically altered, freak of nature like the rest of them. Maybe it's because I am normal old me. Joe Schmo. Maybe it's because I'm the only conscious person in the room who is not a god. Yeah, that may have a little something to do with the whole ambiguity thing. Sorry to fucking let you down.

'So who are you?'

And then I remembered. Clenched my fists and felt the power of what I had now become. I might be the only conscious person in the room who is not a god, but let's not forget that ass-over-head tumble into the tub. My second instar splash. I may not be a god. But I was a demigod. And unlike Lily or Ren or Bee, I took the plunge. I all but drowned in the bloody stuff as the others pushed me in, laughed at me as I thrashed, full-bodied, doused in ick. So beware, you daft old fuck. I'm not slim pickings. I'm the real deal as much as anything.

'Who are you?' Avid Argyle repeated.

I didn't have my weapon of choice, a fist full of brick. So I settled with the marble mortars, each near as big as a baseball bat.

'Who are you?' he said once more.

And I smiled. Me, out of character, cool as a cucumber on ice. 'I'm your worst fucking nightmare.' I thought it sounded cool. I thought those words confirmed it; I'm tough as nails, a real hard badass. But in the end it just made what came next more comical. When I charged towards Avid, speedy with Squidge and duel wielding oversized marble mortars. When I came in for the kill.

And was knocked flat on my ass.

Dispelling my attack, chuckling with relaxed ease, Avid kicked me in the face. And the world went black.

29
THE FINAL BAPTISM

When I came to, the others were already awake. Even Lily. Which had me smiling, but not for long. We were lined up in a row, tied up tight. The rope was thick and well coiled around us. Even as demigods, strong like oxen constructs on a steroids, the bonds held firm against our efforts.

'How are you alive?' I asked Lily without being able to turn enough to face her.

'The glass broke when it hit my rib,' she told me in a ragged breath that did not carry her normal voice. 'It missed my heart, but it punctured a lung.'

'Stop talking,' Bee told her. 'It will make it worse.'

'As if that's going to fucking matter,' she coughed.

'I'm afraid she's right,' Ren said, more matter of fact than somber. He thrust his chin forward to indicate what was being played out before us. And I turned to take in the proceedings of a oddball, freakshow, macabre ritual orchestrated by a raving, batshit, manic, madhouse zealot.

The marble tub was centered before us. Avid was going in and out of the Squidge vaults, trays balanced in hands like a baker with his breads and buns. Except those weren't rolls and croissants he was shoveling into the bathtub. They were first instar squidge wing pupae.

Ten thousand of them. Twenty thousand. Who-the-hell-knows-how-many-thousand of them.

You could see where all the second instar Squidge had been hastily scooped out of the basin, green puddles here and there from our own watered-down baptism. Though ours was more like a trip to the pool. Kids having fun. No religious connotation. No fervid, devout, maniac praises to the fountain of miracles. Nothing like what Avid was doing. Nothing like *this*.

He was naked, as before. His body was aglow with radiance. Ugly colors of radioactive yellow, orange, white and red. Whatever all that first instar Squidge had made him into, god or monster or both, it had turned his skin a mottled patchwork of illuminated grossness. It was revolting and strange. And all the while his scrawny body tore at the seams, blood-red canyons that opened up and healed to close instantaneously. I looked away in revulsion. Then I looked back out of sheer curiosity.

'Into the tub we go, one by one, little wormy wormy worms.' He sang and danced as he went about his creepy business. What the hell was he even doing? Dumping all those first instar worms into the tub, it didn't make any sense. Avid had already undergone the mega dip. The max potency plunge. The ultimate sacrosanct baptism. So what was this? The sequel to a bad movie? Or was he planning to throw us in, ropes and all, as we drowned, like he did, in liquid miracle.

'Ahh,' he gazed my way. Smiled that dazzling, spotlight smile. I had no hands to shield my eyes so I just shut them. Then those raw red flaps of lips must have pressed together to conceal the outpour of light. Even with closed eyes, I could tell the difference. So I opened my peepers and now the mad Doc was standing right in front of me.

'I am pleased you are back with us, Jarred.' Either someone told him my name or he heard them speaking about me.

'Yeah, well, I can't say that makes two of us, Doctor Wackjob.'

He chuckled. 'I like you Jarred. I can see why Bee has taken you under his wing.' He turned to Bee and smiled, blew him a kiss on foul breath.

'Ignore him,' Bee urged.

'Yeah, I'm getting that same idea.' I agreed.

'Oh, a fine team of pesky children you all are,' Avid went on, still looking down over me. 'Jarred,' he singled me out. 'A pretty name. A very lovely name indeed. Were you aware,' He asked, 'that the name Jarred means rose.'

'My momma always told me it meant "descent."'

'Why not both?' He smiled and again I shielded my eyes. 'Why not descend down the mountain to a valley of red roses?' Oddly, I found that sentiment pleasant. But then he turned on his heels and was back to kook times kook, squared. Total batshit. Utterly madhouse.

It was all singing and hooting and bouts of prayer. All the while he squashed those little worms. At one point his flesh tore from ass to neck and he vomited with the pain. His wounds healed in seconds and then he was song and dance and prayer all over again. This went on for a long while. A madman's preparations for the perversion to come.

Then it stopped. The preparation. All was seemingly ready for whatever insane, nut-job ritual awaited. Avid twirled with strange grace, his patchwork of pale colors ugly and mesmerizing. Then he performed a deep, to-the-floor, bow, and shouted out; 'Ta-da!'

'Oh, bravo,' Lily said with an overabundance of sarcasm. 'Good show, you dank tuft of rectal fuzz.'

Avid *tsk, tsk, tsked.* Waggled his finger. Then he marched to the freezer, came back with two fistfuls of larger, fifth instar caterpillars and one by one force-fed Lily, who raged and wiggled against the vice of her bondage. She began to spit and scream but Argyle pressed up beneath her chin, down above her head, forcing her mouth closed to inevitably swallow down a whole lotta icky vibes. When he walked away she wailed, green goo down her chin and tears in her eyes, black trails of mascara like warpaint. 'Go to hell!!' She shouted.

'Oh, I am already there!' He shouted back. And I believed him. His belly flapped open, oozed blood, and closed back up without the slightest of scab or scar. 'Hell is the world we live in. The vile, drab, pimple of a world. All of its festering bile, its oceans of sick. All of its *people*.' He said that last word like it was sin itself. 'But gods are good and gods can mend.' His neck opened up and closed again as he winced. 'Gods are great. And I… I am a god!' The pain was so severe when the next lesion tore up his thigh and across his groin that his stool let loose onto the floor. He kicked yesterday's insta-dins into our faces and all we could do was turn our heads.

Suddenly Argyle became cheery. An absolute 180, attitude change. 'But no matter,' he beamed. 'All is well.' He bent to dip his hand into the first instar sludge that filled to the brim of the bathtub. 'Because here awaits the final baptism. The holy ascension to true divinity. I am a god. And I am great. But I shall be such a god as to make all notions of divinity redefined. I will become the god of all gods. I will be a super god.' He did a little jig, his genitals flapping ungracefully. 'I will be the only thing in the entire universe. I will *be* the universe.' And then he stood up onto the brim of the bathtub, he looked down into the emerald swamp, pinched his nose closed, and with giddy, childlike giggle he jumped into the pool of gore.

We all just watched, tied up and unable to do much else. We couldn't see over the edge of the bathtub but for a while all went quiet and calm.

Then maybe ten, maybe twenty seconds later, gentle splashes, then terrible thrashes, horrific screams and gurgling, stifled cries. It sounded like a portal to hell had been opened up, and from it the sounds of all the many cases of torture, ruin, and demise since the beginning of time. It is a sound that will haunt me until the day that I die. But luckily, mercifully, for us who heard the sound and for he who had been making it, it did not last long. Whatever had gone on within that tub had ended.

So quiet now the room had become that we all presumed what soon we'd determine to be actual fact; Avid Argyle was dead. Killed by his own greed. His attempts to harness a power beyond the stability of his human vessel.

When we did look over the edge of the tub we saw nothing but Squidge. It had taken Avid, mind, body, and soul. It had devoured him. Which in a way, I suppose, it had done since he walked into that field of switchgrass and heather. That impossible little patch of fertile grass. Back on Eight Ball, a dead world of rock. Yes, I think we'd all agree. Squidge had killed Avid long, long ago.

'Motherboard?' Bee reached out on the invisible threads of the digital ether.

'Speak, skin man.'

'You detect my presence?'

'Without effort.'

'Can you please reboot the security protocols of Argyle HQ?'

'Right now?'

'If you would.'

'Done.'

'Thank you, Motherboard.'

'The indoctrinated are one. We of the great network.'

And we all electronically echoed it as one, 'We of the great network.'

The green lasers shot back on and Bee popped up to his feet. All wrapped in rope, like sushi rice in seaweed, he waddled over to the nearest laser and let it singe off his bondage. Then one by one we did the same.

'Come on,' Bee said, 'Lets get the fuck out of here.'

And we didn't even have to take the dunny. We didn't even bother to take the back door. Demigods, as we had become, we walked straight down to the main entrance, tearing apart scores upon scores of android assassins, ninja chimps, and holographic crimson mages along the way. Like it was no big thing. Just another walk in the park.

And I gotta admit, in that moment, I felt kind of cool.

30
A DIFFERENT SORT OF VIBE

We came back a few days later. We walked real casual through the front door. No more need for infiltration. No security to speak of. When we got to the top we killed the green lasers and we did what we came to do.

We gathered all the squidge wing pupae from the Squidge vault. We scooped up as much as the first instar slime that remained in the bathtub along with the liquid remains of Argyle himself. We compiled all of our plunder and we shrunk it down to manageable size.

The day before that we had crashed Repugna's sex party. She was in a good mood with her new pleasure droid. He had been doing his tireless robotic thrust of in and out. And a happy Repugna is a generous Repugna. For a few downloadable drugs she dished out some amber. It was what we needed to get all that Squidge, all of those frozen caterpillars, out of Argyle HQ.

Shrunken down to a backpack-friendly load, we next brought our hoard to the Palindrome dispersers, a center for air filtration, oxygen recycling, and a general, massive system of citywide ventilation which is typically used to disperse calming agents, pacifier drugs, mild sedatives, and other government issued mood-changers to keep the general angst of Nyvyn in check. We loaded up the vast dispersers with all the first instar Squidge. The max potency juice. Then we got our hands dirty with the long, tedious task of crushing all of those caterpillars into liquid Squidge, feeding them all into the massive ventilation system.

Bee sprinkled the amber juju to make what had been shrunken down return back to its normal dimension. A veritable sea of Squidge filled the dispensers, which slowly, over time, would enter the atmosphere of the Drome. The Squidge, vaporized and spread out across citywide margins of mild application, should, over the weeks and months to come, work its miracle to save a doomed city. Bring color and life to a gray, dead wasteland. Nyvyn, the little saint… he may, someday soon, live up to his name.

I met Baby on the fringes of the junkyard district. We picnicked on the riverside of the slow moving Flow. I snacked on leftover insta-dins and she drank white lithium grease from a nearby old tin of pseudo-beans. Baby's new body isn't a combat model like the one before it. But she's still outfitted in pink chrome. She still has those dazzling, marigold bright LEDs.

We kissed a little by the river's edge, but in the end I gently pushed her away. In good faith, and in good graces, I sent out the request to Motherboard via the digital ether. I had the marriage annulled. I wished Baby the very best of luck, and I wished also to remain friends. Through our shared networking devises, the identical microchips within us, we would always remain in contact, and perhaps, from time to time, picnic beside the lazy, brown Flow.

She smiled at my with pretty pearly whites, ceramic pegs as lovely as her last set. She took the annulment like a champ. She understood my feelings and accepted them without an ill thought for me.

'Perhaps my next husband will be a machine, like me.' She wondered aloud. 'Perhaps he will have a processor of super computing capabilities.'

I smiled back. 'Perhaps he may.'

Bee and I went steady for a while. But after a time it petered out. I was maybe just a little too plain Jane. Or, from my perspective, he was just a little too cool for school. Too up on his high horse construct, that brindled mare.

I kind of knew it was over when I dropped the L-bomb one night. When we were heavy-weight pashing, pushing our Squidged-up tongues up against each other's. I said it twice. "I love you, Jarred." And when he didn't say it back, I wasn't hurt. I was sort of relieved. Looking back on it now, I think I was grasping at straws. Just trying to milk something that used to be good. Something that had run its course.

We were no longer *us*. We were just Jarred and Bee. We're still friends. But actually, it's Lily and Ren that I'm closer to these days. They're my best mates. And lucky me, Lily's my boss. Best boss I've ever had. I'm working at the Bee and the Lily. Pulling my own weight. Apprentice to Ren, master barman, cocktail wizard, booze guru.

I was getting to know the local drunks. The regulars. And I've had my eye on one or two luscious lushes. They'd slur sweet serenades of love my way, whispers in my ear and spare keys left on the table with their generous tips. I was loving the attention. And I was loving my life. Something I'd not gotten used to in all my years feeling death might be the better option.

At the end of my shifts I'd wave my goodbyes with a smile. I'd walk home, a few blocks south of where Bee and Lilly and Ren were living large in their flash digs. A ten minute stroll from my friends who were more than friends, that were family. I took in the night air and something about it seemed a little different.

Nyvyn is a real heap of shit. The place I live. The place I was born. The place I didn't want to be. Nyvyn, which means 'little saint,' or 'nephew,' or 'saint worshiper,' was a stack-upon-stack, multi-layer collection of filth and degradation. I loathed it, as did we all.

But it didn't need to be that way. Maybe it wouldn't be like that any longer. Or wouldn't be, in any case, for very much longer. There was a change in the wind. A lightening to the heaviness that weighed down the soul. The smells weren't half so acrid, a quarter so awful. The lesions and sores seemed to fester somewhat less. The roborgs huddled in corners not so filthy. The rats' fur seemed not so greasy. Hell, even the insta-dins tasted a little better.

I looked up to a sky that criss-crossed with the countless silhouettes of metal grating, the cat's cradle of rusted byway. And beyond them, the smog parted to show a streak of night sky. And their they were, sparkling oh-so-dim and anaemic, but bedazzling all the same... *stars.*

I took a deep breath of evening air. I filled my lungs. And I smiled. Something was different. Then it dawned on me. *That's it.*

They were no longer there...

All those icky vibes.